Penny Sumner is an Au... postgraduate student. She did a D.Phil. at Oxford and ... lives in Newcastle upon Tyne, where she teaches creative writing and contemporary literature at the University of Northumbria. Her first publication was a short story in *Reader, I Murdered Him* (The Women's Press, 1989). Another story, 'Dead-Head', which appeared in *Reader, I Murdered Him, Too* (The Women's Press, 1995), was shortlisted for the Crime Writers' Association Short Story Dagger Award. She has written two crime novels, *The End of April* (1993) and *Crosswords* (1995), both published by The Women's Press. She has one son.

Also by Penny Sumner from The Women's Press:

The End of April (1993)
Crosswords (1995)

Penny Sumner, editor

Brought to Book
Murderous Stories from
the Literary World

First published by The Women's Press Ltd, 1998
A member of the Namara Group
34 Great Sutton Street, London EC1V 0DX

British Library Cataloguing-in-Publication Data
A catalogue record for this book is available from the British Library.

ISBN 0 7043 4578 1

Typeset in Bembo 11/13pt by The FSH Group Ltd
Printed and bound in Great Britain by Cox & Wyman Ltd

For my mother, Audrey

Contents

Introduction

Whodunnit? She did, the crime writer. Gave the genre a long, cool look, then proceeded to rework the whole caboodle to suit her own purposes. This process began back in the Golden Age of the twenties and thirties, when Agatha Christie, Dorothy Sayers, and others, challenged the masculine orientation of the genre with strong heroines and more subversive attitudes towards gender than they are sometimes given credit for. Half a century later in the mid 1980s a wholesale demolition was underway, with a new type of female detective taking to the mean streets, and a new generation of writers rediscovering, and remaking, the canon of women's crime.

A number of these new writers were gathered together when The Women's Press brought out one of the pioneering anthologies of feminist crime, *Reader, I Murdered Him* (1989). This very successful collection was followed by *Reader, I Murdered Him, Too* (1995), and now by *Brought to Book*, crime stories set in the world of publishing and the book trade.

A comparison between the stories in *Reader, I Murdered Him* and this collection, indicates the sort of changes that have taken place in women's crime writing and to what extent women crime writers have challenged the traditional formulae and macho mores of the genre. For example, where three-quarters of the stories in the first anthology were concerned with death by violence (despite the title the victims were frequently female), there are far fewer corpses in these pages. And not all the deaths that do happen are the result of calculated murder.

Set in the bookworld, in these stories we meet writers forced to pit their wits, and sometimes more, against unsympathetic agents, editors, prize-awarding committees . . . But equally hard-put are those employed in the industry itself, with harassed publishers facing imminent downsizing on the one hand and the possibly murderous intent of rejected writers on the other, as in Dale Gunthorp's 'Pikeman and the Bagwoman', Barbara Paul's 'Stet', and Joan M Drury's 'Murder at the Sales Meeting'.

In most of these stories, however, the central character is a writer or, like the wonderful narrator in Millie Murray's 'Shame the Devil', is in the process of becoming one. Books are an author's children, as explored in Mary Wings' 'Empty Arms', and writing is central to their life. This centrality is the premise of the first story, the gently humorous but disturbing 'Bad Review' by Susan Dunlap, in which the quality of a woman's art becomes the measure of her life. In this, and in Finola Moorhead's bitter-sweet 'Four Characters, Four Lunches' – in fact in nearly every one of these stories – writing is central to identity. The woman writer no longer agonises about whether she should write, or what she should write about. She *writes*, that's what she does, and who she is. By taking control of their own writing (or, as in Christina Lee's 'Luisa', attempting to take control of what is written about them), the women in these pages take control of their lives.

When her book is attacked the author in Stella Duffy's 'Could Be Better' does not hesitate to retaliate. Crime blurs into fantasy, and what is most evident in this collection is this blurring of genres as social realism gives way to post-modernism, fantasy, magic realism. In Robyn Vinten's witty 'Character Witness' a reviewer confronts a feminist crime writer from the early eighties, appalled by how badly writing has dated, but then finds herself literally drawn into the text, the boundaries between fiction and reality slipping away altogether. Many of the stories in this collection can be described as postmodern, but some are more postmodern than others. Thus Barbara Wilson's translator Cassandra Reilly might be claimed as emblematic of all writing (and reading) being an act of translation; and Margaret Wilkinson's Masha, the splendidly muscular 'printress' of 'A Man's Book', challenges barriers of gender, time, history and profession as she pulls at the heavy levers of her ornamented press.

Most of the stories in *Brought to Book* are optimistic. But they are not complacent. Nor are they about women hitting the mean streets, and getting meaner. In Melissa Chan's delightfully wicked 'At the Premier's Literary Awards' a group of women writers get together and lament the awards the great Australian novelist Christina Stead never won in her lifetime. And then, as a group, decide something must be done about it.

Crime fiction, after all, is set in a world that has been made unjust. And what feminist crime writers are saying is that it's time the perpetrators of injustice were brought to book. Here you'll meet the women to do it.

Penny Sumner

Bad Review
Susan Dunlap

The darker the clouds, the more silvery the lining, or at least so writers believe. Every situation has the potential to drop the story of a lifetime into your waiting computer. That is such a tenet of the craft that we never discussed it. And when we should have focused clearly, when Kay Washburn suggested her pact, she dazzled us with its boldness, and blinded us with her logic. Kay never left a loose end.

I've asked myself whether she had a window to the future, perhaps a leaded-glass affair that let in colours but blurred crisp outlines of events to come. Or was the pact merely a more macabre-than-normal whim of hers? None of us voiced those speculations. The question everyone has asked over and over, that *I*'ve searched my mind for every day for the past two years is this: What possessed Louisa, Cyn, and me – ostensibly three normal middle-aged women – to join in Kay's pact?

I've come up with plenty of explanations, some with more of a ring of truth than others. But whatever our underlying motivation, the fact is that we all did agree on the plan. That was twenty years ago when none of us could have imagined that we'd be famous, rich, or dead, much less that the conditions of the pact would come to pass. Admittedly, Kay had unveiled it after several bottles of Chardonnay at a Monday afternoon lunch. But we were used to the Chardonnay, too. It was as much a ritual as having the lunch on a Monday to celebrate the writer's freedom from the nine to five. What stunned us as much as the pact itself was Kay suggesting aloud that one of us might actually become a literary light. (At that time, affording dental insurance seemed an unattainable goal.)

We rolled the idea of renown and riches around in our mouths as deliciously as we might a black olive before biting into the meat. And being writers we soon narrowed the speculation to a more professional theme – if one of us became really famous, what wonderful book idea would trickle down to the rest? Of course we all had different ideas of what that bestseller would be: *Exposé of Famous Writer? Self-aggrandising Autobiography (ghost-written, of course)? Her and Me?*

Had we been willing to speculate on who might hit number one on the bestseller list, we wouldn't have guessed Kay. My choice would have been Louisa.

Louisa Hammond's novels deal with the loving befuddlement between mothers and daughters. There's a kindness to Louisa's perceptions. It's as if her own body – which now looks like throw pillows sticking to a surprisingly strong frame – took literary form. Like her fictional mothers, she gives and takes, settles and resettles, she reshapes herself, and then just at the point when it appears she'll lose any semblance of herself she stands firm, strong, unyielding, and able to support everyone else.

People tend to underestimate Louisa, to see the pillows and forget the steel frame. I remember the first time I really talked to her about Kay. Louisa was sitting on an old floral couch in her living room, by no means a spectacular room but certainly

better than where she's living now. Then her dark brown hair
– parted in the middle, held back by clips, flopping in loose
waves over her shoulders – was just beginning to grey. She
never fingered that hair or played with it as so many women
do; she wasn't that self-conscious. That day she sat, feet drawn
up under her, drinking not tea as I might have expected but
espresso she'd made with a machine she'd brought back from
Grenoble well before gourmet coffees became a fad. A huge
vase of gladioli, purple hydrangea flowers (the gauzy ones, not
the pompoms), and Queen Anne's lace stood on the hearth,
almost overpowering the small room. Lifting the espresso cup
for a sip, she moved as if both the temperature and humidity
were near one hundred, though, in fact it was cool that spring.
But she kept her gaze on me as if my ruminations were ice
cubes.

'It seems like nothing ever bothers Kay,' I began. 'I can't
recall anything she couldn't handle with that half-smile of hers
and an offhand comment that most often leaves us laughing.
Does anything frighten her?'

'Do you mean does Kay confide in me about her fears? No,
Vivian, not Kay. The Cabots may talk only to the Lodges, and
the Lodges only to God. But I'm sure Kay Washburn wouldn't
put herself at the mercy of any of the three.'

I laughed, but her choice of phrase – *put herself at the mercy*
– is one I haven't forgotten over the years. It didn't enlighten
me about Kay, but it made me a lot less trusting of Louisa
Hammond.

'It says something for Kay,' Louisa went on that day, 'that
even with that brittle reserve she gives us something we
wouldn't want to do without.'

'Us and her readers,' I said.

Louisa nodded, half-smiling, her eyes half-closed, as if she
were sifting all this into herself. 'Her readers and us.' And in the
corrected order of that phrase she summed up what mattered

to Kay. Later I decided that wasn't quite accurate. For Kay, it was her work that was important, and the fact that people read it allowed her to keep writing it. If I had said that to Louisa she would have taken another sip of espresso and said, 'Well, we all feel that way about our writing.' But Louisa, as perceptive as she is about characters and relationships, would have been wrong there. Louisa is committed to the people who people her fiction, those mothers and daughters of hers. At times I know she sees them as more real than we, her friends, are. But with Kay, her characters are just one part of the whole mystique of her books, and it's that mystique that grips her. What Kay truly loves is returning to the manuscript she's had in the works for years. She never talks about it. The rest of us question whether she will ever finish, or if she will polish and repolish it year after year till she's rubbed it entirely away.

Still, if I'd been asked to guess who would make it big, I wouldn't have chosen Kay. I never once pictured myself writing magazine articles entitled 'A Trip Through Kay Washburn's Psyche', or 'Travels with Kay', or penning the best-seller *The Fateful Journey to Kay Washburn's Pact*.

Had I been forced to predict startling success, I would have picked Cyn Ciorrarula. Her heroines were great adventurers, braver than brave, cleverer than even their faithful readers expected, like high jumpers who clear the bar with so many inches to spare we're left wondering how we could possibly have assumed the challenge was worthy of them. Cyn created heroines with long sinewy muscles, control that allowed them to trot across broken rope bridges over Himalayan gulches, and co-ordination worthy of .400 hitters. They were the women we all wanted to be: women who took no shit.

Cyn wasn't young but she was still all angles, and too narrow for her height. It was as if she and Louisa had split two persons' physiques: Louisa'd gotten the softness, Cyn the hard. And she worked at staying in superb shape. It was her heroines' fault, she'd insisted, laughing in that matter-of-fact way of hers – no edge of undelved fear like Kay had. 'Each year it means one more hour in the gym just to keep close enough to imagine how they might feel. Some people write till they die. That won't be what stops me. There'll just come a point when I won't be out of the gym long enough.'

I can still picture her lifting weights or running around a track. But it was a sad moment when I realised she'd never again lope easily along the pine-edged country road where I bicycled beside her a decade ago. I remember how the branches hung over the road, turning the macadam from shining denim blue to black, shifting the temperature ten degrees in a second. Cyn was panting softly with each breath and the wind rustled her short reddish-blonde hair like it would a dog's. Sweat coated her tanned skin, her aquiline nose, and under the awning of the pines she was still steamy and glowing, while I, riding beside her, felt the residual chill even in the sun.

A couple of days before, Kay had given us copies of her latest manuscript before she sent it off to her editor. As Cyn started down an incline I said, 'What do you think possessed Kay to ask for our opinions of her book? It's not like she thinks that my travel articles are on a par with her novels.'

'Or my adventures,' Cyn said in that gravelly voice of hers. 'I'm sure she thinks I write for overaged adolescents.'

'So why does she want our opinions?'

Cyn laughed. 'Maybe she thinks we have the common touch.'

'But "art" is above the common touch. Why does she care?'

'Because,' Cyn said, taking a longer breath as we started up the rise toward the lake where she would end the run, dive in, and swim to the raft. I'll bet she misses that now. I'll bet she's thought of that irony every day for the past two years – if she hadn't kept in such good shape, she could still be swimming in that lake. 'Because,' she repeated then, 'Kay is fanatic about tying up every loose end. She probably wouldn't make a change based on your opinion, but she'd want to be prepared for that criticism. She wouldn't take the chance of your saying it when it was too late for her to do anything about it.'

It occurred to me then that Cyn was not the simple, straightforward, best-way-to-the-goal woman I had assumed. And later when Kay announced that fateful pact, I'll bet Cyn was less shocked than I was.

If the spotlight had shone on Cyn I wouldn't have been surprised. But I doubt any of them ever considered me a possibility for fame. I certainly didn't, which was just as well. You don't become a celebrity writing travel books. Not unless you elect to go places where your roommates have more legs than you do, and the humans' vision of you is in several pieces and ready for the rotisserie. Not for me. I had endured a sepulchralish half-hour in a mud bath wondering just who had been in there before me and how much of their skin was still here touching mine; I'd spent a week in a nunnery in Bali where instead of blessings I'd gotten diarrhoea, fleas, and ring-worm. The sufferings of a travel writer are legion. Indications of sympathy, respect, and adulation are not. I don't go out of my way for adventure like Cyn. My idea of risk is trying kiwi syrup in my mai tai. Bicycling along that country road beside Cyn was as bare bones as I hoped to get.

My dream of fame was that it would befall Cyn, and I would describe the journey through her life to its happy conclusion. For me it would be the chance to translate the micro-novels that make up travel writing to full-blown form, the chance for respect and maybe a soupçon of adulation. My vision ended with me accepting praise and glory in a penthouse suite atop the Four Seasons Hotel.

But if either Cyn or I had had real visions of hitting it big

I can't imagine we'd have come up with the idea of the pact like Kay did.

And Kay was the least likely of any of us to really 'make it'. She wasn't tough like Cyn, or earthy like Louisa, and she certainly didn't have the unpleasantly garnered ability to adjust to the unpalatable situations that I had acquired eating raw worms that didn't quite pass for squid at one hotel on the Pacific.

Kay was a tiny, dark woman with sharp features and a patrician nose down which she observed the world. Only occasionally did I look at her and focus on her pale hazel eyes, which seemed to lurk in the sockets and shift back and forth nervously. Then she reminded me of a chipmunk peering out of its hole into a world of predators, always poised to make a dash to the next safe spot. Kay's novels were seemingly without form, books that demanded all your concentration and still left you feeling like you might be asked to repeat the grade, books that left you laughing so hard you wondered what kind of mind created them. And when you thought about them afterward you realised that, in fact, there was a form supporting the flights of fancy and fear much like the steel bars under the pillows that made up Louisa. When you turned the last page every question was answered, every thread tied up.

If it couldn't have been me who stepped into the spotlight, in one way I'm glad it was Kay. I wouldn't have wanted to live with the thought of Kay, with her biting humour, writing a tell-all about me.

Still, even knowing that side of her, I wouldn't have wanted to do without her at lunch. She was too entertaining. She'd sit there on the deck, silent for long periods, then slice in one soft comment that would ricochet for the next five minutes. Kay was like her books in that sense; they, too, had a final twist, an irony that left you laughing, or gasping, or both.

Besides, Kay's houses, particularly the last one at the top of the mountain, were too magnificent to be missed. And, the unfortunate pact was, in fact, fair and right, and uniquely suited to our foursome.

That's what makes the events of her death so ironic.

We were sitting on her deck that afternoon. This was years before she had the sauna put in and the deck enlarged and edged with lacy trees that filtered the sunlight. Years before the light of fame shone on her and she moved to the top of the mountain. This deck was a few ramshackle square yards of redwood, the table one of those old metal ones with the hole for the beach umbrella. A clear bowl held the remains of shrimp salad, and the knobby end of a baguette lay next to a shapeless mound of butter on a gold-rimmed saucer Kay'd gotten as a gift at her first wedding. Both bottles of Chardonnay stood in the middle of the table, one empty, the other with its wine line hidden behind the label. Kay sat across from me, the shade from the umbrella thrusting half her face into relief, sharpening her cheekbones, darkening the sloughs in the sides of her nose. As she spoke I had the sense that I was seeing her flipping ahead to her last chapter. 'Ladies,' she said, lifting the glass she'd just refilled. 'I propose a pact. A modified tontine. You recall the tontines.' She'd paused here and waited for Louisa to fulfil her responsibility and ask for the working definition. Secure in the cocoon of love and warmth she'd woven around her, Louisa had no qualms about admitting she was hazy on dictionary skills.

'In a tontine the members bequeath their worldly goods to the last surviving member.'

'So that would mean one of us would inherit enough to enable her to continue living indoors?' Cyn laughed. Of course, that was before Kay's film deal and the hilltop villa.

'But what about our children?'

'*Your* children, Louisa,' Kay reminded her. 'We haven't all planned to bequeath to them. As for husbands, Cyn will outlive Jeffrey and anyone she chooses to take on after that.'

'So much for my prospects,' I muttered, but Kay was too engrossed in her presentation to be distracted.

'What I'm suggesting is not a tontine but the reverse of it.'

'An enitnot?' I'm still embarrassed to have said that, as I was then when I saw Kay's nostrils draw inward.

'Despite that,' she persevered, 'I consider you three my dearest friends and the only people I truly trust.'

I was both taken aback and flattered by that designation. For an instant Louisa's face revealed pity, and Cyn's showed nothing so much as a lack of surprise.

Acknowledging none of our reactions, Kay went on. 'My suggestion is that you become my literary conservators.'

'*If* you die before we do, and, Kay . . .'

'I know, Louisa, you wouldn't want to think that. But that's not exactly what I mean.' Kay plucked the butter knife from the yellow mound and tapped her delicate forefinger against it. 'We've all seen women who've lived too long, who are formless shades held up by too-bright rouge, too-yellow hair, who look with watery eyes through holes edged thickly in black.' I remember thinking then that her words didn't sound natural but as if she were reading them off an invisible computer screen, one on which she'd been writing and rewriting. 'They've become parodies of themselves, crones they once would have laughed at.' The butter knife slipped out of her hand and clanked against the metal table. Kay looked down, surprised. It was clear she'd forgotten she was holding it. Picking up her napkin, she wiped the yellow smudge off the table, then put the knife in the salad bowl so carefully it made no sound.

There were no other sounds – no birds, no traffic noises, no hum of distant conversations. It was as if the moment and we in it were frozen, no longer alive. At the time I thought it was in reaction to the painted women clutching their decaying pasts.

Kay waited a moment to let the tension ease. 'Dreadful as it is for those women, they at least are just making spectacles of themselves to their family and friends, the people – as you say, Louisa – who love them.' She paused and looked at each one of us. Her face was dead-white, and it was the first time I noticed wrinkles crowding in on her eyes. 'Think what they would do if they wrote books. They could turn out ninety thousand words that would stamp their memories in purple, or whatever colour humiliation and ridicule wear. They would mock themselves all across the country, day after day, year after year, as long as libraries last.' She swallowed, and then had to swallow again before she could go on. 'And all that because no one cared enough to stop them.'

She drained her wineglass slowly, letting her eyelids close as she drank. No mascara, no shrieking aquamarine eye shadow. I glanced at Cyn in time to see her shiver in the sun. Louisa, sitting on a soft deck-chair with her feet under her, totally in shade, moved her hands as if to draw an imagined shawl tighter around her. The first afternoon breeze blew across my back; or maybe I've just painted that onto my memory of the scene.

When Kay opened her eyes she looked at each one of us and said in that crisp, so logical voice of hers, 'What I propose is an agreement that if any of us should be in that position the others, her dearest friends, the people she trusts the most, would save her.'

'Critique the manuscript? We already do that.' Louisa rubbed her fingers over an African leather bracelet her second daughter had sent her from wherever it was that that one lived. 'If you mean we should tell her the manuscript is a stinker, that's tough, but, well, okay. It's one of those things that has to be done.'

'But what if she doesn't believe you?' I'd asked. 'What if she decides *you*'re the one who's lost her judgement?'

'We're talking group decision, right?' Cyn was sitting up so straight, thighs so tensed that it was fifty-fifty whether she was touching the chair at all. She hated limits and discussions of limits. And criticism.

Kay leaned forward, her face now totally in the shade. Maybe it was that darkness, or maybe I'm painting over the memory, but her pale eyes seemed to be drawn back more than usual, as if she'd seen the snout of a predator halfway down her hole. 'Let's say it's my novel. You three read it. It's trash. Vivian says, "Gee, if Kay weren't so out of it she'd be humiliated to have anyone read this." Cyn agrees, "Suppose someone were willing to publish it. Unlikely, but still . . ." And, Louisa, you say in that sad way you have, "Well, we did tell her." You all agree, "But poor Kay, she can barely remember what she says from one minute to the next; she's dribbling her food down her cleavage. She's past the point of accepting sense. And you know her work is the only thing that matters to her — "'

Louisa gasped, then forced a shrug. As much as she would like to have believed Kay valued friendship — *our* friendship — more than painting a masterpiece with words, even she didn't delude herself enough to protest.

'So?' Cyn or I asked.

'So what I'm asking is that before I commit to a mistake that I — the me you now know and love — should have been sorry for, that would scar my name through eternity, or however long they might mention me in parodies of literature, you stop me. Permanently.'

Again the world seemed silent. I remember thinking that I was stunned, not so much that Kay would ask us to decide if she needed to be killed, much less to commit murder, but that she would even consider having us pass that kind of judgement on her work. It drove home to me how essential her work was to Kay — more essential than she herself.

It was a ridiculous scene — four law-abiding middle-aged

women sitting at a table discussing the fine points of a pact to kill one, or more, of us. Sometimes I can hardly believe we went on with the discussion. How many times have I replayed that scene with a different end, a sensible, happy end? But at the time, with the sun and the wine, and the repartee, Kay's pact didn't seem too odd to consider. Just a little literary insurance policy.

Before any of us could speak, Kay reached into the straw bag she always carried, pulled out a green velvet box, and laid it on the table. The velvet was a dark green, the colour you might find in an English gentleman's library. It looked wildly out of place on the white metal deck table. Kay caught her closely clipped thumbnail under one of the edges and opened the lid.

I don't know what I expected, a poison pen? A switchblade knife? Certainly not baby spoons. Four silver baby spoons lay in a row, their handles widening from the neck up so that near the top there was room for one letter to be monogrammed. L K C V (Louisa, Kay, Cyn, Vivian). Cyn laughed. It was the type of elaborate, prickly joke that was not out of character for Kay.

Kay picked up the spoon marked K and laid it down apart from the others. 'It's clear there is no other way to stop me. I've lost my marbles. My elevator no longer goes to the top floor.'

'You're paying sixty cents on the dollar,' Cyn said, in that gravelly voice. 'Your thermometer stops short of boil.'

Unconsciously Louisa sank back away from them and her brow tightened. She looked at neither Kay nor Cyn, but her expression was what one of her fictional mothers would have had hearing the exploits of an immature offspring. Then, as if to reaffirm the rules of behaviour, she proffered the wine bottle around, and ended up filling only her own glass.

Kay stared at her and then Cyn and me, much as she might control a trio of dogs. When we were still, she said, 'If, in fact, I become hopeless, I am asking you, my friends, to kill me.'

Seemingly, as an afterthought, she added, 'I assume you would want me to do the same for you.'

This was the quintessential Kay, the master of tying up all the ends.

It took another bottle of wine before we all — albeit uncomfortably — agreed to the pact. Death or doddering humiliation? If they were the only two options then what were friends for? Besides, we weren't talking about murdering a friend just because she was senile, she had to be so out of it she'd lost her judgement, yet organised enough to write a one-hundred-thousand-word book.

I had misgivings, to put it mildly, but under the circumstances, it was hard to make a case for producing drivel. And after Kay's total commitment, how embarrassing would it have been to proclaim myself happy as a clam to publish anything that would allow me to spend my declining years on the veranda of the Raffles Hotel in Singapore or a suite at the Top of the Mark in San Francisco, or even some fine nursing home that caters to your every — ever vaguer — whim. Besides, if I started to mix up the Top of the Mark with Motel 6 my friends wouldn't have to kill me to keep me out of print.

'So the question becomes how and who?' Kay went on. 'It's one thing to do your friend a favour, it's another to fry for it.' We'd all laughed then. Clearly, Kay intended to leave no thread hanging. I remember smiling to myself, thinking how ridiculous to imagine that Kay would ever need someone else to make her decisions. I wondered which of us she was really eyeing as the likely incompetent. But I couldn't imagine her deciding a diminution of anyone's work but her own would really matter much.

Louisa drained her wineglass. Cyn perched on her chair, arms clasped around her knees like a kid. I leaned back in the half-shade. Life was beginning to take on that open-ended feeling that an afternoon of sun and wine brings. The pact began to look like a diverting puzzle.

'So we have a little ceremony,' Kay continued. 'We've always liked ceremonies. By this time the recipient – shall we go on saying it is I? – knows she has created dreck.'

'You mean she knows her *friends* think she's created it,' Cyn reminded her.

'Right. At that point I'll know you all scorn my penultimate novel. You'll all have discussed it with me, doubtless at much greater length than I'll want. I'll be appalled. But in the end I'll trust you. If I trust you with this pact, I'll certainly trust you to show literary judgement. So I'll come to lunch, and when we've finished the last shrimp in the salad, polished off the heel of the french bread, when we're sitting here drinking wine just as we are now, one of you – say, you, Vivian – will take out the box. You'll open it. Inside all three of your spoons will be lying just as they are now, bowl down, monogram down. But mine will be reversed, bowl up, monogram showing. I'll look. I won't believe it.' Kay pantomimed her expected horror, eyes and mouth snapping open, hands flying up. But no one laughed. 'Then I remove one of your spoons – it doesn't matter which one – I mix the others, and put them back, bowl down, monogram hidden. One of those three, of course, is mine. I hand the box to each of you in turn and you pick one, keeping the monogram hidden.' She paused till Cyn, Louisa, and I nodded in acknowledgement. 'The one who gets my spoon kills me.'

It was a moment before Louisa said, 'But why the elaborate ceremony?'

'Because, my friend, this way none of you knows who the killer will be. If there's an investigation, the innocent two can't rat on the guilty.'

Cyn glared. 'Thanks a lot.'

Kay laughed and I and then Louisa, and finally even Cyn couldn't help but laugh, too. Ratting was one of the cardinal sins in Cyn's characters' creeds of life. A rat never makes it to the top of Everest. No brass ring for the rat.

There was more discussion, of course. What if the appointed victim was in her right mind but the rest of us went crazy? Odds of that were small. It was worth the risk, Kay insisted. What if the killer tried to carry out her sworn duty, and failed? We talked 'What If's' the rest of the afternoon. And in the next week we must have made sixty phone calls among the four of us. We ended up having dinner the following Monday and it was there that we did finally agree. Now, of course, our handling of the whole thing seems ridiculously cavalier, but at that time death was an unlikely possibility and the idea that anyone would be clamouring to publish an opus of ours that even we found wanting was much less conceivable.

But, in fact, three of Kay's last four books topped the bestseller lists. Critics raved. (And none of these even was her oft-returned-to so-well-polished manuscript still in her drawer.) The books went into fourth and fifth printings. They were translated into French, Spanish, German, Japanese, Norwegian, and languages spoken in places that weren't countries a few years ago. Kay was interviewed on 'Oprah' twice.

Kay had changed by then. Her eyes had sunk farther into the sockets and she'd come to look more like a cornered possum. Those hollows in her cheeks had sagged, the sharp edges of her face dulled, and her observations had changed from rapier blades to gnarled kitchen knives that rasped rather than cut.

She'd moved away from interruption and people, to a house atop a mountain – not a hill but a full-size mountain. The view was great. The privacy was unparalleled, because Kay bought the entire mountain. An unpaved winding one-lane road led up to the gate. But the road washed out with the first heavy rain of winter, leaving her with a whole lot more privacy than I would have found appealing. Even now – when I find myself living with women I would never have chosen as housemates, women who are rarely quiet, and never interesting – Kay's four-month regimen of breaking her fast with dry cereal and powdered milk, closing the day with canned tuna dinners, and no company to look forward to but her own doesn't sound good. But – Cyn, Louisa, and I laughed – surely there she'd finally finish the great manuscript.

The only way up Kay's mountain in the winter was a steep, wet, treacherously slippery, two-mile climb worthy of a Sherpa. Not a prospect to attract visitors, even friends as close as we were. But as Kay said, we cherish our rituals. It was this climb that Cyn made every winter to prove to herself she was still in shape and to experience something of what her latest heroine, an Everest conqueror, might.

Laughingly, Cyn commented that *My Ascent to Kay Washburn's* was as close as she was going to come to the great book dropping in her lap.

Not to be left out of this ritual, Louisa and I created a ceremony to herald Cyn's departure. Louisa made a casserole of Kay's favourites: smoked salmon with fresh vegetables Kay hadn't tasted in weeks. She packed it in Cyn's backpack, along with chocolate bars to keep Cyn going on her climb. At the top, Kay was waiting with hot bath for Cyn, hot oven for the casserole, and plenty of brandy for after dinner. What this meant was that Cyn's descent the next day was frequently more harrowing than her climb. But at the bottom, I completed the ceremony with more brandy and a massage technique I'd learned in Bali.

The trek before last, Cyn said Kay seemed distracted, forgetful, her words out of focus. For the first time Cyn had gone to bed, not exhilarated from the climb, the dinner, and the repartee, but exhausted from her vain effort to get a clear picture of what Kay was saying.

Even so when Kay sent us that last manuscript we were

shocked. After we'd all read it, it was two days before Cyn finally said in uncharacteristic understatement, 'It's not top drawer.' Another day and a half and a bottle of wine passed, and I admitted, 'It's not even in the dresser.'

Then the question of censorship arose. Who were we to pass judgement on Kay's work? If Kay liked it, maybe her readers would, maybe . . . If this was the great manuscript, all those years of polishing had rubbed it down to dross. It was not merely a bad book. It was a bad book, written in a pompous and blowzy style. In it her characters ridiculed all her previous work. And worse yet, ours. There was no chance it would slip quickly into the ditch of well-deserved oblivion. By then a grocery list with Kay's name on it would have been literary news. The world would have gobbled it down. And then spit it back up. Kay's worst nightmare. And, in this case, ours.

The manuscript, alas, fit perfectly into Kay's pact.

We stopped talking about the merits of the book and focused on the pact. The three of us hashed over our decision, trying to find an escape clause that we knew didn't exist. Kay never left loose ends. But still we had to try. You don't decide to commit your first murder, to kill one of your best friends, who disagrees with your decision, when you are not going to inherit her newfound wealth, or even have access to the amenities it provided, without a lot of thought. When Kay died we would lose not only her and her wonderful house to lunch in, but the lunches left to the survivors were hardly a cheerful prospect, to say nothing of the considerable tension we'd feel every time we finished a manuscript.

We suggested to Kay we quash the pact, but Kay insisted it was still valid. There was no give in her position, no wit in her arguments. Kay was impatient. She snapped at Cyn when she disagreed, at me when I criticised her pact. It was Louisa, who'd been the most reluctant about the agreement all along, who finally said to Cyn and me, 'If Kay can't stand criticism of this little ritual of hers, how will she ever live through the reviews she'll get for this book? She'll kill herself. And that will start another round of gossip. In the end her work will be overshadowed by her bizarre death, speculation about it. And she'll be as dead as if we'd gone ahead with the pact and killed her ourselves.'

There was no other choice but to kill her.

It pains me to recall Kay's reaction when I presented her with the green velvet box. I don't know whether it was merely shock, or disbelief that it should be she who ended up on the receiving end of her own pact. She must have had suspicions, after all the discussion and reconsideration of the pact. But, clearly, it had not occurred to her that we found her book so awful we were invoking the pact. But once she did realise that, she pulled herself together and for the first time that day looked like the Kay of old. She never lowered herself to defend her book, much less herself. If there's one thing I'm certain of, it's that if Kay Washburn couldn't write her kind of novel she had nothing to live for.

We drank champagne that day. Kay must have downed a bottle by herself before she opened the green velvet case. Still, her hands shook as she removed one engraved spoon and laid the others bowl-down for us to choose. Purposely, I didn't look at Cyn or Louisa when we drew spoons. I forced myself not to sigh when I checked mine and realised it was not the one with the K, that I would not be Kay's killer.

The next day I considered my options and chose the most cowardly course. I booked a flight to Bali, and spent the following month in that appallingly flea-ridden nunnery. Tempting ringworm, I walked barefoot under the gaze of the Mother Superior, spent days scrubbing outhouses, nights sleeping on a hard pallet. Never once was I free of bugs, busy work, or penitents. After a week I stopped mourning Kay; after two weeks I gave up worrying about Cyn or Louisa. After a month I just wished whichever of them had gotten the damned spoon would get on with her job and let me get out of here. (And, being a writer, I have to admit the thought did occur to me that there wasn't even a chance of writing any kind of article on this place, unless I was doing it for *Microbiology Monthly*.) But the Mother Superior would provide me an unshakable alibi. It wasn't till I got word of Kay's obituary that I flew home.

Needless to say, my trip didn't ingratiate me with Cyn and Louisa. And when the police realised that Kay had been poisoned by eating a casserole made of salmon, corn, potatoes, and enough *amanita viroza balinii* mushrooms to kill a football team, things began to look bad for Louisa.

Amanita viroza, or destroying angel mushrooms, were the method one of those literary daughters of hers had used to dispatch her overbearing mother.

The police surrounded Louisa like blowflies on a corpse. She was terrified. And I was terrified for her. (Especially after my own show of cowardice.) But not so terrified as I soon would be when those same police discovered that the only place *amanita viroza balinii* grow is in Bali.

Blowflies are quite willing to move onto fresher meat. And it was all I could do to convince the police that my old car was hardly in any shape to make it up Kay's hillside in February. Nor, for that matter, was I.

It took them another week to discover Cyn's ritual climb to Kay's retreat, and to posit me giving the mushrooms to Louisa, Louisa adding the salmon, corn, potatoes to the ritual casserole and packing them in Cyn's backpack, and Cyn mountaineering up with her deadly load.

It did stretch credulity to imagine Kay sitting down with one of her murderesses to eat a dish she had delivered. But, of course, I couldn't tell the detective that – not without exposing the pact and making the three of us look a helluva lot more suspicious than we already did.

As it turned out more suspicious would not have been possible. I proved I was out of the country, Cyn swore she hadn't made the trek up the mountain in a year, and Louisa insisted she didn't make the casserole, adding rather charmingly I thought that she would be humiliated to cook with canned corn. It took a jury less than an hour to find us guilty of murder and conspiracy to commit same. The judge had no hesitation about incarcerating us for an unpleasant number of years.

I've been here for two already. Louisa and Cyn are at other ladies' establishments, so, presumably, we won't conspire again. I suppose this place isn't bad as prisons go. Physically, it's better than the nunnery in Bali – no fleas, or outhouses. But every day for the first year I swore I would put up with a camel–load of fleas to get revenge on Cyn or Louisa.

I spent that year alternately trying to figure out which of them was the culprit, and silently berating her selfishness. Could Cyn or Louisa have expropriated some of my Balinese mushrooms? Of course. Could Cyn have cooked the casserole? No chance. Cyn's culinary skills peaked at the can opener. Could Louisa have driven the casserole up the mountain before the snow? No way. And more to the point, Kay would never have eaten it.

The pact was supposed to be foolproof. Kay was a master at tying up loose ends.

Kay had told us that she'd given a lot of thought to the mechanics of our agreement to protect the innocent from endangering the guilty. But, in fact, it was the guilty who'd done in the innocent.

It took me almost the entire next year to realise the truth, the miserable, stinging truth of the only one who could have killed Kay.

We'd all thought of writing *Me and Kay Washburn's Murder*.

I'd envisioned it as the travelogue up to Kay's body. Cyn, I'm sure, had imagined it as the trek to same. And Louisa, a sort of Last Supper, with corpse and recipes.

Louisa would never have gone to print with corn from a can.

I'd like to think it was because Kay changed her mind and saw the wisdom of our decision. But my suspicion is that what she saw was the inevitability of the pact she had instituted. She knew one of us would kill her, so she took the mushrooms, opened cans of salmon and corn, cubed the potatoes she had up there with her, cooked the casserole, and she ate it. And as she lay there dying she must have been smiling at the irony of it all.

I'd like to think that. But the truth is that from the beginning she planned her death and our conspiracy in it. How do I know? Kay's great manuscript, the one she kept polishing all those years, was just published. It is stunning. The characters are, if not flattering, definitely Louisa, Cyn, and me to a T. And none of us will have to scramble to sell our version of *Me and Kay Washburn's Death Pact*, because Kay's brilliantly written book is the final word on it.

Pikeman and the Bagwoman
Dale Gunthorp

Monday 3 February

Friday's diary entry was wrong: I am *not* out of range of the Littlejohn redundancy list. I'm in the line, maybe in the first row. Evidence? Benedict Littlejohn has taken Pikeman away from me.

From this day, Frances Preston is no longer editor of the City's top crime thrillers. She is no more midwife of Pikeman's annual offspring, public voice of the mystery author believed to be at least Chairman of Barings Bank. She is out of the game of billion-dollar fraud in the Square Mile, ejected from the dog-eat-dog society where everybody down to the post-boy is coining it, where nobody has enough honour even to be sleuth, and only the rapacity of greed brings things crashing down.

My life is utterly changed. Yet the change itself was a little thing, just casual seconds of chat. Littlejohn paused at my desk, in passing, and suggested that I let Marketing 'have a go' at the new Pikeman manuscript; Marketing 'has this sense' of what readers want. I noted my place with a pencil, tamped the sheets into a neat stack, and gave him the file. His cufflinks clinked, almost nervously, as if he'd been expecting me to hit him over the head with it. Then he thanked me for the excellent work I'd done, without looking at what that was, and clinked off. For an entire hour afterwards, I sat there, unable to think of anything to do. It was terrifying.

Tant pis, Frances Preston! Every Littlejohn employee is waiting for the bottom line on the Takeover – redundancy. I reckoned Pikeman's editor would be immune. What I didn't reckon was that Pikeman's editor could be someone who wasn't me. This is good news. So why does it depress me?

I won't analyse, for the umpteenth time, why I'd like to go. I won't agonise over how guilty I felt to think I was on dry land when colleagues (no matter how little I care for them) are drowning; won't repeat what I could do with a redundancy package to finance twelve months of freedom; won't even think about the sort of place Littlejohn will be when nobody thinks a book is more than 'product', or sees more to editing than running a spellcheck. What would I want with that species of publishing that consists of Marketing, Design and pickling the judgement of critics in cheap champagne and oysters?

Pikeman doesn't matter to me. If I ever met him, I'd loathe him, as I loathe all his kind. Our relationship consists of little notes ('I *meant* that split infinitive when Johnson sees the bloodstained handprint in the urinal – restore.') For this, and some poor glory reflected from the bestseller list, I give up the best hours of my day, and the best years of my life.

You made this bed, Frances Preston, so lie on it. You've been in this job ten years, to pass the time and pay the rent till the real thing came along. And now your dreaded fortieth is in prospect and what have you to show? Have you mended the leak in the bathroom ceiling? Where's the cat you've wanted for a decade? Why don't you curl your hair, join a singles club; do something? What does it tell you about yourself that the one positive thing that happened today is that you saw a bagwoman?

The Bagwoman. This is her first mention in the diary, though she's been in my world for months. She was on the train again tonight, in my compartment. She gets on at London Bridge. She doesn't sit until an end seat is vacant. She stares out at the racks of office windows, glowing like maturing cheeses, and is staring into the dark when I get off at Lewisham.

Can't remember now when I first became aware of her. These days, I seem to wait for her, as one would wait on an omen. Our first exchange was her sharp hiss when I caught the edge of her shopping trolley with my umbrella. Then she became a discomforting presence – eyes like melting icecubes in the sagging depths of a bundle of old clothes. Last night, I connected: Bagwoman takes the same train, same carriage, same seat; is a person of regular habits. She is like me. This disturbs me. Tomorrow, if she gets my train, I'll drop a coin, maybe even a pound, into her trolley. Sort her out.

Tuesday 4 February

I have a new role, company bouncer. Littlejohn's secretary brought me a great heap of unsoliciteds. 'Benedict wants you to take a glance and send the usual rejection slip.'

Why does *this* depress me? For heaven's sake, I don't want to stay in that place. I don't respect it. Maybe I just don't want to think that my ten years' labour on trashy manuscripts is itself trash. Maybe, on the other hand, I just like being miserable.

However, I did see the Bagwoman, and somehow that cheered me. I even kept her in view, preparing myself to respond to a glance from the melting icecube eyes. She ignored me. However, I observe that she is not old: her hands are chapped, callused and grubby rather than arthritic. Her eyes are too pale and watery for clear vision, but they're loose with despair rather than age. She may not be much older than me. This I do not like. But I had decided what to do, and I did it. I tipped the contents of my purse into my pocket, and left it to impulse to decide what to drop on my way out.

Don't know what effect it had on her, but it was a shock to me to realise that I'd given her a £20 note. Now I'm suffering. My whole week's food allowance! She'll spend it in one night drinking herself blind. Worse, £20 is what Pikeman's crudest villains leave on mantelpieces. I shall take a different train tomorrow.

Wednesday 5 February
I was right about the redundancy. Littlejohn has decided to 'centralise' the Pikeman files. I bundled up all the documentation on schedules, contracts, foreign rights, even Pikeman's little notes explaining the difference between options, derivatives and futures; why asset stripping is acceptable form but insider dealing is not. I came across his formulation, scribbled on the back of a flyer advertising health insurance, of the First Law of Finance: 'wealth is created out of goods by producing more of them; but wealth can only be made out of money by taking it off someone else.' Another said: 'people read crime novels to persuade themselves that only law-breakers are wicked.' I wanted to weep. I didn't know it till now, but he mattered to me. He was so clever about power and fear and why people are greedy, and so obstinate about split infinitives, but he trusted me to sort out the difference between 'there' and 'their', and to know when to put an apostrophe in 'its'.

Why am I being negative? I want freedom. I want to get up late, spend a whole day watching the daisies grow, take myself off whenever I like to walk the cliffs of Cornwall. I want to sort out my bookshelves, put all the novels in alphabetical order of author. I want to learn Russian. I want to play the flute. I want a cat. If I were free I could even, if I wanted to, do voluntary work with derelicts like my Bagwoman. All the things I want to do I can do if I don't have that chain of work round my neck.

So, if it's redundancy, then my only concern is with the size of the package. A bit dumb, not so, to lash out £20 on someone who didn't even say thank you? To avoid Bagwoman, I travelled in the front coach of the train.

Thursday 6 February

Tonight I have almost nothing to say, except that I broke the hearts of another dozen would-be Pikemans, then left early to avoid Bagwoman. It rained all day. The damp patch on the bathroom ceiling is turning mottled black.

Friday 7 February

Today I was so depressed I couldn't even enjoy it being Friday. On autopilot, I got on at Charing Cross and only when the train slid into London Bridge did I remember Bagwoman. I didn't want to see her. I didn't want to face her awkward thanks, or grumpy non-thanks for a whole week of my food money. If she is an omen, she is a bad one. So, when we stopped at London Bridge, I fixed my gaze on the laser-printed text of a manuscript I will reject on Monday.

But, she got on and there was an end seat only two places from mine. I was going to have to squeeze past her on my way out. I glanced at her, working out my escape route. She was staring with hostility at the manuscript on my lap. Approaching Lewisham, I slunk towards the door. She looked up. I was staring into melting icecubes. She opened her mouth. I charged for the exit. But when the train had gone and the platform was quiet, her words were still in my ears:

'Excuse me, madam, if I may . . .' Bagwoman has the perfect teeth of a Tory wife, and her voice is pure BBC World Service.

Now, as I sit over beans that have sprouted with more enthusiasm for this world than can possibly be appropriate and wonder how I can be so cruel as to eat them, I think about this woman. What brought her down? One week ago, I could think: 'there but for the grace of god'; today I wonder if she, not so long ago, used to edit financial crime thrillers, and I wonder how long that grace will be there for me.

Monday 10 February

What is wrong with my mental state right now that I could do nothing at all with the weekend, couldn't even write my diary? If staring would repair a bathroom ceiling, mine would be tight as a ship. I am falling apart. They say redundancy does this to you; if so, God knows what will happen when it actually comes to pass.

At work today, nothing happened. And even that bothered me. Littlejohn clinked past my desk, and back again. I sat there, waiting for him to say something nasty, which didn't happen. Then I sat there worrying about why he was avoiding me. When he paused to complain to Jennifer about the weather, I was in torment.

So I was in no fit state for a put-down from Bagwoman. She got on the train. She eyed me; it was uncomfortable. Then, as I got up at Lewisham, she gripped me with that icy glance. 'You left this behind on Wednesday.' And she thrust at me my £20 note.

I don't need food money. My only use for an oven is somewhere to put my head.

I tried to do something about my mental state. I switched on the television, but couldn't bear all those busy, important people, getting on with their important lives. I begin to envy Bagwoman for the solace she finds in drink. I'm so feeble I can't

even do that: anything beyond a Babycham makes me feel
woozy and then sick. So I had a long bath, and lay contemplat-
ing the stain on the ceiling. It is spreading. Eventually, it will
swallow up the bath, and me in it. I could find comfort in this
thought.

Tuesday 11 February

Today I began my preparations for extinction. I took down
the frieze of book jackets pinned up round my desk, and put
them in a drawer. I put my penholder, Garfield figurines and
emergency cardigan in a plastic bag. Then I looked at the
bookshelves. Anything in those rows of file copies worth
keeping? I've edited better writers than Pikeman, and there's
almost nothing in Pikeman's world I can identify with, but I
put half-a-dozen Pikemans in my bag.

This must have brought me some change of luck. Because
Littlejohn's secretary dropped Pikeman's MS back on my desk.
'Benedict wants you to look at this,' she said. I could have
wept.

Then I did weep. Tucked into the correspondence at the
bottom of the folder was a fax from Pikeman, dated today,
saying that he wanted me (Me!) to check it. Pikeman *values*
me.

I'd read the MS before, of course, but this time I *really* read
it. The story is totally brilliant. It beats Agatha Christie for
precision of clues, Hemingway for macho suspense, Dickens
for insight into human motivation. I have never devoured a
manuscript so greedily. I couldn't be parted from it, and it
came home with me. I was re-reading it on the train, laughing
and mumbling to myself like a bagwoman, when Bagwoman
got on. She sort of winked. I was embarrassed.

When the train stopped at Blackheath, during the exit
scuffle of striped navy suits, umbrellas and briefcases, she
pinned me with the points of her washed-out eyes. 'What so

amuses you about that manuscript?'

It was a shock – not her World Service voice – the aggression in her. I reacted as I would to a flasher. I slammed the folder shut and went cold. Out of some protectiveness, I put my hand over the 'Pikeman' written in two-inch capitals on the cover. 'It's quite good,' I muttered. What I meant was: 'give me time to work out what you are in relation to me so that I can find a safe way for us to communicate.'

'It is rubbish,' she said, giving the 'r' a headmistress snarl.

The authority in her voice overwhelmed me. Instantly, I had doubts about whether Pikeman was as good as he seemed. But only for a second. I collected my wits and analysed the speaker rather than the speech. Bagwoman knew Pikeman's work and had views on financial crime thrillers. This bagwoman was not a complete wreck.

If I had been dealing with an equal, I would have defended Pikeman, said that he had developed his populist style because he wanted to reach everybody, that his cynicism was in part a joke at the expense of expense-account readers, in part protest; that he was a master of his chosen genre, and had a message – that the world should not be a place where cruelty and wickedness are allowed to triumph. But I was brought up not to talk to strangers, and any woman living alone in London knows why. Also to know that when dealing with someone unknown and possibly dangerous – as all outsiders must be till proven otherwise – one does not engage in argument; it allows the other to respond. So, if they attack, you back off, leave no opening for violence or abuse. 'I take your point,' I said, holding on to the folder on my lap.

3 a.m., Wednesday 12 February
Woke with the most hideous shock. I suddenly got it: Bagwoman is Pikeman. Pikeman is Bagwoman. How have I not recognised this before? When I'd cleared my panic with a

mug of tea, two scenarios became possible.

Scenario 1: Bagwoman is Pikeman in disguise. Pikeman's current joke is to trail his desk editor while she's working on his text. That's why he made Littlejohn give me back the MS. I will appear as some half-wit in the next MS. Pikeman is exploiting me and mocking me.

Scenario 2: Pikeman is Bagwoman in disguise. Pikeman's novels are actually written by this woman, maybe eccentric, maybe genuinely mad. She dresses like a tramp because she likes to feel invisible, and spends her days snooping around London Bridge, the *Financial Times*, Lloyds and the Stock Exchange, picking up snippets of gossip from the idiots in pinstripe suits. She was genuinely amused to stumble on the editor of her texts, and maybe she even rather likes me. If Pikeman is Bagwoman, Pikeman himself is one of Pikeman's best jokes.

Now I must really try to get some sleep.

Wednesday 12 February, the usual evening entry
What a day! Whether I'm Pikeman's ally or Pikeman's dupe, I was exhausted but inspired. Marketing's committee has produced a blurb for the new Pikeman. It says he's 'slick', 'fast' and 'funny', the City's biggest mole. It was written out of the dictionary of clichés. No committee could understand Pikeman, recognise the greatest satirist since Jonathan Swift, the greatest writer of melodrama since Daphne du Maurier. In fury, I wrote another blurb. It's the best I've ever done. When I was through, I knew which of my two scenarios was the real Pikeman: Pikeman is a woman, and she is my friend. I faxed it to her directly.

At lunch time, I was still re-touching this blurb. It got longer. Within the hour, I could see there was a big story here; I had the germ of a biography.

But no Bagwoman on my train tonight. No matter, she is so present in my mind it would be almost disappointing to have

an ordinary real-life conversation with her. Anyway, I couldn't
show her my draft. I'm nowhere near ready for a battle over
split infinitives.

Must rush this diary entry, as I have a thousand new ideas
for the biography.

Friday 14 February
No time for diary over past two days – just rush home and
write. Alas, no sign of Bagwoman. I even got out at London
Bridge to search for her.

What an amazing place London Bridge Station is. Heaps of
builders' rubble, ineffectually screened by the kind of plastic
tape they use to mark off pile-ups on the motorway. Long dark
brick-lined dripping tunnels, identified by a few collapsing
signposts giving wrong information, leading to cold windy
platforms where lost souls await orders from crackling
electronic noticeboards. This place, only a stone's throw from
the postmodernist City plated with gold, is a vast sewer
swarming with human rats. Some clip by armed with furled
umbrellas, some totter on chilblained feet swathed in strips of
old blankets. Bagwoman's station.

I see it so clearly now, how she hovers, hands clutched round
a cup of polystyrene coffee, eavesdropping on the City's dark
secrets, creating the characters for her novels. I've had curious
insights, too, into the rest of her life. She stays on that slow train
all the way to her ramshackle house in Rye. She spends
evenings at her kitchen table, her computer perched between
big sleepy cats, while her Aga cooker purrs, and she laughs and
drinks, recalling the folly of the City, and pushes another cat off
the keyboard to write. Very late, she goes to bed, lighting her
way with a candle. She has little use for baths, but does enjoy
her bathroom. It is a grotto festooned with fungoid growths
over the ceiling and walls, sprouting flowers of iridescent
orange and purple, rich as shot silk. I hugely admire her.

Sunday night
I spent the entire weekend on Bagwoman's story. I wasn't
writing it. I was transcribing something given to me. She was
christened Monica Geraldine. Her younger brother, who
inherited the family estate, is a total pig. He works in the City,
making fortunes (for himself) and losing them (for other
people). Bowler hat pulled over his eyes, he passes her twice a
day, at London Bridge Station. Every time she sees him, she
laughs. I have written almost 50,000 words.

Friday 28 February
Pikeman has rejected Marketing's blurb in favour of mine. I
wanted to be gracious about it, but couldn't keep the 3-foot
grin off my face when I showed the fax to Littlejohn. Pikeman
and I are now in regular communication. I haven't yet broken
the news that I am writing her life, but we are having a
thrilling contretemps about the subjunctive. I wonder if she
realises that I am falling in love with her.

The redundancy notices came out today. Jennifer got hers
and went home in tears. I didn't get mine. So I barged in on
Littlejohn (Bagwoman has made me bold) to complain. He,
looking astonished, said I was staying on, to be the core of a
new department, Creative Editorial. My main job would be to
invent future Pikemans.

I demurred. My only wish now is time to finish Bagwoman's biography, but to do that, I need the redundancy
package. Pikeman's spirit directed me: I resigned. I hope she
knows what she's doing with me. She's made me leave empty-
handed. She'd better have a good stack of £20 notes.

Friday 14 March
Pikeman's new novel went off to the printers today, but I have
two more weeks at Littlejohn. Jennifer and the other
redundancees may leave at their convenience, but I must serve

my notice. So I shall spend my last fortnight working on Bagwoman's biography. Littlejohn seems to think I'm doing something for the firm. Wrong! They're not even going to have the chance to bid for Bagwoman's story. He also asked me to reconsider my resignation, to call him Benedict, and to allow him to organise a farewell party for me. I've become sociable these days, and agreed to the third request.

But something is missing in my life. Bagwoman has avoided me ever since I started on her biography. I languish for those icecube eyes, that World Service voice, the shopping trolley. I'm tempted to fax the entire draft biography to her, but modesty restrains me. It is just too brilliant. I can see now exactly how she caused the stock exchange crash of 1987.

Friday 28 March
My last day. The draft of the biography (these days I call it a novel) is done. In six months, or maybe less, I'll have a showable text.

Then came the party: most of the redundancees turned up, looking miserable since none of them has found another job. Jennifer says she's taken to drink, and proved it by jabbing a pineapple at Littlejohn's crotch.

I was feeling a bit crazy myself, and got talking to a City man. Predictable: tall, skinny and overbred; looks sixty and is probably forty; fob-watch, hair in lank grey strands; sticks out his jaw and runs his finger round the inside of his starched collar as he talks. Littlejohn introduced him as Lord Buccleach, partner in de Hoeg's Bank, owner of half a county. I've read too much Pikeman to be impressed by his sort, so I teased him in a patronising sort of way, asking him if his job was as interesting as mine.

He isn't a cheerful conversationalist. Said, no, his job was hard, boring and very stressful. Money excites people, he said, and so people think they love it, when in fact they are terrified of it, and he was one particularly easily scared. He added that it was only some scribbling he did on the side that kept him sane.

We got talking about Pikeman. I was impressed by the extent of his knowledge of Pikeman's work, but disappointed by its lack of depth. 'That stuff's all right, as entertainment,' he muttered. 'Real crime is deeper; it arises out of the way things are set up. Real crime is what is happening at Littlejohn.'

I hastened to point out the amazing moral subtlety of Pikeman's social analysis. On each point, he scratched at his collar and said, 'Well, I never thought of that,' or 'I suppose it can bear that interpretation.' I came close to telling him about the Pikeman biography.

Just as well I didn't. Because when I said he ought to re-read all the early Pikemans, he said, 'I'm not sure I like them now. Once they possessed me in a mad infatuation – but only while I was writing them.'

In shock, I downed an entire glass of red wine. My face was burning, my lips were numb, and I was deprived of the power of speech.

He took my hand. 'Latterly, Miss Preston,' he said, 'I think I've been writing them for you. With your departure from Littlejohn, I shall have lost my Muse.' His eyes, till then glinting like hard-frozen icecubes, began to soften. Fazed as I was, I recognised these phrases: all Pikeman's gentleman fraudsters long for a muse, a guardian angel, some moral force in the form of a loving woman.

Was this possible? Could I transfer my passion to a different Pikeman? I looked at his professionally shaved jutting chin, and thought of my Bagwoman's grief-ridden eyes, and knew I could not. 'I'm sorry,' I said, 'but I am not and never will be the person you want me to be.'

He stayed on for another half-hour, chatting languidly to Littlejohn (not Benedict, of course, Big Daddy Littlejohn), and

though I truly was sorry, I didn't wish to recant. Bagwoman is
my mind's freedom, and Buccleach would be its gaoler – not
because he is a bad person but because of the way things are
set up.

After the party, and tiddly for the first time in my life, I
scoured London Bridge Station. There were tramps, rough
sleepers, junkies and drunks by the score, but she wasn't there.
But she wouldn't be, half an hour after midnight; she'd be
wherever it is she goes on the 6.30 train. Whoever she is, I will
finish her biography, because I'm writing it for her, it's the life
that might have been hers, if life itself weren't set up on crime.
I'll get a fancy publisher (anybody but Littlejohn) and then I'll
track her down. I'll follow her when she leaves the train, and
at the right moment, approach her. Perhaps she'll be with a
knot of winos, at a wasteland fire; perhaps holding court at a
Salvation Army hostel. I shall invite her and all her friends to
the launch of her book. And I'll be disappointed if she doesn't
call it rubbish.

Luisa
Christina Lee

I lost touch with Louise after we left school. Yes, I know I should call her Luisa, but I still think of her as Louise. No, I never asked about the new name. It didn't seem polite, like bringing up some awfully embarrassing thing that someone did when they were twelve. Anyway, she did Arts at Sydney Uni and I was going out to Lidcombe every day for the physio course, and we just never saw each other. When I met her again she was Luisa.

It was at Jacquie and Belinda's party. I'd actually met Jacquie as a patient. Lateral ligament, left ankle, quite a nasty sprain. It's a classic netball injury but in her case it was line dancing. I'd never even heard of it then, can you believe? Well, I'd led a pretty sheltered life. The physio course was pretty demanding, and then when you graduated it was all shift work and long hours and you tended only to socialise with other physios. That's how I met Mark, of course. Physios are very nice people but I suppose Jacquie would say we're a bit straight. Certainly we seemed to live in a different world from her and Belinda.

I don't usually socialise with patients, but Jacquie was lovely and it turned out that she and her friend Belinda lived just around the corner. And the ankle had healed up beautifully, she wasn't an ongoing case or anything. Besides, most of a physio's patients are about ninety, people tend to think we spend our days treating football players for groin injuries and massaging Olympic swimmers and so on, but in fact it's mostly strokes, and rheumatoid arthritis, and post-surgical. So Jacquie made a nice change. She used to giggle if it hurt and tell me funny stories about her job and her flatmate and so on. Which certainly made a change.

So I said yes, we'd love to come, though I was a bit doubtful about how Mark would take it, going to a party with a bunch of people we didn't know. In the end, though, he had a marvellous time, even though − well − I know I should have twigged after all the stories Jacquie had told me about Belinda this and Belinda that and the things they did together, trekking in Nepal and backpacking in Europe and all the rest of it. But as I said, I do lead a fairly conventional life and it really wasn't until we got to the party and they were standing there arm-in-arm that I realised.

I mean, it's not like I'd never met a gay person or anything. Now I come to think of it, I'm sure a couple of the girls in my year were lesbians. But you didn't talk about that sort of thing, so I suppose it never occurred to me. I don't really see why it should be such a big thing, I mean you're there to do a job and what you do in your own time is your own business, isn't it?

Anyway, Mark took it all in his stride. He kissed them both on the hand and turned on the smile and in about two seconds they were running around finding him a glass of champagne and taking his new distressed leather jacket off to the coat heap in the bedroom and introducing him to people left, right and centre.

So I turned around and there was Louise. Of course she'd

changed a lot. When we were at school she had long bunches
of fat white ringlets and lots of pimples. Now she was very
tanned and athletic-looking, and she had a sophisticated
cropped haircut and one of those short slim little dresses that
just yelled at you that here was a girl who grew up on the
North Shore and whose daddy gave her a monthly clothing
allowance.

'Jane,' she said to me. 'What a surprise. Have you got a
drink?'

So she got me a drink and we caught up on what had
happened to us. For me, of course, it was pretty simple, physio,
six months working in London, back here to marry Mark and
a job at the Prince of Wales. For her, as you might have
expected, there was rather more to tell, and I must confess that
I never really did get the whole story straight. The arts degree,
yes, but all the sailing in the Med with Jean Paul and skiing at
Val d'Isere with Claudio and the study exchange in Padua and
the part-time job in Seville got a bit complicated. Anyway she
said she was a freelance writer, which confirmed my suspicion
that her daddy was paying her an allowance, and she lived in
the flat next door and knew Jacquie and Belinda from a
publishing party. Most of the people at this party were in
publishing or writing, because Jacquie is an editor at a big
publishing house and Belinda tutors in Creative Writing, so of
course most of their friends are writers and things.

Well, after we'd got all that sorted out, she looked over my
shoulder and asked me to introduce her to Mark because she
was really looking forward to talking to someone who wasn't
a friend of Dorothy's for a change. I didn't know Dorothy
either, and I was going to say so. But she was the sort of
woman who, when she said 'someone', you knew that other
women didn't count.

So I took her over to Mark and she held out her hand and
said, 'Hi, I'm Luisa.' That was the first I heard of this Luisa

business, and I was going to ask, but just then Jacquie came bouncing up and dragged me off to look at the knee of a friend who'd fallen off his high heels. And the friend's knee turned out to be perfectly all right, he just wanted a photo of himself in drag having his leg massaged. So we had a lot of champagne and he and his friend kept taking photos of people doing outrageous things, which made them do even more outrageous things, and next time I looked at my watch it was half past one and we had to go.

Mark was still talking to Louise, and he kept saying how wonderful it was that she and I had met up again after so long and we would have to keep in touch, and the friend with the knee took a photo of me hugging Louise and another of Mark and Jacquie drinking champagne out of each other's glasses. It wasn't at all the sort of party we usually go to.

Well I dropped over a couple of days later with some flowers to say thank you, and Louise was there, sitting at the kitchen table drinking peppermint tea, and I wound up staying talking for hours. After that it just became a habit. I had a early shift most Wednesdays and Mark was hardly ever home, he had a private sports physio business as well as the hospital job, so there was nothing much to hurry home for.

I would buy a few Hungarian cakes and then go to Jacquie and Belinda's. We'd have tea and cakes, and then they'd sit at the kitchen table writing or talking and I'd cook and then we'd all eat. Luisa wasn't there all that often after the first time, and usually she didn't stay long if she was. She said she was very busy on a writing project, but Jacquie said that she had been saying that ever since she moved in next door and as far as she knew Luisa had never published anything.

They talked a lot about books. Belinda wrote short stories and reviews and magazine articles, and she always had stacks of creative writing exercises to mark, and of course both of them read all the time. It was very different from our place, we had a lot of books too but of course they were mostly anatomy textbooks and things like that.

One week, Belinda asked me if I'd read a story she had just had published in a short-story magazine. She'd never shown me anything she'd written before and I was quite flattered to be asked. So I sat there and tried to concentrate while she pottered around the kitchen making curry.

It was about a physiotherapist called Madeleine who falls in love with a patient, who's a woman, but the woman's got this great boyfriend and isn't interested. At the end the boyfriend turns out to be the physio's ex-husband. So this woman she's got so keen on is the same person as the bitch who stole her husband.

It sounds rather ordinary like that, but it was a lovely story. The physio realises that she's been feeling sorry for herself, and she's been blaming the new girlfriend for her own misery without even knowing her. And she realises it's time she got on with her own life.

The disturbing thing, though, was that it was about me. Well, not about me, I mean nothing like that has ever happened to me, but it was me all the same.

When I'd finished, Belinda turned around from the stove and said, 'What do you think?'

I must have looked a bit shocked, because she said, 'Oh no, I've upset you, haven't I?'

I said, 'It's me, isn't it?'

She said, 'Umm . . . in a way.'

And I said, 'But I'm not like that. I haven't got a thing about an old boyfriend and . . .' and I stopped, because I was going to say I wouldn't fall in love with a woman, but I couldn't think of a way to say that to Belinda without sounding rude.

And she poured me a drink and said, 'But that's what writing's all about, you start with something real and you think, what if this happened or that happened, and it turns into something else. You were telling me once about touching people who were very unattractive and how you coped with it. So I started thinking about how a physio would cope with having to touch someone she found very attractive, and it grew from there.'

I was a bit puzzled. I understood what she meant all right, but I wasn't too sure about it. I suppose I'd never thought about where writers got their ideas from. But of course, what else could they possibly do, they take incidents from other people's lives and turn them into something else. But when you read something you don't think about the friend, or whoever started the whole thing, and how maybe they feel about it.

It felt a bit uncomfortable, but I couldn't really see what she had done wrong. Anyway, just then Jacquie came in and we wound up having a really interesting talk about writers and how they steal events out of their friends' lives or things they read in the paper or conversations they overhear on the train.

'That's what creative writing is all about,' said Jacquie, pouring us all another drink. 'Taking things that you hear about and turning them into something different, something that expresses a new truth.' She talked like that sometimes.

I still wasn't too sure about it all, but when I told Mark about it, later that night, he couldn't see what the problem was.

'She wrote a story about a physio. You're not the only physio in the world. What's the big deal?' he said. 'She met you, it made her think about physios, she wrote a story. She's a writer.' And he turned over and went to sleep.

Put like that, it sounded pretty reasonable. But it wasn't just a story about physios, it was a story about me. Once I got over the initial shock, though, I decided it was quite flattering. I mean, how many other people have had stories written about them? So the next week I took her a bunch of orchids. To say thank you, or sorry, or something.

And so life went on. Mark was working long hours, and I found myself looking forward more and more to seeing Jacquie and Belinda each Wednesday. Sometimes we'd go out together on a Saturday too, to big raucous pubs or little jazz clubs. Luisa came along every now and then, but not all that often. I had a feeling that she saw us as a fallback option, for nights when she didn't have a date with some man.

Anyway, it was all very settled. Like family, really. So when I came into the flat one afternoon with my bag of sticky cakes and found the two of them just sitting, in this awful oppressive silence, with no books on the table and no drinks or snacks or newspapers or any of the usual clutter, I got this heart-in-my-mouth feeling and stopped in the doorway. At first I thought that somebody must have died, except that they were both looking angry rather than sad, so then I wondered if they had had a fight.

Jacquie looked up and I could see that she was making a big effort to pretend that everything was okay and that she was just about to offer to put the kettle on or something. But if they were upset about something then as a friend I should ask about it, so I put my bag down and asked what was wrong.

Belinda sort of groaned and ran her hand over her face as if she had to do that to stop herself hitting something, and Jacquie went over and picked up a book that was lying on the floor. That was odd in itself, because they were very careful about books. They certainly never left them on the floor. And there was something about the way this one was lying that gave the distinct impression that it had been thrown.

'What do you think of this?' she asked in a grim sort of voice.

It was a paperback with a sort of medieval-looking wood-cut of four women dancing together on the cover, done in purple and green and with the two colours printed crooked, so it was like seeing double. *Pretty Maids All In A Row*, it said, by Luisa Mayfield. And underneath, in smaller writing, 'the book that lifts the lid on lesbian Sydney'.

'Luisa's book,' I said stupidly. 'She's finished it.'

I looked at the two of them, who glared back at me.

'But . . .' I persisted, dropping my eyes to the book again. The blurb on the back described it as a rollicking lesbian love story set in the pubs, clubs and back lanes of Paddinghurst. There was a black-and-white photo of Luisa sitting in a café wearing a grunge cardigan and smoking, which I had never seen her do, and underneath it said 'a witty, fast-paced *tour de force*'.

I looked back at the two of them. I didn't know what to say. I suppose I'd expected them to be pleased that Luisa had got her novel published, they were always pleased when their other friends had things published, but obviously there was something terribly wrong.

'Oh, Jane,' said Belinda. 'For heaven's sake. I know you're naive but you're not stupid. Can't you see how insulting it is? That girl is not a lesbian, she's got absolutely no understanding of what's important. How dare she write a book about it?'

'But,' I said, and then stopped, because I didn't know what to say next. Fortunately I had a bottle of wine in my bag, so I pulled it out, opened it, and poured us all a glass. We all drank and I thought they'd both calmed down. Jacquie certainly seemed happier, she got a bowl of olives and feta cheese out of the fridge and things started to feel almost normal again.

'Stupid girl,' she said in a dismissive sort of way and I had the feeling that whatever it was about was over. Boy, was I wrong.

'Explain it to me,' I persisted. They usually liked me asking dumb questions. 'Why shouldn't she write about lesbians? I mean, can't people write about whatever they like?'

Well, that was entirely the wrong thing to say. Or perhaps the right thing, I don't know. Belinda was still absolutely hopping mad, and I really set her off. The arrogation of the subjective experiences of an oppressed societal group by a member of the oppressors, a woman who spent her entire life chasing men while ridiculing other women, exploiting her few female friendships, using a false voice to give the wider public a distorted view of Luisa Mayfield and a distorted view of lesbian life.

'And this thing that really hurts,' added Jacquie, who had got steamed up again while she was listening to Belinda, 'is that there she is, right next door, and did she ever talk to us about it? Did she ever discuss her ideas with us? Did she ever tell us her plans? Did she even have the decency to show us a copy? Oh no, this just turned up on my desk at work. In the recent-publications-from-rival-publishers heap. That's the first I knew that our precious Luisa was actually putting pen to paper instead of just talking about it.'

A few months ago I would have been really intimidated by the amount of anger that was flying around in that kitchen, but they were always telling me that society tried to control women by making them afraid of negative emotions and that one had to have the courage to face anger and learn to deal with it. So I gritted my teeth and kept right on going.

'Well,' I said, 'I can see you're both terribly upset.' Jacquie had told me that acknowledging another's negative feelings was often a good way of neutralising them, so I thought I'd give that a go too. 'And I know you wouldn't be upset without good reason. But I don't understand. Isn't this what a writer does, taking what she sees and turning it into a story?'

'There's taking and then there's taking,' said Belinda. 'The thing is, lesbians, genuine lesbians, have fought for the right to have our voice heard. And now here she is, never had to fight for anything in her life, calmly taking that voice and using it, not in solidarity, but to exploit an oppressed group of women, to use us to further her so-called career as a so-called writer.'

Well. It was one of those nights when we drank and talked until two in the morning. I could sort of see what Belinda was getting at, though I still wasn't sure how it was different from her writing about a physio when she wasn't one. Although of course physios have never had to pretend to be something else, or be insulted in public. Belinda talked a lot about what it was like, how hard it was, how her parents didn't understand and some of her oldest friends wouldn't bring their children to visit. I must say I had no idea, I mean why would anyone care about what other people do at home in private?

Anyway, we wound up deciding that Luisa could do whatever she wanted, why should we care, and I slept the night on the couch. When I got home at about eight the next morning, Mark was hopping mad. He said he'd been really really worried about me, and how was he to know where I'd been, and he'd been that close to calling the police. So I told him all about it. I suppose it was bad timing more than anything, he must have been really worried and upset and obviously he can't have slept properly, because he called them a couple of stupid bitches and said he thought they were just jealous that Luisa had written something good enough to get published. Then he grabbed his distressed leather jacket and said he'd be home late, and pushed off.

Well of course that wasn't much help, but it had been a bit stupid of me not to call and let him know where I was, of course he would have been worried. But I had to get to work too, so there was no time to think about sorting things out with Mark till later. And then later that day I heard the news on the radio in the hospital cafeteria. I don't usually bother too much about the news, but the name Luisa Mayfield caught my attention while I was having lunch.

Louise had won a prize. The Voices of Diversity Award for New Literature.

Well. At least I had some idea what to expect when I got

round to Belinda and Jacquie's this time, but even so it was a bit of a shock. Luisa had dropped in to see them, she'd wanted to borrow Jacquie's 'Reclaim The Night' T-shirt for a television interview, and Belinda had screamed at her, and Luisa had screamed right back, and now Belinda was sobbing quietly in a corner and Jacquie was planning some horrid revenge.

I didn't stay long, I don't think I could ever get to like that sort of atmosphere whatever Belinda says about how liberating it is, and anyway I wanted to be home when Mark got in. Only he didn't get in until midnight, which meant I wound up seeing Luisa on the television. She was wearing a pink triangle T-shirt, and the interviewer was gushing about her wonderful book and the film rights and the overseas rights. Luisa didn't get a chance to say much but she was looking pretty pleased with herself.

The next few days I seemed to see Luisa everywhere I looked. The bookshop next to the bus stop had a huge window display of her books, with big photos of her and blow-ups of the cover, and there were articles in the newspapers about her novel, which everyone said was daring and fresh and exciting. I started wondering whether I ought to buy a copy, since it did sound rather good.

I hadn't seen a lot of Jacquie and Belinda because I was trying to get things back on a better footing with Mark. He really couldn't see what Jacquie and Belinda were so upset about, he just kept saying that Luisa could write about lesbians if she wanted, it was only a novel after all. He actually had a copy of the book, though neither of us read it. It was hidden away in his underwear drawer, which I thought was pretty odd but I supposed that it was just his way of avoiding even more conflict. And it did seem silly, for us to be fighting over something that Luisa had done.

The next thing I knew, there was this huge feature article in the *Sydney Morning Herald*. 'Will the Real Luisa Mayfield

Please Stand Up?' written by Belinda. It was brilliant. All those things she'd said to me, about betrayal and dishonesty and bad faith and so on, all turned into this really good argument about how outrageous it was and how nobody should buy the book because it exploited lesbians.

I read the article in the cafeteria at lunchtime, and I went straight over that night to the flat and told Belinda how good it was. She gave me a hug and said, 'I'm glad you're back on our side,' which I wasn't too sure how to take, but I hugged her back and she cracked some champagne. Quite like old times.

Anyway, as you know, things really heated up after that. Louise just disappeared, the papers said she had gone to the Blue Mountains but of course I found out later that she was still around.

But lots of other people jumped into the argument. The people who had decided on the prize said that they didn't care whether she was a lesbian or not, they couldn't see that it changed the quality of the book, they thought it was a good book, and a group called the Sydney Attack Lesbians said that this just showed that the judges were a bunch of doddery old heterosexual fools and that lesbian writing should only be read by lesbians. And some other people said that a novel was fiction, Luisa had the right to write fiction about people who were different from herself if she wanted, and at least it wasn't a boring thinly disguised autobiography like most first novels.

And a couple of academics wrote articles saying that it was exactly the same issue as with B Wongar, only since I'd never heard of B Wongar it didn't really shed much light on the situation for me. And sales of Louise's book kept going up, they brought out a new edition with 'the most controversial book of the decade' across the front. I kept dropping in at Belinda and Jacquie's flat, which had become a sort of a nucleus for the anti-Luisa camp, and then going home to Mark, who kept

saying that there was no such thing as bad publicity and that
Luisa should dedicate her next book to Belinda, with thanks
for all her help, and that Belinda was taking the whole thing
far too personally, the book was being read by lots of people
who didn't know Belinda from a bar of soap and didn't care
whether Luisa was a lesbian or not, so what was she worried
about. I was pretty confused.

In the meantime I actually read it, and I must say it was
really good. Very funny, with lots of action. I didn't tell Jacquie
or Belinda that. But of course that wasn't what they were upset
about anyway.

Well, after a bit things started to die down. Novels aren't the
most exciting thing in the world, and there was an election
coming up and more stuff about police corruption, and it all
sort of quietened down. Luisa's publisher sold the US rights to
Pretty Maids All In A Row for some enormous amount of
money but nobody except Luisa really cared.

Belinda still used to make comments about Luisa, but more
out of habit than anything else. She was editing a book of
poems to come out during the Mardi Gras, and that was taking
lots of her time. Jacquie was busy too. And I was worried about
Mark, who hardly ever seemed to be home these days and
who always seemed really tired. I wanted him to ease off on
the extra work but he said he was really starting to get
somewhere with the sports physio and he didn't have time to
ease off. But he didn't seem happy, and I had this feeling that
our marriage was going through a bad patch, so I was trying
as hard as I could to be there as much as possible.

But tonight he was out, so I was cutting onions for a curry
in Jacquie and Belinda's kitchen when Belinda walked in and
handed me this magazine. There was a photo of Louise on the
cover and the blurb said, 'Luisa Mayfield Tells: My Secret
Lesbian Lover'.

I couldn't believe my eyes. It was me.

There were two pictures. One was at that party where we'd met again, and there I was, looking pretty drunk actually, with Luisa giving me a big hug and some man dressed in feathers in the background. It was the other that really shocked me, because it was a photo of me at the beach, lying on my front with my bikini straps all undone and sort of laughing up at the camera. You could see about a mile of cleavage and I was looking awfully relaxed and happy. Of course the implication was that I was looking at Luisa, only of course I hadn't been, I'd been looking at Mark.

I just saw red. How dare she? I didn't know what was worse, coming around and stealing my photos, or telling these terrible lies about me. I didn't even put the onion knife down, I just walked straight across the landing to her flat.

It's exactly the same as Jacquie and Belinda's flat, only mirror image, you walk straight in and turn left and here you are in the kitchen. She wasn't here and I was so upset that for a moment I didn't even stop to wonder what Mark's distressed leather jacket was doing hanging over that chair, it was such a familiar jacket and the kitchen was so familiar that it seemed perfectly natural. In fact it wasn't until I went down the passage and into the bedroom that I realised. I realised a lot of things all of a sudden. Why Mark was always so tired, why he was out so late, why Luisa used to nip off as soon as I turned up anywhere, how she had got my photo for that filthy magazine article.

And now I've got blood all over my work clothes.

Could Be Better
Stella Duffy

She walked to the post office that afternoon. Light-headed, sure-footed. Each easy step a small dance, her feet hovering over the pavement barely touching it, too perfect to be affected by the grime of the street, too joyous to notice the broken and bloody glass beneath. She handed over her baby and wrote her editor's name with care and delicacy and the flourish of finished. And then she went home alone to celebrate and congratulate and wait.

The manuscript came back from her editor three weeks later. She opened the grimy biked envelope in anticipatory delight. This one she knew was right. This baby was beyond compare. With this one she had finally done it, had achieved all she was capable of. The months of work, days locked in her silent office, nights where she slave-laboured herself to sleep. Her sustenance the pure glow of the screen saver that held each single thought moving gently as the digital clock ticked silent. This was the one. The seventh book, the last of the series. Seventh child of a seventh child, this one was blessed.

The final magic of the completed jigsaw and every word she knew to be perfect. All she awaited for final confirmation was his agreement. The tick from the teacher that would fill in her report card, matriculating her merit from potential to reality. Seven years of work. One new book each year and every cell completely regenerated in that time. Her entire body remade by her own effort. Nourishment from life and brain growth and heart growth through the real people she had made conjured from thin ether.

This one, she knew to be absolute. Sure, the others had been work. As this baby had been work, but they were not born perfect, had needed re-writing, time to grow beyond their own gestation and help from the midheaven midhusbandry of his editing. This creation she had birthed all alone and pure. Brand new, whole and fully formed with no need of intervening surgical skill. This baby, this seventh daughter, was already perfect and he would think so too.

Except he didn't.

The virgin pages were slashed through with red ink. Shattered with barely legible phrases of 'really?' and 'this makes no sense' and 'too much, you are saying too much'.

How could that be? She could not be saying too much, she was saying every word there was. Every word there had to be. And after trawling through the four hundred pages, each one splattered with his belligerence and belittling she came to the last page. And there, under her coda, beneath the last dying dialogue was his final damning indictment.

'Could be better.'

No. It could not be better. There was no better to be. Good, better, best. She had done it. This was her last good deed. This was all she had to give, all she had to do. This was all the better she could attain.

And there followed a day of tears and gin and then a night of acrid burning. Swimming through a fog of thick whiskey

coffees at eight in the morning until late at night and attacking
the perfect and beating down the flawless and dismembering
the child. Recreating the already created and remodelling,
reforming until what had been the ultimate parthenogenesis
became just another ordinary baby made by two. Just another
one of many. And now she was applauded and now he
begrudged her a final 'this will do' and now she was a good girl.

And now she was a bad girl because 'could be better' wasn't
good enough for her. Because 'could be better' held no compas-
sion, no awareness, no understanding. Because 'could be better'
was a red rag to a bull, was an incitement to this mad cow, was
really a very thrilling challenge and so she took it up and took
him in. Because 'could be better' was not just for her. 'Could be
better' was everybody's. Of course it was. And there had to be
something he could do better. Maybe even many things. So she
started to look. And where before she was just writer and hack,
now she was real spy and flesh sleuth and blood detective and
she was the stalker and she hunted him down and she taped him
and she screened him and yes, the intuition was right. Her
educated, 'could be better' guess was right.

Because there were one or two things he was doing very
badly indeed.

She looked first at his wife. The mouse girl, mother woman,
small and pale with wash-stand hands and lank thin hair and
she decided yes, he could do better than that. And so she
placed in his way a temptress of her acquaintance. A friend, a
helpmate who would give up her time and energy to help the
wounded woman and play the role. She played it very well.
Was harlot, tart, the come-hither babe. A really very good fuck
and he ran right for it. He ran from the pale wife and target-
ready fell straight into the arms, the legs, the sex and the
candid camera of her lust. Those three days and stolen nights
of passion would have been sufficient in themselves, certainly
the four rolls of film caused consternation enough in the High

Street, but she was not done. She had only just begun.

The children next. And first they visited Daddy every weekend, because even an angry mouse Mummy knows that little baby mice need their Daddy to play with. To help them grow big and strong. And even if Daddy doesn't love Mummy he still loves all the little babies, will never stop loving all the little babies. Of course he loves them. But maybe he loves his work more? And suddenly it is all he has. Daddy's work is too precious and she sends him envelope after envelope and, with her impassioned encouragement, so do all the others and then he is swimming in a sea of words and paragraphs and pages and chapters and on every one there is a 'could be better', 'try again'. He is working so hard his red pen has run dry and how could everyone but him become so stupid so quickly? He has much to do, much to fix. He is so very necessary. And then there was no time and the clock ticked right through babies' birthdays and Christmas and holidays and the mountain of papers hid the calendar and silenced the alarm. He forgot. He was neglectful and oh so unintentionally hurtful and the children grew bitter and resented him and when they were adults they paid their therapists far too much just to be allowed to say 'he should have done better, he could have been better' and the therapists smiled and soothed and agreed and quickly pocketed the cash.

Then there was his home. And with no wife to share it and no children to play in it, what did he need with a three-bedroom house in the rich leafy suburb with twenty-foot garden and high, hiding walls? What indeed? This beautiful home of ivory tower proportions is not real life, she thought to herself. I must give him experience of the true people, the wind and the rain and the street. I must help him closer to the real. He can certainly do better than this stifling rag-rolled shell. And under her guidance the trees grew faster, the rain fell heavier and the very foundations crumbled more swiftly than the stilton he and mouse wife had loved to nibble. And the bricks and mortar toppled around him and the equity stabbed with its negative bite. And he was out at last. Into the street and back to the world he thought he had left behind with education and occupation. Bedsitland held out its welcoming hand and took him into its thin candlewick bedspreads and nylon sheets and now she was feeling much happier. But not quite done. Not just yet.

And of course his work suffered. So very sadly his work suffered and one day it came time to tell the truth and he admitted it was all too much. He could no longer cope. Could no longer manage. The fact was, he could be no better. He had no better left to be. She heard the story related in whispers down crackling telephone lines. And for a whole moment she was sorry, for the entire age of a blink of time she regretted her action and pitied him. Wondered if it had all been just that little bit too much. Then she turned to the shelf and saw her seventh baby. Saw the adulterated cover and the watered down words and remembered him as he was then and she walked out into the street and found him.

There was a park bench and there was a fine mist and he sat entranced by the warm alcohol in his hand. She was beside him and held him and he leaned his tired head on her shoulder and almost remembered her, nearly knew her and, just as he struggled with the name, she smiled and stood. He lost balance and crumpled heavily, falling to his knees before her. Blood ran scratching from one gravel-grazed hand and she looked down and she saw him cry and she saw the mess as he fell before her and she shook her head and smiled and helped him back to the seat.

'There now,' she whispered gently, 'you can be better than this, can't you?'

And when she went home she was very happy. Very wicked, but very happy.

Shame the Devil
Millie Murray

'Whatever is in darkness will surely come to light.' Dat saying has been around from before me was born, an yu know someting – it's true. Let me show yu how me know. Once me did lost one beautiful brooch me Mudda did give me, it was cut-glass, but me did inform all and sundry sey it was diamond – anyhow me remember taking off de brooch and putting it down on de dresser (or so me did tink) and when me ready now fi wear it – cyann find it. Me look from roof to foundation an not a ting me uncover. Me ball me ball me ball, til me Mudda fling one lick pon me dat me have fi go lie down. Still no brooch. Den how much years later, me a sweep out de yard, an me see someting a sparkle an a shine, me turn round fi check dat nobody an peek pon me an me swoop down and pick it up. Imagine, one piece a shock did tek me. Is me long lost brooch! Dis time now, some of de 'diamond' did drop out and de mount a nyam out with rust, but me so happy dat me did find it, even dough me cyann wear it.

Yu see, if yu cast yur bread pon de water, after many days it must return to yu.

A lot of these sayings yu hear bout de place is built pon true experience yu know.

No matter what part of de world yu live in (an me live inna de London Borough of Hackney, an me love it) de sayings apply!

When me did live in one lickle village in Westmoreland, Jamaica all de while me a chat to meself an mek promise say 'Dorcas Thomas, one day, yur dream is coming true dat 'Yu a go England a live, not America, England,' cos me know dat, 'where dere is a will, dere is a way'.

An every day me a sey 'me a go a England, me a go a England' an some people laugh, some sey me crazy, but me never did worry bout people, all me know sey is dat one fine day, me will arrive in London. An look now, is over forty someting years me is here yu know, time fly eh?

Right now me just turn sixty-six (but everybody sey me look inna me early fifties) anyhow, me and me two friend dem (dere used to be four a we Joan Hailey, but she died),Vi Palmer and Orla Smythe who both come up wid me from Jamaica, find sey now we retire what can we do?

We try fi come up wid ideas:

'How bout flower arranging?' Dis is from Orla, who ever since dat bottle of fruit she was soaking in some rum did drop off de shelf an lick her inna headtop, she can come out wid some strange tings.

'Is how yu mean flower arranging, me fed up wid flower anyhows. Me granny backyard did full wid flowers and bush, me nar interested in any ting like dat.' SeyVi.

'But me like flowers an . . .'

'Hush yu mout.'

Me never did hot pon de idea too, but me never say nutting.

But Vi suggestion even worse, 'Me tink sey we should join a swimming club.'

'Me nar like water,' Orla did moan.

Dis time me did have fi sey someting.

'Yu mad?'

'But swimming will mek we healthy and lose weight and bring down any high blood pressure,' Vi a look pon me.

'If swim yu want swim, me is happy fi yu, but count me out.'

Let me just tell yu bout dis two women.

First off, Orla is a big brown-skin woman. Her waist, bust an hips all one size, but she good looking. She nar have much hair, so most time she wear a wig, she must have over two dozen, long, short, curly, straight, every one different. She have three pickney all grown up an but she an her husband bust up as soon as dem did marry, an she a live with a next man (for over thirty years!) sey she never trust a man fi marry again. Me love off Orla like a sister, only ting dat since dat fruit jar did lick her inna her head she talk de wrong ting at de wrong time and she always seem to get inna trouble. Poor ting.

Den come Madame Vi. She red like de sunset and small and marga. No matter how much she nyam, she cyann put on weight (de opposite is true fi me). She is a woman not to mess wid. She have a streak inna her if yu vex her up she could strangle yu wid her bare hand. True yu know, she can be deadly. De man dat she did follow fi come a Britain fi marry, she never marry after all (which did shock out me an Orla, cos Vi did tell we how much she love off Kennett an life is not worth de living wid out him), instead she did marry three times an de man she wid now is not her husband, an she have four daughters and one 'precious bwoy' so she sey, but we all know sey Rudy is out of order, fiesty and rude! Hmm. Is only me still wid me husband Freddy. Me did have one pickney bwoy Tony, an him did have six pickney fi two women, so indirectly me did have a big family.

It was Orla granddaughter who sey 'You ladies have lived such full lives you should write them down.' Me did bust out laughing 'write which down' me did laugh cos me writing is not so hot, an me spelling even worse. But dis granddaughter hang on to we three bout dis writing business til we change we mind.

Orla sey 'Sheri,' is de granddaughter name, 'find out bout a writing class fi retired persons.' Orla tink sey she talk better than me, 'An me ting it would be educationally benefit fi us.'

Me wasn't eager fi get involved, but when Vi sey she wants to try it out, me tink bout it, den me did agree.

Me did start build up a dread fi go a writing class, an when de time did come me feel sick wid all de fretting. What a waste a energy.

Hmm, talk bout don't judge a book by its cover, de first afternoon we start de class de teacher, Trevor Harris, did not look right. Him a wear one shirt, which iron never reach, same wid him jeans. Him have matta in him eye. Dis me could never unnerstand, cos de class start at two o'clock, dat must mean him only just get up an him must never pass lickle water cross him face. Nasty. Me tink him only shave bout once or twice a month and never on a Wednesday (dat's de day of we class).

Me did glad sey me did sit at de opposite side of de circle to him, because me did reckon sey, if him never wash him face, den what chance has him teet have of getting brushed?

Me cyann stand de stale breath.

Anyhows, he was a very nice man. Him have one squeaky voice, but even me know sey him a educated man. When we start, me was a lickle fraid cos of me bad writing, but Trev sey, 'Listen folks, this class is not about how wonderful your handwriting is or the fact that you can spell every word in the Oxford dictionary, it's about what is important to you, and what you want to say.'

Me start relax now.

Everybody had to introduce demself, and me surprise when a few of dem sey how dem reading an writing not so good. So when me turn did come, same ting me sey. By de end of de class me did consider how much me enjoy meself, dat me already looking forward to next week.

On de Sunday after de first Wednesday class, we three a discuss what Trev say:

'I imagine,' sey Orla, 'de stories dat we writing will appear in our own book.'

Trev say it no terrible cos we nar have no big name like Jackie Collins. Him sey de way foreward is fi everybody inna de community fi gather round and organise demself an publish dem own ting. Hmm, Trev is well smart. Dis is how de future will be an we will beat de big time publishers at dem own game.

'Well, me decide sey me a go write bout when me first come a England and how everyting grey and cold, an me did feel homesick fi Jamaica,' sey Vi. Orla an me did agree sey dat is a good idea, but Vi quick fi sey, 'Nar bother follow me yu know, find someting else fi write bout.'

Orla did turn up her lip, cos me feel sey she did want fi write bout de same ting.

Every day me a struggle fi tink bout someting to write. When me in Rigley Road market a shop all me tink bout is, 'What can me write bout?' Me start get so confuse, dat when we go fi buy me meat, me did purchase some beef, instead of mutton. Me vex yu see, cos me waste me money pon de BSE beef, an me have fi dash it way out de street fi some dog to nyam it up.

It wasn't til me was sewing up some night dresses me did mek fi two a me lickle granddaughters, dat de idea hit me.

'Me a go write bout me grand pickney dem.' It come in like somebody did turn on de light 'click' cos as me tink it me know sey it is going to be a good story. De only problem was me reading an writing. Everyting me want to write down is in me head, but somehow me cyann get it down pon de paper.

Me so glad Wednesday come cos me really want fi do de story now, an me want Trev to help me (me will just have fi cark up me nose when him come near me).

It was fifteen minutes after de hour of two o'clock pon de Wednesday an de three a we still a reel an a roll from de shock, well, more so Vi really.

When we did turn up at de class, we just a expect de people fi turn up as de week before, but dere was a few new faces, and one not so new. What a ting, imagine after all dese years, who should we meet up wid and in such a circumstance, but Kennett, Vi's old time man. He look fit an hearty an next to him was a white woman who inform us sey, 'I'm Ken's wife Gloria, and we've been married for,' she looked to him an smile an him did grin him teet at her and whispered someting, she den sey, 'fifteen years, it seems like only yesterday.' Some of her teet did look rotten, an her hair come in like straw dat yu fed horse wid, and her dress and shoes did look too small and her lips too red, but Ken seem to love it up. De two hours did fly by so quick, de class de come in like a dream.

Afterwards Kennett come up to we three. 'Hi girls, how's life?'

Me just mumble 'fine', Vi tell him sey 'Me life has gone very well, better dan it woulda done if me did stay wid yu.'

Orla she did launch pon one big everlasting long story bout her life and loves and troubles and trial, dat she was got so carried away dat she never even realise dat Kennett wasn't pay-ing her one piece of attention. All de while him a stare out Vi and she him.

Mek me unnerstand dat dere is some unfinish business between de two a dem.

Anyways we did sey we goodbyes, except for did Gloria, she must a suss out de situation between her husband an Vi, an she did twist up her face, an cross her arms. Hmm. Could be trouble.

Well, all de next week me a try fi work out me story. Freddy did get fed up wid me.

'Freddy how yu spell cantankerous?'

'Woman nar bother me, go look it up.'

Another time me ask him, 'Freddy how yu spell pregnancy?'

'Dorcas, what me know bout how fi spell it eh, me only know bout how it happen.'

Dat did vex me.

It funny yu know, every time me try fi do some work pon me story de phone ring, or somebody knock de door, or me we just too tired. Writing story is hard work yu know. Everytime me write down two words, me have to have someting to eat. So me start put on lickle weight which upset me, cos me doctor sey me have fi lose it cos of de 'pressure'. It start mek me feel all twist up inside, dat when me son come one evening me ask him fi one a him cigarettes.

'Don't make me laugh Mum, you don't even smoke.' Him start laugh. 'One little story and you want to get on the tobacco trail.' Him laugh even harder. 'Next thing you know, you'll be drinking rum.'

Him can laugh de thought de cross me mind bout de rum, but when me open up de bottle de smell a de rum nearly knock me out, dat me did have fi go an lie down.

By de Wednesday me just manage to write down two pages. Dis writing business is worse dan giving birth!

De class same as last week. Dis time Kennett have a briefcase, me have fi grin an sey to meself if him tief it.

Trev asked, 'Who would like to read out their story so far?' Him eyes roam round de class but nobody respond.

'Do you want me to pick someone?' Dis mek me fraid. Me was just tinking bout going to de toilet when Kennett wife Gloria shoot up her hand.

'I'll go first.'

'That's great. Go ahead then,' sey Trev.

She stand up an straighten out her skirt an clear her throat. By de time she finish (it come in like an hour) Vi mout twist up over her can a Diet Coke an Kennett have one smile dat did go right round to him neck back!

Yu see, de story was all bout him, and how wonderful and loving and generous him is. Lie. Leopard never change him spots, an dere is no way yu can teach a ole dog new tricks.

By de time she sit down, one a few people de clap. Me an Vie never bother cos we know sey she only write rubbish. But, fool-fool Orla a laugh an a grin an a sey, 'Dat was so good it touch me heart.' Now an again she need a few tumps in her head fi straighten her out!

If dat was a surprise, de next story was a volcanic eruption, earthquaking shock.

Orla's story.

When time come fi Orla fi read it out, she stand up an put on her glasses, touch up her hair (wig), clear her throat, and fool around. Me was ready fi tell her sey, 'sit down' but she beat me to it.

'Dis story is sorta true to life. It happen long long ago, but is still fresh inna me mind.'

She start.

'Once upon a time,' everyone bust out laughing. Me wanted to tell Orla, fi hush up an sit down.

She start again. 'Once upon a time, inna lickle town in Jamaica dere was a beautiful young woman name Jane. She was very talented. She could sew, cook, an she always have time fi everyone. But de ting dat she was especially noted for, was her singing voice. Dat young woman could out sing any man, woman or bird.'

As Orla continue wid her story, me start fi shift inna me seat. Me wanted to stop Orla reading out de story. When me look from Kennett to Vi, me could see sey dem very very uncomfortable.

Yu see, we all unnerstand sey dat Orla story is bout we friend Joan. Everyting she sey bout her so far is true. De ting is, remember me did sey dat Joan did died, well, de true story is dat somebody did kill her.

'. . . Many many people did envy Jane. She did have one handsome bwoyfriend called Keith . . .'

One very true seying did pop inna me mind just as me see Vi fling her drink of Diet Coke pon Orla dress who did jump up like kangaroo, 'He dat keepth his tongue, keepth his life.'

Orla start fi ball bout de coke will stain de dress she a wear. If Vi sey she sorry once to Orla, she sey it a million times. All dis did make time run on an poor Orla never did finish her story.

What a piece of adventure!

When de class done, Orla approach Trev an ask if she can read out her story again. Me could see sey Trev not too happy wid her question but she sey, 'It's very important to me Trev, it is someting dat me needs to bury, yu know to rest in peace once me finish it off, please?'

What could de man sey. Him look soft anyways.

'All right Orla. Leave it for a couple of weeks, go over it again and then you can read it out to the class.'

'Tank yu, tank yu Trev.' She lean over an kiss him pon de cheek.

She so extra. All me coulda do was squeeze up me face, cos it look like dis day was not de day dat Trev did wash himself. Hmm.

By now, me an Orla a look fi Vi, but de classroom empty. Dis come in like a puzzle.

'Where is Vi?'

We hurry out to de gate, an de puzzle completed. Vi a inna one big conversation wid de one Kennett. Him wife Gloria was in dem car nearby looking like she did want to murder somebody, but de two a dem too hot inna dem talking fi paid her attention.

Orla burst out to dem, 'Did yu like me story?'

If looks could kill, is dead she would be dead, right dere pon de ground. Up til now dem never did answer her.

Me hang on pon Orla arm an start fi pull her to de gate. 'Come.'

She is very hard a hearing. 'But me did want to tell dem both someting.'

'Woman, leave dem be. Come.'

One piece a strugglin between me an Orla. Finally Kennett come over an sey, 'Eh Orla, what yu doing next week?'

Her eyeball pop up. 'Nuttin.'

'Well how would yu like fi come fi dinner wid me an me wife?'

She carry on like she did have fi consider, but she quickly sey, 'Me accept yur enquiry.' She mean invitation, hmm.

'Fine.' Him turn an walk to him car.

Vi link her arm inna Orla's an de two a dem did walk off leave me. It never did worry me, cos it did give me time to ponder pon de situation.

All dat day me mind did a work overtime. Come de next morning me did have one terrible, awful dream at night bout Orla, dat de sweat me did run off me like Dunn's river waterfall.

One ting me did realise, me have fi warn Orla.

Yu see, dis story of Orla's is true. Its bout we friend Joan. At de time we four was schoolfriend, but it was Orla and Joan dat was very very close, an it was Kennett who was first Joan's bwoyfriend. All de bwoys did love off Joan cos she was beautiful and she dress good. All de gal dem was red-eye after her, but she never did paid dem any mind. It happen dat all de schools inna de parish was offered two scholarship, one fi a bwoy and de other fi a gal, fi go a America fi study. Me never even bother fi apply, but Joan an Vi did. Nobody was too shock when Joan get it. Her mudda did love fi boast an she run go tell everybody she meet sey her daughter a go a 'Merica. Dere was some people vex up sey Joan get it, but dat never trouble Joan. She start mek up dresses and pack up tings fi tek wid her.

Kennett was not too pleased. All him coulda sey was, 'What bout me Joan?' an 'Me really love yu Joan, don't leave me.' Me never did trust him, ole goat, but one ting me did remember, Vi an him did become good good friend.

It happened de day before Joan was due to go. Me never know too too much, but what me did know as dat, one day Joan was alive an well, an de next day she dead, dead, dead.

Somebody, we never did clearly find out who, did give her a couple a patty fi eat pon de plane, but she did nyam it dat night, an it did have in some root-juice or someting which did mek her belly swell up like she havin baby. It did kill her off. What a ting. Her mudda nearly go mad, in fact she was never too right from den onwards. All de investigations bout who de give her de patties dem, never turn up anyting.

But, it was Orla dat did tell me sey she did pass by Vi's house dat very day an she was baking patty? Me did just dismiss it. She sey how Kennett was sitting in Vi's kitchen a laugh an a joke wid her. Me was too distress fi really tek in de information, an even much later me could not believe it, so dat was dat.

Til dat fruit jar lick Orla inna her head.

Straight way, me ring Orla an tell her me did have one bad dream bout her an if me was she, we woulda stop home an not go to Kennett's.

'Oh but Dorcas, dem especially want me.'

'Yes me know dat, but don't go.'

She pause an me feel sey she was considering what me seying. Den she sey, 'Yu jealous.'

'Me sey yu's mad. Jealous fi what? Listen do what yu want.'

Me fling down de phone. But me did feel bad, so me did call out to Master God, fi not let stupid Orla go to Kennett fi dinner.

De Lawd did answer me prayers.

Apparently, as Orla step off de bus hear Kennett's house, some body did bust her head wid stick and try fi tief her handbag. Hmm, Orla never eat up her dumplings, rice and pea fi nuttin, she sey she give de man one kick, he did fly into de air, and de lick to her head, never do much cose she was wearing one tick, tick wig.

She was saved dis time.

By de follow Wednesday, Orla never turn up fi class at first, den half way thru, she a hobble in, wid one big big plaster cast pon her foot, an two crutches. 'Sorry me late Trev, when me was standing at de crossing near de station yesterday a car come straight at me. Me so fraid me could not move an it run cross me foot.'

'You must be in a lot of pain Orla, you shouldn't have bothered to come in.'

'Oh no Trev, me was determined to come today. Me still writing out me story.'

'Okay then, take a seat.'

One and few people get up and mek way fi Orla.

All de while me a check out Vi an Kennett. Dem a look pon dem one anudda like two ole sly fox, but me see dem.

All dis cause me fi worry. Me start lose lickle weight wid de fretting. Freddy sey, 'Me cyann unnerstand why yu tek up Orla problem. Yu know sey she never did born wid much sense from time, yet yu a carry her burden.'

'But Freddy, she need help.'

'De best help she can have is when Kennett and de wicked Vi kill her off an she nar be a trouble to yu or anyone else.'

Me start fi ball. Much as me love me husband, him is like most man – dem nar have much feeling.

Me start fi tink sey if me should contact Scotland Yard (but nar leave me name) an tell dem what me suspect. Every time me go fi phone dem, me get afraid.

Again me dream bout Orla, it was worse den de first one.

Me tell her me see her tongue swell up, an den her head chop off.

Hear her tell me now, 'Yu musta eat some cheese last night Dorcas, or did yu see a bad film? Yu need fi rest more.'

What a ting. Me a fret meself bout her, an she a more or less sey, is me dat did have di problem.

Yu know dat action speak louder dan words.

'If yu cyann get Harry, yu can get him shirt,' dat's what me sey when me hear dat Sheri, Orla granddaughter, get stab up at college. Orla did phone me late late Friday night, a ball.

'Dorcas, Dorcas. Me poor granddaughter dere a hospital, dem stab her up.'

By de time Orla finish de everlastingly long story, it turn out tings not as bad as dat, but dem is bad enough.

De granddaughter an one next gal, did get into one piece of fighting. De gal have one friend who have knife an chop Sheri one blow wid de knife. It cut her arm an she have fi have some stitches.

'So what de police sey?' me ask.

'Dem a investigate, an a inquiry.'

'Dem never arrest anyone?'

'Yu never hear me sey dem still have tings fi sort out.'

'But . . .'

'Dorcas, listen. One ting me granddaughter did sey was dat thru all de ruckus she sey she tink she hear somebody sey someting bout "tell granny fi stop de story". Imagine dat.'

She stop talk.

Me never sey nuttin, me a wait.

Den Orla speak. 'Eh, yu never tink it mean me?'

Me did hear a lickle shaky shake in her voice. Is fraid she fraid now. Hmm.

'Dorcas, what yu tink?'

'If yu tek me foolish advice, not only stop de story, but completely forget yu know anyting bout it.'

She never sey nuttin, at first, but me never mind cos she phone me an is her phone bill dat is running up.

'Okay. Me stopping.'

Me did heave a big sigh of relief. At last de stubborn woman hear.

De booklet de class did published was entitled: *Tell The Truth (and shame the devil)*.

Mine was de last story fi go in, on account dat it did tek me de longest fi write.

Trev organise a lickle party when de booklet done, an de *Hackney Gazette* come an tek pictures of de class.

Yu know in life yu have times when yu feel proud, dis was one of mine. An yu know how much me writing improve, so much so dat Trev encourage me fi start write a book. What a ting, a whole book. Him sey dat him will help me all him can. Just now me a tink bout de subject matter.

Every body inna de class manage to write a lickle someting. Except for Orla: When she tell me she stopping de story, she did not mean just den, it was only when 'dem' lick out all her windows, mash up her man car, lick down a few of her family members, an den try fi burn up her house, dat she stop!

What a woman!

Two people stop coming to de class.

Kennett stop coming. What come round go round. Him was having dinner wid him wife, an Vi, an a few friends an him did eat two patty as well as a lot of odda tings.

Him dead.

When dem cut him open and tek out de food him eat from him belly, dem sey de patty dem have some funny substance dem not sure bout, an up til now dem a still investigate.

An Vi stop coming. After dat dinner she leave de man she was living wid and run off wid a next one to Miami, Florida, fi live out de rest a her days.

Empty Arms
Mary Wings

Tenant, Apt. 4D, Upper West Side, New York City
Christopher Robin breaks the egg, an omelette for Barbar!
Soon, it will happen – soon! I will call him Christopher
Robin. I know it's a boy. Don't ask me how. I just know these
things. I am very good at planning. I plan everything in
advance. Not like my publishers!

They want the manuscript yesterday and I don't hear from
them in a year of tomorrows. My editor always takes my calls,
but what to say? They never know the sales figures, it seems.
Not until it suits their purposes. And I'm up for contract!

Christopher Robin if I don't hear from them soon I'll go
out of my mind!

Oh, how my arms ache! The crib must have adjustable rails,
an adjustable mattress, to raise and lower, the easier to pick him
up, put him down, keep him safe. Safe. Absolutely safe.

To hold him! To watch him grow! Those perfect little hands!
I will wake up every morning – and probably several times
during the night – and I will count his little fingers, his little

toes and make sure that there are ten. And I will never stop counting.

I'll have one of those low to the ground rockers, perfect for mothers, white. With a rush seat. Some kind of painted decoration – I haven't decided about that yet. Which childhood motif? Common memories of all those delightful characters. Beatrix Potter? Winnie the Pooh? Pooh! Everything will be white in this nursery. That's it. With a few attendant blue notes of course. But I want some toddler furniture. Something really beautiful and fun that we can look forward to when he's old enough.

My god, I'd better call my agent. She said it was my year. She said she was going to break me through! She also said she'd get me a fifty-thousand dollar advance. And I sure could use the money. But they're all full of promises in the beginning.

Time to get his layette ready! I want everything in sixes. The tiny undershirts with the little satin bows, diaper covers, stretch sleepers. I'll have a little dresser, white wicker, the drawers running on smooth runners. I will fold the tiny items and put them in. Then I will take them out and fold them again and put them back. Glorious repetition! Horrible waiting! How empty my arms feel. I want the nursery to be perfect. It has to have a theme. Mary Poppins? That bitch? Pat the Bunny. Better.

The christening robe, the fabulous outfits for showing him off, if only to myself. Italian organdy! White lawn! All to be hung on miniature stain-padded hangers. I can do a bit of embroidery myself, handy with a needle, I am. The beginning of a mother's skill. My arms positively tingle in longing. Every piece shall have his initial, to show he's mine, mine alone. And with each stitch, a moment of my love before he comes. I'll do up a perfect pillow, velvet embroidered chenille studded with pearls, spelling out the arrival date, his name. All will be trimmed in frothy lace, fairy fine.

Knit, pearl, the tiny cuffs for those perfect little hands. Soft booties, soft for a baby's feet. Hard to cover up those tiny toes! Must be done! Every day! My arms ache so, as if he's here already, as if, as if I've been holding him for hours. For years . . . What will be that nursery motif?

Silver! Silver for my baby boy. Porringers, cups, even a silver rattle, with tiny little silver beads decorating the bells at either end. Silver knives and forks, baby bowls. Handles shaped like bunnies . . . bunnies! That's it! That's the theme park for Christopher Robin. I want bunnies and rabbits for my boy. They'll hop away with him into realms of fantasy.

What will he remember of this room when he's older? Will it be the smiling faces of rabbits, the curling initial, a stitch of a mother's love? Because of course, that's all there will be. A Mother's love. Bye bye baby bunting. Daddy hasn't gone hunting. He's left us in the lurch that bastard.

Fuck the book business. And soon the aching in my arms will stop.

Mrs Harriet Fant, Salesperson, Tot Trifles, East 97th Street, New York City

Sure I checked out her credit card limit, what do you think I am, stupid? I do that sort of thing with every purchase. But especially with these kind of custom orders. We're talking custom designs from Milan, you don't want to screw up or have any misunderstandings about anything that gets shipped over the ocean. Believe me. She said she was a children's book author. Never heard of her.

She went for the most expensive Italian hand-painted designs. We have a whole catalogue right here, look. Raggedy Ann chairs, hearts on her cheeks, a trademarked design, I want you to know. We have elephants, moon and star (very popular with the baby boomers right now, sort of psychedelic), Puss N'

Boots, but no, she didn't want any of that. Flipped through
page after page, getting more and more frustrated. Couldn't
find what she wanted. I thought she was going to tear the
perforated holes in one of the plastic display sheets, in such a
hurry, she was. These sample books aren't easy to get you
know, all the way from Milan.

Irritating customer, I tell you, but just like every customer,
always right. There she was flipping through the Mother
Goose section, and she gets the idea. Rabbits! Bunnies. That's
what's going to do it for this lady.

Okay, fine. She wanted the backs of the chairs painted like
rabbits. Mr Tollini, I'm telling you, he can do anything, I
assured the lady. I showed her the Alice and Wonderland Tea
Ensemble just in case she might have missed that page, but she
would have none of it. I told her I would fax Mr Tollini and
have the preliminary sketches made up for her approval. I
warned her it would be costly, but she just waved that credit
card and told me it had better be express. She didn't like to
wait. She was the kind who planned everything well in
advance.

So three weeks later the initial sketches for the Custom
Made Tea Ensemble arrived.

The back of each chair painted just like a fully dressed
rabbit, waiting politely for tea to be served. Huge long ears
grew out of the back of the chairs. Some of them were flopped
over. Cute rabbit faces, little pink triangular noses, softly
brushed fur. Realistic touches, like pink eyes with little tear
ducts in the corner. You know the Italians. So good at these
things. The sketch itself was suitable for framing.

And the table! A checkerboard with faux tea cups, tea cakes,
petit fours, even little sugar cubes with rosebuds painted on!
That's standard, actually, with the Granny Goose Ensemble you
get that too. She came into the store and loved it. Do it up, she
said, have Tollini build it and paint it and put it on a plane.

And then she set out to order the rest of the furniture. She ordered the white muslin curtains with the ribbon threaded eyelet trim at the bottom. Also custom. And she even had a valance embroidered with small rabbit faces, ordered through Pickering Company of Somerset. I'm telling you, this lady went all out, price apparently being no object for her.

She didn't go for plated either. Her silver had to be solid. We don't ask questions here. But how can the kid tell the difference? Half the time it's going to be full of egg yolks. And you can't put solid in the dishwasher. Whatever.

The rest was all going to be Victorian Wicker. White. She ordered a cane woven suspension cradle. With wheels. That way the mother can take the infant into whichever room she wants. Over the basket where the baby lays – you understand we use German hardware, everything is stainless steel ball bearings – there is a crown of white broderie anglaise, a curtain of lace to protect the infant's skin from you know, any harsh rays. The mother can add extra layers to the crown for immediately after the birth, if she so desires. The nursery should be kept dim anyway the first few weeks. Not that this mother was going to miss a trick. We do special hand weaving, should the client prefer, and of course she did. The hand-woven fibres come in beautiful lily patterns, this particular cradle is called the 'Victoria Regina'. It's a copy from an 1851 piece. Woven into shapes reminiscent of the Queen Victoria's own lily, the largest waterlily in the world discovered by Mr Livingstone, I presume, in Africa. This stuff has history!

People love the Victorian look. So romantic. That's when lace baby clothes really came into popularity. Among the upper classes of course. Of course, it was quite an indulgence in those sentimental times. A lot of laundry. So many infants died, you know. Mothers too, in childbirth. Not anymore, thank God.

Tenant, Apt. 4D, Upper West Side, New York City

My agent called. The sales figures are down! As am I. Our conversation was shorter than the first print run of my book.

My god, all the furniture came today. In one load. I won't think about how I'm going to pay for it all.

I was up late, scrubbing the floor (after my agent, the movers called. They said delivery would be this morning – but I didn't expect it to be so early). It's almost ready now, the nursery.

The little rabbit faces, they look like rabbits sitting in chairs, on either side of the table, painted with its tea service already brewing and steaming. The light, long layers of white curtains, shot with the blue ribbon. Rows of bunting, Daddy's gone a hunting –

Fuck, there's the doorbell. Shit.

I cannot tear myself away from this room, my own little universe of perfection. Not like anything, anyone, that rings on the phone. A story between two covers that no one ever bothered to read, apparently.

Stop ringing!

Oh, they know I'm home. I have to give up. Close the door on this lovely land here.

Goddamn! Stop that ringing! I'm coming, I'm coming.

My publishers should be so interested in me.

Probably that Rosalind and her girl Angelica. I like Rosalind, as much as I like anybody these days. But I wish she'd shut up about Angelica. A thoroughly unremarkable child!

I showed Rosalind the book when it first came out. She smiled and said she liked the pictures. And then she let Angelica touch it with grubby fingers. She never read the story but I could tell she was impressed. Everyone is impressed by published authors. You can see your stock go up by the look in their eyes. But I may never have another book. I may never need to write again.

Bye bye Christopher Robin Room. I'll come back and see you soon.

'Coming!'

Mrs Rosalind Churry, neighbour
If you ask me, she didn't like children. Why the way she went after Angelica, when all the child wanted to do was take a peek into the room! What did she expect, the hallway all piled up outside her door with cartons. And packing materials of all kinds still on the carpet. Don't tell me kids don't notice that stuff. Angelica notices everything. Excelsior, styrofoam popcorn, bits of it were floating all over the floor when we stopped by to see her.

She was an interesting enough woman, very creative, writing those children's books, and all. I felt a little sorry for her. She seemed so isolated. I guess writers are like that. Children seemed to make her nervous. Her husband, I think, left her some time ago. She never mentioned it. Kept to herself. It was hard to get close. But writers must be like that, mustn't they? I mean, they choose to lock themselves up with their fantasies.

I kept on coming by. A habit. Stay in touch with neighbours in times of trouble. That's the way I was brought up.

Probably too smart for her own good. You know, I try to get to know people in the building. She showed me the book she wrote. About a little baby boy that was found under a leaf. And a fairy godmother took him home. I didn't see why it couldn't be about a little girl. I'm tired of finding books about little boys. Angelica needs someone to identify with in a story. Not a baby boy sleeping under a leaf.

She kept more to herself after her husband disappeared. I understand, people have tragedies and tragedies can rip the union of marriage asunder. People lose jobs, parents, children. Some couples just never get past the troubled times.

But that was no reason for her to go after Angelica like that.

We'd just sat down to tea when my daughter toddled over to the door and reached for the shiny knob. Why, there was a noise hardly human! Our neighbour screamed – no – she roared! for to Angelica to stop.

I never want to hear her raise her voice again to my daughter. I'm never going back, I don't care how tragic the whole thing has been. Writers are weird. Maybe next time she'll write about a baby girl. Hope she isn't a foundling, dumped in a fairy forest. Or a dumpster.

Tenant, Apt. 4D, Upper West Side, New York City

Thank god she's gone. She was politely inquiring about my work. My work! As if I have had time to make up a pleasant fantasy. Reality, except for my publishers, will be much more pleasant. It will be endearing. Enduring. Unconditional.

It's time to get ready. Of course I'm nervous. It's just like before. I have the overnight bag packed. Everything is white, this time, I made sure. I have the soft-soled shoes, starched and pressed linen. I am going to do this right this time!

I'll call a taxi. No, wait, I think I'll walk. That's it. The exercise will do me good. Allow me to prepare. I'll start the breathing exercises now.

Nurse Annette Tropi, St Luke's Hospital

Motherhood. I have seen it all here. And it isn't just roses and mottos embroidered on pillowcases.

Yes, there is the wonder of birth, of new life, but babies emerge coated with placenta, and they have to be spanked to get their lungs in gear. I know, there's women giving birth in hot tubs and in darkened rooms. But don't put me there. I want to assist in a sterile environment.

And Mother is something you suddenly are. Not everybody takes it so well, believe me. All this stuff about the Natural

Mother, I'm sorry. I don't care what the anthropologists say. Mothers are made and not born. It's a hell of a lot of work from the first contraction. Worth it? yeah, sure. Been going on for centuries. Hey, did I say it wasn't worth it? I wouldn't be working on this ward if I didn't enjoy the assisting in birth. The baby's job is easy.

The women have to become Mothers. I've mostly seen people happy to be bringing new life into the world. But there are those Mothers who are afraid of their babies. Are they going to make a mistake? What does the baby want? Why doesn't she eat?

And there are the Mothers who have post partum depression. I've seen Mothers reject their babies altogether. I have seen it!

No, enough of the Natural Mother. They all learn it eventually. What's natural for them.

Tenant, Apt. 4D, at St Luke's Hospital
St Luke's Hospital! How I remember it.

Birthplace of Christopher Robin.

I'm nervous, even though I've been there twice before. Once was purely research. Getting used to the layout. Breathe deeply.

Inside the doors I see a friendly elderly gentleman at the information counter. A volunteer no doubt. He's busy and overwhelmed as he can't figure out the telephone system. Now where are those elevators again? I was too sedated last time. This time I'm going to keep my wits about me.

Elevator bank. A quiet, uneventful ride to the top where the nurseries are. I'm tense, shaking even. It doesn't matter. So is everybody else. Is that an expectant Father there? Why isn't he by her side? They let men into the delivery room now. I should know.

Bing! Ninth Floor. We all step out, me with my little overnight bag and my wide brimmed hat. I make for the bathroom.

Damn, these nurses uniforms have a lot of buttons. Right now I want nothing more than a good stiff drink. Never helped with the writing. Might help now. Have to wait.

White stockings, shit, I got them twisted. It would be a disaster to have a run. There, completed. The thick-soled shoes. The jaunty nurse's cap placed just so. I even have a little name tag. Copied it off one I saw a nurse wearing on my research expedition.

A look in the mirror. Perfect for the part.

Nurse Annette Tropi, St Luke's Hospital

I can't believe it happened on my shift. I just can't believe it.

That Mother is so distraught. Out of her mind. My god! Oh my fucking god!

Tenant, Apt. 4D, at St Luke's Hospital

It was easy. I glided down the hall quietly in the heavily treaded shoes issued to nurses. I kept my eyes to the ground. Everyone was so busy, with something in hand, a test tube, a cart, an infant.

An infant. Jesus. Here's the viewing room. Keep back.

There they are inside that window. All those new little lives, just beginning. Beautiful. But which one?

Who knows? They are all there. One of them is him.

A nurse, talking to someone, in a corner.

The room is dark, dim.

The nurse, she'd stopped talking. She knits her eyebrows. There's a problem. She gets up as if to leave the nursery.

I'm praying. She's walking now, towards the door, with her colleague who's making gestures. She shrugs her shoulders and walks through the door – through the door! She's out!

There's a backward glance at the nursery, I'm flattened in a doorway now, she can't see me and then she's around the corner. Christ, I'm going to make it.

The nursery! I run in. Babies! There are so many, in so many colours! I hadn't thought about that.

He must be here. He knew I was coming.

The babies have started crying now. One has set off another, like howling dogs, there is a squalling.

But it didn't keep me from hearing the noise. The tiny suckling sounds of Christopher Robin. Or who will grow up to be Christopher Robin.

'Thank you for waiting for me, darling!' I say, picking him up and carrying him quickly back down the hallway to the bathroom, where my overcoat waits in one of the stalls. I need never write a book again.

EPILOGUE

Police Officer, Laura DeLeuse

We had the profile of course. Everybody knows it. That wasn't the surprise.

We were looking for a woman in her mid twenties to late thirties who had recently lost a child. That's standard.

Of course, we check the hospital records for all the women that have lost children at that hospital. It's a pretty exhaustive search, and not likely to get results.

The best thing going for us in this situation is the media. 'Baby Carrie,' 'Baby Eddie,' the parents giving heart-wrenching interviews, that kind of thing. Networks eat it up. And everybody gets to play a bit part. There is no more public outcry than around the situation of a baby stolen from its Mother.

Basically, we almost always solve the case on a tip from a neighbour. Women who suddenly have babies in their households. Tend to act very secretive, but do you know how hard it is to hide a baby?

Think about it. The crying alone is one big baby alarm. And

a baby's crying knows no clock. Not to mention the disposable diaper boxes, or a diaper service, what have you. Babies are really hard to hide. Especially in a city like New York.

So we found her. Neighbour's tip. Mrs Rosalind Churry noticed the baby crying. Pamper boxes. Quite a little nursery too. Said she didn't want to call the police. Felt sorry for the woman. I recognised her name. She wrote a book I gave to my nephew last year. A baby boy found under a leaf. Not a lot of action, but that's the way I prefer my off-duty hours.

Arresting anyone isn't fun. Arresting the disturbed has a distinct, poignant quality about it. They don't belong in handcuffs, but that's my job.

She didn't put up a fuss. It'll be a psychiatric defence. Good lawyer too.

Parents united with baby. End of story. Almost.

Because this woman was a published author there was a certain amount of notoriety to the case. People re-read her book, and read a lot into the story about the baby found under the leaf. I guess she's going to write another one.

My sheriff pal tells me she's been a model prisoner. She's fallen into the rhythm of the institution well. She loves to clean and scrub. Well, she came to the right place.

I heard that the TV crews came into the jail to interview her. After they got all the permissions, taped down the wires, pulled in all the lighting and the camera's, our model prisoner talked to them through a wire mesh screen.

She didn't cry. She didn't insist upon her innocence, as most of the prisoners do. Her fingers curled around the wires, like she was desperate to explain herself, to get her point across. A lot of the prisoners seem to do that, especially when the media get involved.

She said was going to write about women who commit this kind of crime. And she's going to give all the profits to a foundation for lost children.

Babynapping. It's sometimes not the crime that everyone thinks it is. She talked about how she'd received a lot of mail while waiting for the trial. I remember, we forwarded a good three bags to the jail. The writers, apparently, were all women who had something in common.

They had all lost children through miscarriage. Although not moved to crime their letters all recounted the same phenomenon that had set our kidnapper off. Sometimes it's the result – hormonal, chemical, psychological, call it what you want – of miscarriages. There was a specific physical symptom that was present in each case. And it was physical.

Can't wait to read it. I guess her agent visits her cell, trying to pep up the suspense bits. At least that's what my sheriff friend tells me. But our prisoner is busy scrubbing floors and compiling statistics. She tries to keep her hands busy, she told the interviewers. It's all because of the physical symptom, you see. After their miscarriages, they all felt that their arms were suddenly empty. And ached.

And I guess it's the title of her book, too.

Empty Arms, The Feeling That Never Goes Away.

Well, they all have an excuse, don't they?

At the Premier's Literary Awards
Melissa Chan

The Great Hall at the Art Gallery was filling slowly. The officer from Premier's, responsible for organising the Premier's Literary Awards Dinner, stood back, admiring her handiwork. Sixty or so tables, their cloths pristine white and table silver sparkling under the high, stained-glass roof, waited expectantly. Place cards were set at each chair. The arrangement of table seating had been carried out with immense care.

Could Tanya James, the columnist and theatre critic, be seated anywhere near Roger Soames, playwright? Having savaged his most recent drama, and its having subsequently played to swiftly decreasing numbers of theatre patrons at the Athenaeum in Collins Street, Ms James might better be placed as far away as possible.

Would it be wise to position Jack Starkey alongside Maya Trelowthan? Better not: at the last Premier's Literary Awards Dinner the two had talked (and more) all night. At least all through the dinner, to the annoyance of their respective

partners. Their *then* respective partners. Others at the table had
exchanged glances of relief when Jack's erstwhile mate, Mary
Tuck, had ostentatiously gathered up purse, shawl and
complete table setting, in the pause between main course and
dessert, to sweep across to the other side of the hall, depositing
herself at another table and loudly requesting one of the diners
to fetch her a chair. They had sympathetically but thankfully
bidden good night to Simmond Hughes, Maya Trelowthan's
live-in-partner-that-now-was, when he rose bitterly from the
meal to announce another pressing engagement. But, the
rumour mill now disclosed, the Maya Trelowthan-Jack Starkey
liaison had been relatively short-lived. It had ended, as so often
those mad, passionate, eyes-for-no-one-else affairs in the art-
world and world-of-literature do, in whopping rows; pouting,
grimacing silences; charges and counter charges; makings-up;
fallings-out; recriminations; wild, known-to-the-world
comings-together; equally wild, known-to-the-world partings;
then, the affair played out for every possible emotional point
and counterpoint, the *coup de grace*. A severing of ties. An
announcement, almost, to the literary pages of the *Australian*
and the *Age* or the *Sunday Herald* (or even the lesser read art
sections of the *Sunday Herald* and the *Herald Sun*), that the
couple was no longer a couple, the partnership dead, finished,
gone as though never been. And on to the next . . .

Mmm, no, separate tables for those two.

Roly Dangerfield, on the other hand, ever considerate, had
made it easy. Well, easier. He had written to the Premier
demanding that he not be seated anywhere near – and reeled
off a list of six or so authors, twenty-four critics of various
hues, and every woman with whom he had ever had an affair,
a passing fancy, or a snub.

Of the latter, his being what he was, the list was not
inconsiderable.

The only problem Roly Dangerfield presented was where

to sit him. For it was not only he who wrote demanding a placing not alongside various denizens of the literature and allied fields. Many had indicated their desire not to share a table with him. The telephone had rung constantly in the weeks leading up to the event, many of the calls being from writers, critics, members of various literature and associated bodies, and others, whose select list of table companions did not include Roly. Indeed, specifically ruled him out.

So it was repeated every year, at the Premier's Literary Awards Dinner. The writer who refused point blank to sit near – anywhere near – the critic who had for personal reasons of spite (so it was said) written an unforgivable piece on the author's latest book in the *Australian Book Review* or *Arena* or some other publication. The critic who couldn't abide some poet or playwright or novelist or short story writer. Or someone. The numerous authors, from all categories of writing, contributors in every genre, demanding placement away from numerous other authors. Endless demands. And contradictory, from one year to the next, as relations in Melbourne's literary ranks ebbed and flowed, swayed and soared, swept back and forth in an unbounded state of flux.

Majorie Robbins, resilient in her Premier's role, coped with it all.

At Rhumbaralla's in Fitzroy, however, another sort of rebellion had been at hand.

'I tell you, I'm sick of it,' says Constance Bryant, flourishing a champagne glass. 'How come the men always take out the prizes, or most of them? How come if women get a few look-ins, there are cries of favouritism and a women's take-over? I know that it isn't as if women haven't got a bit of a go at literary prizes, at least in recent years. But even more have lost out – to lesser examples of writing by – yes, you guessed it, the men. And when a woman does win, it's usually associated with some sort of drama, some controversy as if to lessen deliberately the joy of winning and acclamation for women's writing.'

Drury Martin thrusts a fork into a steaming plate of pasta. 'Like the time they awarded the top prize to Christina Stead's *Oceans of Story* – then took it back because she was dead. As if that makes any difference to whether or not your writing's worthy of an award or not.'

'Anyway, dead or alive Christina Stead's worth a dozen men!'

'Pity she didn't get the prize when she was alive, though,' says Constance. 'She lived long enough.'

They are silent for a moment, glowering.

Next Grace Fulford butts in. 'What about the time it went to Genevieve O'Rourke's *First Person*. Then the speech made it clear there was really a tussle between the judges about Roger Brown's *Gloria Utopia* and something by Jane Ransome, and the winner was some sort of salvageable compromise. Appalling.'

'We've got to do something about it,' says Kate Smithers, knitting her eyebrows as she spreads butter on a piece of breadroll. 'I agree with all of you. Astonishing how if men sweep the board – or scoop the pool, or whatever cliché you want to put on it – it's taken as natural or not even really commented upon. Whereas if women get any more than minor representation, even in the shortlists, there are cries of bias and reverse discrimination.'

'Come to think of it, you lot,' says Constance Bryant, refilling her glass and handing the bottle to Grace Fulford to pass around the table, 'even talking about reverse discrimination they give themselves away. If there's reverse discrimination in women getting some share of the awards, it must mean that there's pro discrimination favouring male authors, when they continually take out the top possies.'

A lull falls as all eyes turned to Marjorie Robbins.

'Well, Marjorie, what about it?' Grace Fulford looks up from her plate of dips and crunchy toast. 'There must be something we can do about it.'

Six weeks later. Six-thirty in the evening at Rhumbaralla's on Brunswick Street. The women at the table towards the back of the restaurant have put in their usual orders, and a bottle of champagne and the antipasto have already arrived. But unlike the usual animation that centres on the group, the faces of the five women are glum.

'It is hard not to be cynical,' says Marjorie Robbins. 'Especially when every prize, apart from the Nettie Palmer, is named after a man!'

'You'd think women wrote hardly a thing,' exclaims Grace Fulford, swallowing a mouthful of champagne quickly, and almost choking. Recovering after Kate Smithers has thumped her comfortingly on the back, she intones, 'Vance Palmer award for fiction. CJ Dennis prize for poetry. Louis Esson prize for drama. A A Phillips prize for Australian studies. CJ Dennis poetry prize. Allan Marshall prize for children's books. Why, they wouldn't even let some woman have the glory of a children's literature prize being named after her. And there's heaps of women writers in that field. Look at May Gibbs and the gum nut fairies. Mary Grant Bruce. We could go on all night.'

'Mmmm,' sighs Constance Bryant. 'And the other one's neutral. ANZ new writer's award. You'd think the head of the bank could've at least named the award after his wife.'

Rarely dispirited for long, the table is now surging with renewed energy. 'At least the Nettie Palmer prize for non-fiction is worth the same as the Vance Palmer. Fifteen thousand dollars,' says Marjorie Robbins. She pauses, thumping her hand on the table with such force that the glasses bounce, one jangling noisily against the champagne bottle that stands, half empty, near Constance's left elbow.

'Look, it's too early to give up.'

She thumps the tabletop again. 'We haven't sat around this table every week for the past three months without having a host of good ideas – brilliant ideas, I might say. It'll just take a bit of working out, and we'll get there.'

'Another bottle of champagne?' asks a voice at Drury's side. 'I think this table ordered it?'

Wine was flowing at the tables set around the spacious expanse of the Great Hall. Wine had been flowing for some hours, with a number of the revellers noticeably affected.

It seemed to be those seated at tables together with Constance Bryant, Kate Smithers, Grace Fulford, Drury Martin or Marjorie Robbins who were most boisterous, their glass-filled hands waving, their eyes shining, their words slurring – just a little. But then – several of those seated with the members of the Allan Marshall prize for children's literature were laughing and joking with extra loud voices, too.

Barry Cremona and Robert Hodgkin, two members of the Premier's Awards Committee, appeared to be definitely under the weather. Robert sat with Constance Bryant at his left hand. On this occasion, had her behaviour been closely observed, those who knew her well might have been not a little surprised. Rather than joining in the revelry by matching Robert Hodgkin glass for glass (a Brown Brothers' Riesling, extra dry), Constance had exercised a deal of short-term self-denial and altruism all night. Upon Robert's glass being emptied of a few mouthfuls by the man himself, Constance gaily filled it with wine from her own. She had long since lost count of the number of times she had done so, just as she had lost count of the number of times the wine waiter had approached their table and filled both her glass and Robert's – unknowingly adding doubly to Robert's intake. At the neighbouring table, Barry Cremona was being well served by Kate Smithers, though Kate's deprivation was far less: a nondrinker she, Kate was able to maintain two glasses at her table setting, a glass of iced-water standing beside one regularly filled with wine by the waiter and just as regularly emptied, by herself, into Barry Cremona's ever-filled glass.

Just below and to the right of the rostrum, where Stafford Truex was conducting proceedings as Master of Ceremonies, Pedro d'Arbo of the non-fiction judging panel sat snoring gently, hands clasped on rotund waistcoat, chins resting on sunken chest. Carolyn Noble of the children's literature panel glanced across at Grace Fulford, who sat at the next table. Grace raised her eyebrows. Carolyn Noble nodded back.

Next to Grace, Adam Flannigan, third male member of the Premier's Awards Committee, was sunk low in his chair. As she looked, Carolyn saw him slide gently under the table. The feat was achieved with hardly a sound, hardly a pause at the table. No one really noticed, apart from Grace Fulford who, with a deftness born of her previous career as nursing sister at St Vincent's, swished the table cloth expertly above Adam Flannigan's now supine body. White cloth subsided gently, hanging straight from the tabletop. An acute ear might hear a slight rumbling noise from below as Adam's chest rose and fell in the calm innocent sleep of the well-fed, well-drunk *homo sapiens*. But even the most penetrating of eye would miss his well-concealed body at Grace Fulford's feet.

Drury Martin was faring less well with Dixon Webb of the poetry judging panel. She had engaged his attention all night, rather more than she had intended. But he had laughingly caught her wrist each time she had attempted to fill his emptying glass from hers. She glanced at her watch. It was almost time for the winner of last year's Vance Palmer award to move to the microphone at the conclusion of Stafford Truex's laboured introduction. Once his speech was completed, it was time for the announcement of this year's awards. It was imperative that Drury should divert Dixon Webb, whether by drink or (the thought was unwelcome, but born of necessity) other means, before the list of prize winners was read by the Premier and the winning writers took the rostrum to speak their thanks.

At a nearby table Sally Moon, a second member of the children's judging panel (who had turned up one evening, fortuitously, at Rhumbaralla's, and been welcomed at the table at the back, where champagne flowed, breadrolls were broken and buttered, and antipasto, pasta and dips devoured with a will), was in some difficulty, too. David Rue of the fiction panel and Danton Crisp of non-fiction were seated on either side of her. Danton Crisp had drunk well, but Sally Moon had not been able to keep up the flow of wine to David. In the end, she had decided to concentrate on Danton Crisp's glass, whilst her mind worked rapidly to determine upon a solution to David Rue's comparative sobriety. Perhaps she could persuade him his bladder called urgently, immediately prior to the announcement of the winner of the fiction award?

Positioned close to the dais so she could observe the proceedings and step in should anything go wrong, Marjorie Robbins sat, casually glancing around the hall. Far over to the left she saw Sarah Hinks, with an empty chair beside her.

Another under the table? Her eye ran down the list of table-seatings she had placed beside her dinner plate. Ah! It must be Grant Boyston of the fiction panel. Dreadful man. Terribly opinionated. They were well rid of him if he had slid, circulation drowning in Riesling, under the large, circular top of the table. She caught Sarah's eye. Even from that distance, she detected a slow, glittering wink. Yes! Definitely another destined for a heavy hangover in the morning. How would they get him out from under, to shoehorn him into a taxi that one or other of them surely could flag down when the night was over? That could wait for later.

'And it is imperative.' There was a long pause. It was

Dunkley Dater, winner of last year's Premier's Award for
fiction, who was speaking. His delivery was dour, his
concentration on his own words monumental. He was making
a point.

'It is imperative. That we recognise. The multicultural value.
Of Australian writing . . . And that we not,' he thundered, his
eyebrows curling down towards his watery blue eyes, 'and that
we not resile from the position. That we now hold. On the
world stage.' Major pause.

'Governments must recognise. The value of the Australian
arts community. Governments must acknowledge. The un-
matched contribution. Made to the Australian character. To the
Australian identity. By the novelists. Poets. Dramatists. Essayists.
Now making Australia known. Overseas.'

His hand swept to his forehead, swishing back the rapidly
diminishing locks.

'Governments must give. I say, they *must* give. Increased
subsidies. Adequate incomes. To our writers.'

He paused, sipping at the glass he had carried with him,
shaking slightly in nervous hand, to the platform. Now for the
denouement.

'My books are now. Sold. In every. English speaking.
Country. *Perishing Valley Twilight* reached. The bestseller list. In
the US. Last week. My agent in New York tells me it's-bound-
to-stay-there-for-the-next-ten-weeks.'

The last sentence came rushing out, the author suddenly
childishly excited, unable to refrain from the lilting gallop of
his own words as they tripped off his honeyed tongue . . .

What he thought of as his honeyed tongue. And so, too, did
someone sitting at the table at which he had sat all evening,
who gazed up at his gangling form at the rostrum, eyes wide,
face openly admiring in worshipful adulation. How could
anyone not, the eyes gazing at him seemed to be saying.
Admire. Dunkley Dater?

It was Dunkley Dater. Author of *Perishing Valley Twilight*, the bestseller. And *Fruit Bowl*, winner of last year's Vance Palmer award. He had sat at this table all night and he was delivering the speech of his lifetime. The adoring eyes widened further.

Clapping burst forth from the assembled throng.

At one of the tables, Colin Fen of the poetry judging panel was rising to stagger from the room, his face ashen, his hands clutching at his mouth.

Obviously drunk too much, thought Marjorie Robbins as she watched his shuffling walk from the hall. Then her attention was caught by a movement at a table to her right. Graeme Easton and Serge Cartier, members of the Louis Esson drama award panel, had been imbibing well, too. At the height of the clapping, one grabbed the other by the necktie and Marjorie saw his lips move in what appeared to be a threatening expletive. She glanced down at the others seated at their table. Grace Fulford was there. She had moved over, giving up on any possibility of scintillating conversation with Adam Flannigan upon his disappearance floorwards. Serge Cartier and Graeme Easton had, predictably, been fertile ground.

Marjorie looked over at Grace's now deserted chair. No sign of Adam. Still sleeping it off, cosily curled under the clean white protection of the crisp linen tablecloth. But it was back to Grace Fulford's new table companions. They hadn't lasted long, either. Marjorie Robbins saw their departing backs disappearing out to the toilets – or perhaps to St Kilda Road, for fisticuffs? Oh dear. And the Premier just now moving to the microphone to begin the announcement of the awards.

Stafford Truex was feeling slightly uncomfortable. He was not quite sure why. Couldn't put his finger on it. Thought there was something wrong. But what was it?

He had performed brilliantly all night as Master of Ceremonies, even if he did say so himself. Introduced the head of the Premier's Awards Committee with his usual aplomb. Waited the appropriate length of time before moving, without the audience noticing, not at all, toward the rostrum again, to nudge the speaker gently from the microphone. Persuaded all the speakers to speak sharply, to the point, not too long, not too involved. Moved them on.

He moved the head of the committee on. Then – after the leek and leaf spinach soup with goat's cheese and pinenut parcel – he had, with the appropriate touch of deference combined with a practised air of 'boys together', announced the Premier for his welcoming address. And, after a suitable pause in which the Premier spoke, Stafford Truex had moved, gently but inexorably, to resume the rostrum and microphone.

Following the breast of chicken in puff crust with an avocado mousse filling and tomato hollandaise, Stafford Truex had announced the guest speaker, Dunkley Dater. And had borne, with exceptional spirit, he thought, the speech that came forth. With enormous fortitude, he had listened for the appropriate length of time, then moved smoothly and surely to regain the central position. There, in full view of the sea of tables filling the hall, he had called for the Premier once more, this time to present the awards.

And so, as with every year, the presentation of prizes began. First, the Vance Palmer award for fiction. Cherry Mae Bryant, for her novel *Bitter Gratitude*.

A short, crisp speech from the winner, slightly stumbling, a little as if unprepared. When after all, thought Stafford Truex to himself, they all know they've won before they come here. At least – I thought they did? Don't they let the winners know in advance so they can prepare their spontaneous speeches? And why not Bradley Dickson, for *Living on the Edge of War*?

He glanced across to where Bradley Dickson was sitting, next to the Premier's wife. Bradley Dickson's mouth was open, his eyes glassy. He was noticeably moved, made as if to stand, then slumped in his seat, his hand to his brow. Before his eyes disappeared behind his fleshy palm they had registered shock and bewilderment.

Yes, thought Stafford Truex, his head full of support for the drop-jawed author of *Living on the Edge* . . . Then, he pulled himself together. He must stay aware of what was happening, so he could step in to take over at the appropriate moment. Ah well, suppose the women have to win something.

Next, the Nettie Palmer award for non-fiction. Candace Rush, for her study of feminist politics in the 1960s and '70s – what was it called? Something about personal . . . Ah, yes. *Personal and Public Politics: A Mind for the '90s.* Whatever that meant.

So, let the ladies have their day, thought Truex, as he mused on. Yet the uneasiness he had felt earlier persisted.

Australian studies award. Decided by the same judging panel as the Nettie Palmer. Jesse Watson. *Sixty Thousand Years – Murri Women of the North.* Short speech. Well received. What was it? The never-forgotten truths of Aboriginal women, was it? Murris. And women. Never knew what these groups were wanting to be called, now. Couldn't be 'ladies' any more. Or 'girls'. What a man had to get used to . . .

Stafford Truex was brought sharply back to the present. Time for the announcement of the winner of the Louis Esson. Drama. He was sure Dan Herlihy would win it. He had had a bet on that one, with some of the fellows down at the ABC. What was that play he had written – for stage, but adapted for the big screen . . . Joint Australia-Hollywood production . . . Bringing Australia to the attention of the real professionals . . .

Again, he was drawn back with a shock. There was a woman on the rostrum. 'Another one,' he thought, suddenly realising he was beginning to feel angry. What was she doing there?

Janice Greenmore was making her speech of thanks for the

playwrights award, for her play dealing with the politics of genetic engineering and scientific fraud. Saying she hadn't been able to stage it, apart from several playreadings. But with the prize, and the recognition, she was sure it would be performed not only in Victoria, but nationally.

Stafford Truex's anger did not abate. His mind ran back over the winners already announced – Vance Palmer: Cherry Mae Bryant; Nettie Palmer: Candace Rush; Australian Studies: Jesse Watson; Louis Esson: Janice Greenmore. Women! All women! Every one a woman!

He knew now why he had felt uneasy. What had got into the judging panels this time? What were David Rue and Grant Boyston thinking about in naming a woman as prize winner of fiction? God! You could always count on their good sense – and good taste. Well, he had always thought you could. Pedro d'Arbo and Benjamin Dent. They were on the non-fiction. And who else – yes. Danton Crisp. Sound. All of them sound. Couldn't believe they'd pick a woman. Woman writer of non-fiction? Fifteen thousand dollars for a woman's book! Something on feminism – politics – God! His usually inventive mind, his ordinarily admirable grasp of language, was leaving him. He pulled himself together. The Louis Esson ... Graeme Easton and Serge Cartier? Surely he could have counted on their granting the prize to Dan Herlihy's *Up There, Castor.* Greatest stage play to come out of Australia, he thought. And being filmed, right this instant, here in Melbourne, with various scenes in the bush. What had gone wrong? *What – had – gone – wrong?*

He glanced again at the rostrum. Another woman. Poetry, this one. *Gambling Between Two Worlds*, was it? And who was it? Luisa Boero? And who the hell was she, anyway?

The new writer's award. A woman. And next? Children's. Oh, well, what could anyone expect. A woman. Of course.

Head sunk in chest, Stafford Truex made his way slowly back to the microphone. The Premier had just completed his wrap-up. Stafford had been too busy with his own thoughts to judge the timing – whether the speeches had gone on too long, whether the audience had been restive, whether he was keeping up with his professional intervention just to keep the show on the road. All he could recall, now, of the evening, was the clapping that greeted every announcement. Even some stamping of feet, he reflected.

He looked around. How could the men on the judging panels let him down like that. Let the world of art down like that? Because it was not only the glory of winning, of being rewarded in recognition. There was the money, too: fifteen thousand for some, seven thousand five hundred dollars for others. The prize winnings should go to writers. Not *women*. And this time – it had all – *all* gone to women!

Glancing across at the entrance to the hall, he noticed David Rue looking somewhat truculent, a glass in his hand and a woman by his side, holding him up. Wasn't it – yes, one of the women on the children's book award panel. What was her name? Caroline – Carolyn – Noble, that was it. What had David been doing during the evening?

Looks as if he's a bit worse for wear, thought Stafford Truex, his inventiveness finally leaving him altogether, cliché coming readily to his lips.

And behind them? Benjamin Dent – and another of those women judges from the children's award. Sally – Sarah? Hinks? Hicks? Oh, what did it matter. The men had stuffed it up. Well and truly stuffed it up. And none of them that he could see – and come to think of it he couldn't see many of them – looked as if they would be able to hold a decent conversation, much less answer for this débâcle.

Stafford Truex dejectedly made his way from the platform to his table beneath the rostrum and to his dish of crème caramel. Morosely, he began spooning the concoction between his trembling lips.

'But – but – I hadn't realised the Louis Esson had gone to Janice Greenmore,' stuttered Margaret Gibson to Pearl Whitburn, a fellow member of the Premier's Awards Committee. 'What happened? Remember. Wasn't Susy Bonham so mad that she lost out to those two – those two – men! The report came back to us from the panel that it was Dan Herlihy.'

'I know.' Pearl Whitburn was looking half shocked, half victorious. 'Something happened between the names coming to us and their being typed into the envelopes. Something wonderful?'

Suddenly, she began shaking, her eyes lighting with laughter. Her shoulders heaved. Staggering, she turned to look at Genevieve Pounder, another committee member, who had come up behind her, grabbing at her arm. 'Pearl. I thought – we know – it wasn't meant to be Cherry Mae Bryant at all. Constance was so mad that Grant Boyston and David Rue wanted *Living on the Edge* – Bradley Dickson, that they overruled her. Or am I . . .

Then Genevieve Pounder had joined in. The table rushed and roared with noise, the laughter rising to the stained glass ceiling. Suddenly, the entire Premier's Awards Committee had gathered – well, all except Adam Flannigan, Robert Hodgkin and Barry Cremona, who had long since begun sleeping the sleep of the well-imbibed. The prize giving and speeches had flowed on without them.

A month after the night of the Premier's Literary Awards: the women have expanded to two noisy tables at Rhumbaralla's. There is talking over one another, laughter flowing between the emptying champagne bottles and platters of antipasto.

'They couldn't – they couldn't say – do – anything,' says Pearl Whitburn, between gulps. 'It was just too ridiculous – couldn't admit that when the prizes were announced they were under the table or out in St Kilda Road bashing each other up.'

'And being picked up by the cops.'

'I heard Graeme Easton and Serge Cartier had more to worry about than who won the Louis Esson award,' says Constance Bryant. 'They ended up at Russell Street, then slept it off in the cells.'

'What about the fiction lot, Constance?' asks Margaret Gibson, her eyebrows raising as she clutches her shaking sides.

'David Rue was so mad at being turned down by Carolyn, he couldn't speak for a week, much less protest,' returns Constance, waving her glass as she speaks.

'Bradley Dickson tried to get him to do something on the night, but he couldn't take it in,' she adds. 'That almost ended in a fight, too.'

'Until the Premier's minders stepped in, and that was the end of that,' chimes in Marjorie.

Constance nods, looking down the long table fashioned from two pushed together. 'And,' she says, triumphant. 'None of them could admit they were finessed by a bunch of women!'

They sip champagne.

'But what about next year,' says one.

Marjorie Robbins looks over the rim of her glass.

She waits for a moment whilst she selects the biggest, fattest, blackest olive from the plate in front of her.

'What about the Mary Grant Bruce award for writing for teenagers. And the Mary Fortune prize for crime writing? The Acting Premier's agreed. It's only awaiting the announcement.'

'*And* the Vida Goldstein women and politics prize,' says Constance Bryant.

In a spontaneous gesture borne of long habit, they raise their glasses.

'To the Christina Stead prize for the living.'

Wie Bitte?
Barbara Wilson

Quickborn.

Schlump.

Poppenbüttel.

I stared at a map of Hamburg's subway system. My destination was one stop beyond Schlump, Marianne had said. Marianne Schnackenbusch was a translator acquaintance I'd run into at the Frankfurt Book Fair a week ago. When she heard that we were both translating Gloria de los Angeles' latest collection of short stories, she into German, me into English, she'd generously told me that I must come to stay with her after the fair in Hamburg. She and her partner Elke had loads of room and I could stay as long as I liked.

It sounded perfect. I had a brief engagement in Paris first, but after that I was at a loose end. My translation was due at the end of November, and I didn't have the money to go anywhere splendid to finish it. Certainly I could have stayed in my small attic room in Nicola's house in London, but in truth I'd been rather avoiding Nicola since the arrival of the

Croatian lesbian commune last summer. How was I to know that my blithe offer many years ago to reciprocate their hospitality in Zagreb meant that all six of them would turn up on Nicola's doorstep in July?

Marianne and Elke's flat was in an old area of the city called the Schanzenviertel. Leafy streets, tall graceful apartment buildings, graffiti, bikes everywhere, Turkish and Greek shops just opening up. I'd taken a night train from Paris and it was still early.

Marianne embraced me heartily at the door. 'Please sit down, sit down and eat. You must be starving, all night on the train. You should have told us when you were coming. We could have picked you up.'

She was a big woman, with a mane of hennaed red-purple hair around a broad, eager face. She was barefoot and wearing a red silk robe. I knew from our brief talks at bookfairs that she was the daughter of a German Communist who had fled to Chile before the war, and a Chilean mother. She had told me that in addition to translating she also was a lecturer at the university in Latin American literature. I could see from the hallway that translation and teaching must pay better in Germany than in Britain: the flat looked enormous and was full of Oriental carpets and big leather sofas and chairs. There were bookshelves up to the tall ceilings.

'She's a bit overwhelming,' my friend Lucinda in Paris had told me. 'A combination of Latin American vivacity and Prussian forcefulness. But she's generous to a fault; she'll take care of you well.' Lucinda was as poor as I was and knew the value of visits to people with washer-driers and fax machines. Lucinda sublet a studio about the size of an elevator carriage, and practised one of the few literary occupations to pay less than translation: poetry.

Elke was already sitting at the kitchen table, which was spread with a huge number of plates of meats and cheeses and

jars of spreads and preserves. She was much frailer looking than
Marianne, and older too, with narrow shoulders, short grey-
blonde hair and round small glasses. If you didn't see her
wrinkles, she would remind you of a boyish Bolshevik in a
Hollywood film about the Russian Revolution.

'Just coffee for now,' I said.

'No, no,' said Marianne, pushing all manner of things
towards me, and settling herself. 'No, you must eat. This is so
exciting for me, having Gloria's English translator here. There's
so much I want to talk over with you. I'm enjoying the stories
so much; they just go like the breeze.'

I looked across the table in astonishment. We hadn't had
time in Frankfurt to discuss the literary value of Gloria's work.
I had only assumed she felt the same ambivalence I did. 'Well,
I always find Gloria to be fairly easy to translate,' I said
cautiously. 'There is a certain . . . similarity in all her work.'

'Yes,' said Marianne, delicately spreading layers of soft cheese
on half a roll and then devouring it in a gulp. 'That's what I
enjoy so much, how you can always count on her to write so
lusciously. Other writers seem dry next to her, while she is
sensual, opulent, rich and vivid. I just sink into her books like
a big feather bed, like a warm bath with perfume.'

'They do tend to have something of a bathetic effect,' I
murmured.

'Yes, exactly,' said Marianne, but Elke said, 'Cassandra means
they're sentimental drivel, my friend. And I'm afraid I agree.'

'No, she doesn't mean that,' Marianne said good-
humouredly. 'After all, Cassandra has translated all Gloria's
books into English.'

Elke fortunately changed the subject. 'I must be off soon to
work. I wish I could stay and help Marianne show you around
the city. But we have some problems at work that are rather
worrisome.'

'Not just the usual problems between the bosses and

workers,' said Marianne indignantly. 'Threats. Terrible threats.'

'But don't you work in a bird-watching society?' I asked, uncertain if Marianne had given me the right information or if I'd understood it properly.

'Yes, yes,' said Elke. 'Well, that's what it was when it was originally founded. Sort of like your Audubon Society in America, I think. But you can't watch birds nowadays without seeing how they are threatened by the loss of their habitats and so forth, and that has made some of the members very activist. We are trying to purchase land and writing letters to the politicians, as well as planning a big demonstration in two weeks. And of course some members are nervous about all this activism, which to them is like confrontation with the state.'

'But who is threatening whom?'

'Our whole organisation got a threat in the mail, several threats. The first two weeks ago, and another last week, and yesterday one more. It's about the cause we are working on now, trying to save a stretch of the Elbe River. It used to be that this section, not so far from Hamburg, marked the boundary between East and West Germany, and so it was never developed. If you go there, you see old farms and very little else. But now, with reunification, they want to build on either side, and worse, from our point of view, from the birds' point of view that is, they want to dredge the river to make it deeper, and make concrete sides and so forth, for shipping.'

Elke got up. 'We don't want this to happen, of course. There is very little left in Europe of undeveloped land, especially wetlands. So we're fighting.' She wrapped a scarf several times around her neck and put on her jacket. 'And someone doesn't like it.'

As soon as she left Marianne was back to Gloria's writing. 'Just now I'm translating the story of the servant girl and the colonel,' she said.

'Oh yes, that one.'

'What a sly sense of humour Gloria has, don't you think?'

'Well . . .'

'But that's what I admire so much about Gloria. She is capable of slyness and subtlety, and also of great exuberance and broad strokes. She has such a large talent.'

'Broad strokes, yes,' I said weakly.

Marianne polished off the rest of the rolls and several more cups of coffee, chattering all the while about Gloria. She then showed me to my room, which was large and light. It over-looked an interior garden where the lindens and ashes were turning gold and yellow. 'And here is the desk where you will work,' she said, and it was old-fashioned and walnut, a desk I had always dreamed of, with green blotting paper and a desk lamp with a warm brown paper shade. A tall bookshelf along one wall was filled with novels in French and Spanish. There was a red Turkish rug on the floor and a daybed covered with pillows.

'I hope this is all right,' Marianne said anxiously.

'It's wonderful!'

'And the best thing is, at night, after you are finished translating your Gloria and I am finished translating my Gloria, we will have long evenings to discuss her.'

But today there was to be no work. Today Marianne had decided to show me the city of Hamburg. She drove me by the university and through parks with lakes and parks with statues. She bought me an expensive lunch at a restaurant just off the Rathaus Square and told me everything she knew about Hamburg's history, which was quite a lot.

The stories she told me were reflected in the layers of the city: the few timbered buildings with a medieval touch, the tall, narrow buildings along Dutch-looking canals, squeezed in among modern offices in the international style. The city had a grandeur that was more in its substantialness than in any great elegance. It looked like a city where business was done and had always been done. It looked solid, commercial, successful. And yet this air of solidity and permanence was illusory too. For since the Middle Ages the city had been destroyed over and over by fire, and during the last war the Allied bombings had flattened huge sections of it.

The harbour, the heart of Hamburg, where Marianne was taking me now, had been practically destroyed in those bombings. You would not guess it now. Huge container ships from around the world snaked slowly by, escorted by pilot boats. Around them, smaller working and pleasure boats churned up the river water, that on this bright fall day and from this distance, looked blue-green and sparkling. We strolled along the promenade and came to the inner harbour, where Marianne said she had a surprise for me.

'It's funny,' I said, looking around me at the huge brick warehouses and the multitude of wooden docks, 'I've never been here, and yet it seems familiar.'

'A dream?'

'No,' I said, suddenly remembering, 'It was . . . it was a language course, on British TV, oh, about twenty years ago, when I was first in London. It wasn't an ordinary language course; it had a continuing plot, and it took place in Hamburg, around the red-light district, and the harbour.'

'So you do know German!'

'*Wie bitte?*' That was the name of the programme, which translated as simply, 'Please?' or 'How's that Again?'

I admitted, 'Actually, I didn't progress very far with the lessons. I would usually get too caught up in the plot to remember that I was supposed to be listening for grammatical constructs. So then, after fifteen minutes of action, there would be questions – "What was Peter doing in the red-light district that evening?" "What did Astrid say when the killer pulled out his gun and shoved her in the back of the boat?" – I could never answer them.'

'But your German will come back if we practice it,' said
Marianne, as she marched me down a flight of metal stairs to
a wooden dock alongside one of the harbour walls. 'Here it is.'
She stopped in front of a boat called *The Juliette*. 'It's Elke's
boat. Actually, Elke owns it with some others, all of whom
work for the bird-watching society. It's become the official
ship of their movement. They take it out on the Elbe with
banners and invite journalists and TV stations.'

We stepped down onto the boat and Marianne unlocked
the cabin. It was a beautiful old cruiser, roomy enough for ten
or twelve people, with a small sleeping area and a miniscule
toilet behind the pilot's cabin.

'I wish the others who used the boat would pick up after
themselves a bit better,' said Marianne, reaching for a bucket
and rope that had been left in the middle of the captain's
room. 'Elke always leaves it spotless.'

'Oh no,' she said, when she saw the contents of the bucket.
It was a seagull with its neck twisted by a metal coil. A piece
of paper was attached to the metal, but its message was so wet
with blood it was hardly decipherable.

Marianne turned the colour of her hair. 'This is really the
limit. I don't think they should be trying to keep this quiet
anymore. They should call the media right away.'

'What about the police?'

'Yes, them too. Not that I trust them to be helpful.'

I watched as Marianne put the bucket on the dock. I
expected that we would follow it, and that she would start
looking for the nearest phone booth. But instead she turned
the key in the engine, which started up with a promising
rumble.

'If they think they're going to destroy my pleasure in
showing my friend the harbour and the river, they're mistaken.
We'll deal with this when we return.'

It was an amazing thing to be out on the river among all the

other boats. The container ships towered above us like apartment buildings and even the tugboats seemed five times as
large. The water, close now, was pale green, slightly dirty, with
a smell that was more river than salt. We cruised past the
promenade above us and the port of Hamburg buildings, very
grand and rounded, and then past the city, in the direction of
the faraway sea and Marianne pointed out restaurants and
villas, beaches where there had once been swimming, and the
large brightly painted asylum ships that held foreigners who
had come to Germany hoping for refuge or economic
opportunity.

Outward bound Marianne was in determinedly high spirits,
telling stories of the river and trips they'd made, relating
political problems with gusto and anger, and turning the
subject again and again back to Gloria de los Angeles, and her
large talent.

'I tell you,' she said over the roar of the engine, 'I have very
little patience for some of these fiction writers who are
deliberately obscure. I grew up in a very political family, my
father was friends with Neruda, and I have always believed that
writing should serve the people and be very accessible. There's
a Latin American woman writer, for example, who some
people rave about, but who I have absolutely no time for. They
have asked me to translate her books, and I tell them, Why
bother? She is self-indulgent and obtuse for no reason. I hope
she never gets translated into German. We have enough of
those kinds of writers already.'

'You don't mean Luisa Montiflores?'

'Exactly! You know her?'

'She . . .' Actually, I had received a letter from Luisa only a
few days ago. She'd found out from Nicola that I was in
Germany and was demanding my help in finding a German
translator. 'Since you're there, you must have contacts,' she
wrote.

'Hey! Look out! Get out of our way! Whew. Now would you like a lesson in steering?'

That took all our energy for a while, and in truth, I found it exhilarating, if a bit terrifying, piloting *The Juliette* along the huge waterway. But as we came back into the inner harbour, I could see that Marianne was brooding more and more about the bird with the broken neck.

'Whoever these people are, they're monsters,' she burst out finally.

'Who is it who wants to develop that stretch of the Elbe?'

'That's just it. Many corporations, shippers, industrialists stand to gain from it. They're so powerful anyway, why would they resort to such cheap, ugly tricks?'

'They must be more afraid of Elke and her group than you realise.'

'Well, I'm calling Elke and getting her to stage a press conference with that poor bird. As soon as we get back.'

But when we returned to *The Juliette*'s berth, the bucket had vanished.

That evening there was a meeting in Marianne and Elke's flat, attended by eight of the core bird-watchers. Several were mild-looking older people, and only one was under thirty, a quiet, bald-headed woman with astonishing tattoos. Two men came together, one very tall and one very round, and a middle-aged couple with a new baby. They were the only two whose names I caught, Karin and Helmut. The baby was named Sappho, which seemed promising, though she did have an uncommonly pointed head. Marianne decided to take part in the meeting, but I retired to my room so as not to be in the way, and was soon working on my translation under the light of the lamp at the beautiful desk. Maybe I *was* too much of an élitist. Gloria's books had reached millions of people and given them a great deal of enjoyment. Who was I to judge? Maybe my long years of association with Luisa Montiflores, who hated Gloria de los Angeles and everything she stood for with a terrible passion, had made it impossible for me to look at Gloria objectively. I re-read the paragraph I was translating:

He took her passionately; she responded as if in a dream. They coupled frenetically, hour after hour, without eating, without drinking any more than each other's torrid sweat. Days passed, weeks. One day he got up, as if an alarm clock had rung. He looked at his beard in the mirror, at his wasted feverish limbs. And he left.

It was sort of like a warm bath, scented with patchouli oil. But it was not great literature. I must hold my ground. Actually, I must state my true opinion before I could hold it. But I trembled.

About an hour into the meeting baby Sappho began crying, a noise that started far off down the hall in the living room and came closer, until it remained outside my closed door. In between the shrieks were the voices of her two parents, who started out trying to calm her down, but seemed to move into another topic: problems with the way the bird-watchers meeting was going. Helmut, who had seemed sweet and eager to please when I met him, the very picture of a proud, forty-five-year-old father, sounded very aggrieved indeed, though it was hard, because of my limited German, to understand why. Karin seemed defensive. The only words I caught were 'capitalists', and '*politizei*'.

Too bad I hadn't paid more attention long ago to that *Wie Bitte* series. Why not? I willed myself back many years ago, to Bayswater, to the small shabby parlour of the house where I'd been staying with a girlfriend and her mother (right from the beginning, no place of my own!). I'd met the girl in Madrid and had followed her to London. She was working as a translator, which I thought so fascinating that I decided to try it myself.

She was actually quite a boring girl. Her idea of a good time
was to sit at home watching language programmes. My idea of
a good time was to figure out how to get her mind off
television. Her mother had eventually asked me to leave – when
the series wasn't even over yet!

Sappho finally calmed down and the pair went back to the
meeting. Eventually everyone left and it sounded like even
Elke and Marianne had gone to bed. But to my surprise I ran
into Elke on my way to the bathroom, and she was dressed to
go out. It was almost midnight. She looked more like a
Russian revolutionary than ever, in her black leather jacket,
Palestinian scarf and leather cap.

'I'm going to sleep on the boat tonight with one of the
others,' she explained. 'We want to make sure that nothing
happens to *The Juliette*. We're planning a demonstration this
weekend on the Elbe with several boats, and *The Juliette* is to
lead them.'

'What is the nature of the threatening letters?' I asked. 'Has
the group been able to come up with any ideas about who has
written them?'

'*Who* has written them and who they want us to think has
written them might be two very different things.'

'What do you mean?'

'They seem to me to be written by an educated person
trying to sound simple-minded. Computer typed, but with a
few words misspelled. Come,' she said, and led me back into
the comfortable living room where Marianne was listening to
the stereo with earphones on and a pile of papers beside her.
She looked like a large red bear in her dressing gown. 'I'm
reading student translations,' she shouted happily.

Elke took up a folder from the coffee table and pulled out
a computer-printed letter. 'Here's the first one: BIRD–LOVERS
BEWAR. YOU CAN NEVER WIN AGAINST US. GIVE UP BEFORE YOU
ARE SORRY.'

She held up another. 'And later on they write, IF YOU GO ON WITH THE PLANED DEMONSTRASION, YOU WILL REGRET IT.'

'They seem sort of fake, don't they?' I agreed. 'But how did he or she know about the demonstration?'

'A good question, since we had at that point not made a public announcement. Still, it was no great secret.'

'Could it be a spy or infiltrator?'

'We don't want to say this, but some of us believe it is someone in the group, maybe not the core group, but the larger one. Big corporations don't send little notes saying, *Drop this cause or you'll be sorry*. They have lawyers and money to bribe the politicians. Why would they strangle a seagull and put it on our boat? It's quite childish, really.'

'Have you raised the issue in the core group? At the meeting tonight?'

'No ...'

'Why not?'

'Because it is so much easier and more usual to see evil outside oneself. Everyone says we must be vigilant and sooner or later the culprit will reveal himself.'

That sounded like a line from *Wie Bitte*. And suddenly I had a dream-like flash of disaster in a dark harbour, of someone being knocked on the head and thrown into the water. The lesson on indirect objects perhaps.

But as Elke went out the door, I thought, if a child strangled a seagull we would not call it childish. We would find it most disturbing.

The next days fell into a pattern. At seven every morning (Marianne was under the impression that since I had arrived on the night train from Paris that I was an early riser, which was far from the truth), Marianne would give a crisp rap to my door and call out, 'Breakfast, Cassandra,' or alternatively, '*Frühstück*, Cassandra.' Since hearing about *Wie Bitte* she had begun playfully to test my knowledge of German by throwing words into our Spanish and English conversation. The more words I knew the more she threw. 'By the end of your visit we'll be speaking German all the time.'

In theory I had the days to myself, in my lovely peaceful room, but Marianne was always knocking and breaking into my thoughts, asking if I wanted more coffee, bringing in little trays with snacks, telling me she was going out shopping – did I want to come and choose my favourite foods, oh yes, it would be amusing, wouldn't it, for me to visit one of the little Turkish shops in the neighbourhood, and important too, to meet some Turks face to face, they were having such a hard time in this terrible place, she had experienced it herself, growing up in Santiago among free-spirited Communists and then coming to the university here and having to make her way, having to become more German than the Germans, but, oh, she really shouldn't be interrupting me, and she closed the door softly and apologetically, tip-toeing away. Half an hour later she would be back, wanting to show me an interview with Gloria in a Berlin newspaper, or an article in a Chilean journal or a xeroxed copy of a speech Neruda gave from exile. Sometimes the flat would fill with music from her expensive CD player. Stravinksy's *Rite of Spring* was a great favourite of hers.

She was so good-natured and enthusiastic, so clearly pleased to have me as a visitor, that I felt churlish turning her invitations down or pretending that I didn't hear her calling me, or even fantasising about locking my door. Still, when Elke asked me one day if I'd like to go on a local bird-watching expedition, I responded so willingly that she was taken aback. If my friend Lucy Hernandez had been there she would have been quite surprised. She'd tried for years to put a pair of binoculars in my hands and to explain to me that a robin and a sparrow were not the same thing.

'It's not a serious trip,' Elke warned me. 'But every month Karin takes a group to one or another of Hamburg's parks and points out local birds and discusses some topic, like nest-building or migratory patterns. It's nice for beginners and for parents with children.'

'I'm dying to go,' I assured her.

A few hours later I was sitting on a bench with Karin in a park thick with golden-leafed trees while she breastfed baby Sappho. I had learned the difference between a robin and a sparrow, had even learned their German names. That would show Lucy. The rest of the small group was wandering around a small pond, staring at the ducks and, in the case of the children, feeding them.

'Is it your first?' I asked Karin. In the bright daylight she looked older than she had at the evening meeting. Well over forty, with grey streaks in her dark hair.

'Yes. Is it so obvious? I keep wanting to pretend to everyone that it's dead easy, though clearly it would have been much easier had it been fifteen years ago! Helmut is even worse, of course. We're trying to share childcare, in the progressive fashion. Which means that each of us is convinced the other doesn't do it quite correctly.'

She yawned. The autumn sunlight stopped pleasantly short of being hot, but it was still sleepy-making. 'Just last night, in fact,' Karin said, 'we were having a fight. We were up late discussing this whole business again of the threats to the group. Helmut takes it very seriously. He doesn't want me to take the baby on the demonstration for fear of violence.'

'Are you expecting violence?'

'Oh, there's always something with the police,' Karin said, shrugging. 'I've been in demonstrations over the years where I narrowly escaped being beaten badly. But of course I plan to keep the baby well away from any of that. It's important that we have babies and children at the demonstration. We want to show how destroying the wetlands and bird habitats will affect their future.'

'How did the bird-watching go?' Elke asked when I returned. Marianne was mercifully at the university, no doubt lecturing her adoring students about Gloria de los Angeles. Elke poured me a glass of wine and I sank into one of the huge leather sofas.

'It was wonderful to be outside, out of the house,' I said. 'Elke, are you expecting violence at the demonstration? A real confrontation with the police?'

'We're not going to instigate it. It may be provoked.' She sipped her wine thoughtfully, the sober Bolshevik.

'By the police?'

'Possibly. But to tell you the truth, I'm also a bit worried by a few people in the core group, not the older ones, but that young woman with the tattoos who says so little, Astrid, for instance. She is an environmental scientist and understands a tremendous amount about biological diversity, but other than that I don't know much about her. She is a bit vague about her past.'

'I like the DNA spiral up her arm,' I admitted, and Elke smiled. 'Well, Astrid did tell me she thought you looked intriguing.'

'What about those two men in the leather jackets, Tall and Round?'

'I know them pretty well,' Elke said. 'The tall one, Peter, I worked with long ago on anti-nuclear issues. He was quite combative then. Sometimes I've wondered if Peter is trying to push our group into a stronger and more aggressive stance. But at other times I think he is very clear-sighted about our difficulties, and that's good.'

'And the round one?'

'Until now Kurt hasn't been very politically active. I think he just follows Peter's lead. But he is quite sincere in his interest in birds. He is a very enthusiastic volunteer.'

'What about Karin?'

'Karin used to be a heavy-duty politico, but all that's changed now she's with Helmut. He was never involved in anything during the seventies and eighties, though how that's possible, I don't know.'

'Karin said he's nervous about the demonstration.'

'I can't imagine him strangling a seagull,' Elke said. 'He's not that type.'

'Could any of them have written those letters?' I persisted. 'And why?'

Elke shook her head. 'Anyone *could* have done it. Why, I don't know. They may have wanted to create a feeling of threat. So that our group would feel more isolated, more fearful, and would be easier to manipulate. It's happened before.'

I was going to press her further, but the door swung open and Marianne, arms full of papers, books and groceries, burst in. 'Tonight I'm going to make Chilean food,' she said radiantly and gave both of us kisses. You really couldn't dislike her. Even though you knew she was going to keep you up half the night.

A week passed, two. I began to suspect that Marianne did not sleep, for I rarely saw her working. She was forever in my room or catching me in long conversations when I was on my way to the bathroom. I wrote to Lucinda that perhaps one should make a new vow: never to stay with strangers just to use their washer-driers. I wrote to Nicola, hinting that I might be willing to return to London sooner than expected. I wrote to my editor Simon saying the translation was going a little more slowly than I'd planned. On the other hand, my German was improving.

The night watches at *The Juliette* seemed to be having their effect. There had been no more incidents and only one letter, which the bird-watchers had promptly turned over to the press. The media had become involved now and everyone was expecting a great deal of publicity for the demonstration on Saturday. All Friday was taken up with preparations, sign-making, phone calls, xeroxing of fact sheets.

Friday evening, when Karin called to say that Sappho was under the weather and she wouldn't be able to spend the night on *The Juliette*, I saw my chance. Elke had asked Astrid to substitute. I'd been wanting to see where that DNA spiral ended up.

'Why don't I come too?' I offered.

'What a good idea,' said Marianne instantly. 'Astrid, Elke, Cassandra, me, we'll all spend the night there. It will be such fun, like a party.'

We arrived about eleven, Elke in black leather, Marianne in a big quilted jacket and a dozen scarves, and me in some scavenged warm clothes. Astrid was planning to meet us there. There was a thick fog over the river and a smell of oil and fish. The docks were lit, with weak, eerie yellow lamps, but there were few people about. Water slapped against the docks and intermittently came the hollow blast of a fog horn, lonely and yet warning of danger.

The Juliette looked normal, untampered with, as we unrolled our sleeping bags and lit the lantern. Elke poured us some tea from a thermos and Marianne chattered.

'Last night I translated the story about the married woman and the servant boy, Cassandra. Isn't it a good one?'

'Is that the one where they couple frenetically or where they frenetically couple?' I said.

Elke laughed and then turned it into a cough.

'I admit,' said Marianne without blushing, 'that there is a certain amount of heterosexual romance in the stories, but . . .'

'Romance!' said Elke. 'It's nothing but soft pornography in the tropics!'

'It's not! It's beautiful writing. Help me, Cassandra. Help me defend Gloria from my unromantic girlfriend.'

'It's not beautiful,' I mumbled, thinking, Now I have to leave Hamburg by the morning train. I'm glad my clothes are all washed.

'What?' said Marianne. '*Wie bitte?* I didn't hear you.'

'What's that noise?' said Elke, sitting bolt upright.

'Where?'

'On the dock, coming down the dock. Is it footsteps?'

'It's just Astrid,' said Marianne. 'Astrid,' she called out, but there was no answer.

The footsteps stopped, not far away. They didn't move away again.

'You'd better call some of the others on the cellular phone,' I said.

'Yes.' But Elke searched and could not find it. 'We must have forgotten it.' She took the flashlight and shone it out on the dock. There was not a sound.

'Probably just rats,' said Marianne determinedly. 'Now, Cassandra, tell me what you were saying. I didn't hear it . . . about Gloria . . .'

'I'm going out to investigate,' Elke said.

'No, Elke,' said Marianne, but Elke slipped up the short ladder and onto the dock. We saw her light flicker down the dock and then disappear.

'Elke!' Marianne shouted. There was only the sound of the fog horn.

'I'll go see what's happening.' I said.

'Don't leave me alone, Cassandra!'

'I'll be back in a second.'

I crawled out of the boat on my hands and knees, keeping my flashlight extinguished. I made my way over to the harbour wall and inched along it in the direction that Elke had disappeared. The cement was cold and clammy. The fog was by this time so thick I could see almost nothing. Not even the boat I'd just left.

My nerves were wound to the highest degree, so that when I heard the thump of someone leaping onto the boat, and Marianne's shriek, cut off, I froze and couldn't move. Who was more important for me to save, Elke or Marianne? Let me rephrase that: Who, given the fact that my feet seemed to be stuck to the wet wooden planks of the dock, could I save?

The question soon became more than academic. There was nothing more to be heard from Marianne, except some banging on wood – had he – she? – shoved her in the tiny WC? But after a few minutes the boat's engine started up. Was he planning to steal the boat with Marianne on it? Was he planning to dump her into the river somewhere?

Adrenaline finally unlocked my knees and I fell forward and started creeping back on my belly over the dock to *The Juliette*. Whoever was driving the boat didn't seem terribly practised; he manoeuvred clumsily away from the berth, knocking against the pilings. Just as the boat began to pull away, I jumped as quietly as I could into the stern, which was open and had a table and built-in seats. I barked my knee sharply on one of the seats.

Limping and crawling, I made my way to the door that connected the back of the boat with the middle sleeping cabin. It was locked. I would have to squeeze around the side of the boat to the pilot's cabin in front. But the boat was hardly stable enough at the moment for any tricky manoeuvres. I hung on as the unknown pilot made an ungainly turn away from the other berths, putting us in the direction of the river. I thought of those huge container ships out there somewhere in the fog. This idiot hadn't even put on any lights.

Very faintly, from the dock that had completely disappeared in the thick white mist I heard feet running and a thin cry, 'Marianne! Cassandra!' Well, at least Elke was safe, and could get help. Hopefully before we sank or were involved in a major collision.

For we were heading out of the inner harbour into the huge, invisible river.

Now it was time to move. I inched as slowly and carefully as I could along the right side of the boat, trying not to look down into what seemed awfully black, cold-looking water. Forward, forward, I thought. Just think forward. Around us there seemed to be nothing but a damp brackish cloud. Finally I squeezed to the right-hand door. How could I possibly get in without being seen? I peeked through the window. No sign of Marianne. At the wheel on the other side of the cabin was a figure all in black, with a ski mask, not exactly a sight to inspire confidence. I thought it was a he, but couldn't tell much more in the shadows. Was it Tall or Round? Was it Astrid?

A fog horn went off somewhere close-by and I almost lost my balance and toppled into the water. I grabbed the doorhandle and it turned and gave, propelling me into the little cabin and straight at the figure at the wheel.

'You will pay for this,' I unexpectedly said in German (*Wie Bitte*'s lesson on future tense maybe?), and grabbed the wheel and gave it a sharp turn. The boat made an abrupt change of direction and the momentum knocked the figure out through the other side of the boat, through the left door, which had swung open in the turn.

I waited for the splash and looked around frantically for the life-preserver. Some lighted shape, a buoy I hoped, since we ran into it, appeared and disappeared. I struggled to recall my very brief lesson in river piloting from Marianne.

Yes, Marianne. I had to get her out of the toilet, but I was afraid to let go of the wheel. In fact my hands were now frozen fast to the wheel. And meanwhile, where was that life-preserver? Where was, in fact, that splash of a human body hitting water?

Out of the corner of my eye I saw a shape clinging to the side of the boat. He, for now he was not just provisionally, but actually masculine, had managed not to fall, but to hold on to the left side just as I had on to the right. I couldn't see him well, still, and was afraid to turn my eyes from the window in front of me, though I could see very little in that direction either. He was shouting to me in German.

'Speak English!' I shouted back.

But if he could, his brain was as jammed as mine was, and it wouldn't come out.

I forced myself to remember some basic conversation. 'What's your name, please?'

'Helmut.'

'Helmut. The father of Sappho?'

'Yes, yes.'

'What are you doing?'

But I couldn't understand his response. '*Wie bitte?*' I shouted back, seeing something boat-shaped on the right, and jerking the wheel so that we missed it by inches.

'I only wanted. Only wanted to scare Karin. Not to go to the demonstration. I hate violence.'

'What about that seagull?'

'A mistake. I'm sorry.'

Should I believe him? My mind said yes, but my instincts were still all wrapped up with that damned television programme, once forgotten in my memory bank, now resurrected and imposing itself on reality.

There was the harbour at night. There was a murderer on the loose. There was a boat and a man overboard. There was a chase. There were a lot of people crying, '*Halt! Politzei!*' There was a big crash, and just before the crash had been the Imperative. Watch out for that boat up ahead. Turn! Turn!

What the hell was he saying now? I could barely hear for the banging on the WC door behind me. 'Hold on, Marianne!'

I called, and then to Helmut, '*Wie bitte?*'

'Turn!' he was suddenly screaming in English.

'Well, why didn't you say so in the first place?' I wrenched the wheel around, but not quite quick enough. And that's all I remember for a while.

I had a mild concussion, but the doctor said I didn't have to stay in the hospital long. Bed rest for a week or two and then I should be able to return to normal. Marianne was of course pleased to nurse me. She came into my lovely guestroom every half hour to see how I was doing and to chat. Helmut had been taken into custody but had been released. After his wild ride on the side of the boat he was only too happy to confess to the police boat that had caught up with us and that, in fact, I seemed to have run straight into. He'd been worried about Karin as he said. He'd told her he wouldn't be home in time for her to go stay on *The Juliette* with Elke. He thought only Elke would be on the boat and that if he lured her off, he could take *The Juliette* up the river and then sink her somewhere. Not very nice, but it could have been worse. For him, of course, it was worse, since they wanted to charge him with kidnapping and reckless endangerment of life. But the bird-watchers refused to press charges. Their demonstration had gone off splendidly, with only a little healthy bashing here and there, and there was hope for the future that the Elbe wetlands might be saved.

'Of course Karin is not speaking to him at the moment,' Marianne reported. 'But in the end she'll probably forgive him.' She looked wistfully at me from the side of the bed. 'If only I hadn't been locked in the toilet. I could have helped you, Cassandra. I could have steered us to safety.'

I had been let off with only a very stern warning never *never ever* to attempt to pilot a boat in the Hamburg harbour again.

My punishment was to lie in bed at Marianne's and have her

read Gloria de los Angeles to me, first in Spanish, and then, to
improve my German, in her translated version. When I got
better, however, Astrid took me out one day to the banks of
the Elbe and showed me how to identify the birds that lived
on the river and in the marshes. I tried to get her to show me
the full extent of her tattoos, and finally, in reluctance and
pleasure, she did. But the next time I saw her she was with
Karin, who had not taken up with Helmut after all. They
planned to struggle for the ecological revolution and to bring
up little Sappho together.

I forgot the difference between a robin and a sparrow.

Days passed. Weeks. One day I got up, as if an alarm clock
had rung. I looked in the mirror at my forehead, the bump
now turning a mellow jonquil–plum colour, and I saw my
wasted limbs. And then I took the boat train to London.

Character Witness
Robyn Vinten

It was my most important interview ever, with the queen of lesbian pulp crime fiction, Prudence Silverstone, and it was going terribly wrong.

Firstly I was late. I had stayed up till four reading her books and overslept. There had been no time to iron the shirt I wanted to wear, instead I threw on what I was wearing the day before, jeans, a T-shirt, albeit a Calvin Klein T-shirt, and my leather jacket. I had meant to wash my hair too, but there was no time for that. I ran some gel through it, it was so short that it made no difference, except to make it look dirty brown, rather than dirty blonde. Still, I thought, I was there to interview her, not seduce her.

Then there was the room, in a small hotel opposite Hyde Park. It had looked perfectly normal when I went in, but as I sat there it took on a strange two-dimensional feel, like a B-movie set. And it might have been my imagination, or the fact that I had stayed up so late, but Prudence seemed rather flat herself.

Finally my carefully prepared list of questions, they suddenly seemed trivial. Did it matter that it wasn't possible to survive 70 per cent burns, never mind return to work a week after they had been inflicted? Or that a normal person falling four stories would do more than twist their ankle?

I found myself asking instead if she liked London. And as she smiled at me, Prudence's face started to change. Before my very eyes, her jaw strengthened, her hair straightened and deepened in colour to the 'warm chestnut' that was the trademark of Melissa Martin, the heroine of all her books.

I shook my head to try and clear my vision. She smiled at me again, her voice was deeper and fuller than it had been.

'Are you all right, Jude, my dear?' Her eyes were clear green now, where they had been a nondescript brown.

'Too late a night,' I mumbled. Reading too many of your bloody books, I thought. So many books, so many clichés. I skimmed through all fifteen of them. One to four were quite good, five to ten were starting to wear thin, eleven to fourteen were getting more and more improbable, and fifteen, her latest and the reason she was here in England, was just plain ridiculous.

I was having trouble breathing and my head started to spin.

'Are you sure you're all right?'

'Please help me.' I heard myself whisper. It sounded oddly familiar.

'Of course my dear, if I can.' She patted my hand. I sat up straight: Prudence's touch had stopped the room tilting, but I felt suddenly nervous, like something was about to happen. Sure enough it did.

Behind me the door flew open and four or five policemen stood in the doorway. A man in a suit pushed through them and flashed a badge.

'Ms Martin.' He tipped his hat up with the corner of his badge. 'I'm afraid we're going to have to arrest this young lady.'

Book seven, I thought. *Murder on the Thames.* No, that wasn't it. The plain-clothed cop had his hand on my arm. *Murder at the Savoy? Murder on the Nile? Murder . . .*

'Don't make this harder than it needs to be.' The cop had pulled me to my feet before I realised it was me he wanted to arrest.

'But . . .' He dragged me to the door.

'Don't worry, dear,' Melissa called after me. 'I'll sort it out.'

The cops handcuffed me, bundled me out the door and down the front steps to the waiting paddy wagon. I looked back up to the window of the room we had been in. Melissa was standing at the window watching. She waved.

All the way to the station I racked my brains. *Murder on the What?* If only I could remember. The cop in the back with me stared straight ahead. I thought about engaging him in conversation to try and get some information out of him. But I couldn't think of what to ask, or how to phrase a question without sounding totally potty.

'Nice day,' I tried, but he just sat there. I didn't smoke usually, but the desire for nicotine suddenly swept over me.

'You got any cigarettes?' I must be a journalist in this, they were always chain-smoking, black-coffee-drinking characters. Even as I thought it, my hands started to shake from caffeine withdrawal. The cop didn't answer.

Murder on the bloody what?

At the station they took my photo and my fingerprints. In the rush out of the hotel I had left my bag behind, or did I remember Melissa putting it out of sight when the cops arrived? They went through my pockets; lots of loose change, house keys and a silver lighter, which wasn't mine. They put them in a plastic bag and took them away, then they put me in a cell.

I sat there for some time, not thinking about anything in particular, except how much I wanted a cigarette and how odd that felt, and whether I liked the feeling or not. Then I remembered I was supposed to get one phone call. I banged on the door, after a while a bored looking cop stuck his head through the hatch in the door.

'What?'

'Don't I get a phone call?'

'Maybe.'

'I want my phone call.'

His face disappeared and I heard the sound of the door being unlocked. When he opened it, he looked me up and down and then shrugged, like I was just what he'd expect for someone accused of whatever it was I was being accused of. Murder I supposed, the book was called Murder in the something, they all were.

He ushered me along a cold, grey corridor to the phone, then stood uncomfortably close behind me while I decided who I should ring. He shuffled impatiently. I dialled my own home number, I don't know what I expected, I certainly didn't expect someone to answer.

'Hello.'

'Who's that?' I asked.

'Who wants to know?' It was my own voice.

'It's . . . it's . . .' I hung up. I didn't even know what my name was supposed to be.

'Well, that was worth getting off the John for.' The cop pushed me back in the direction of my cell.

'But . . .'

'That's your lot. One call, and boy did you blow it.' He gave me an extra little shove back into the cell. Just before he closed the door, I put my foot in it.

'You haven't got a cigarette?' I asked sheepishly. He laughed and slammed the door. Then after he had locked it, he opened the hatch and tossed one through.

I picked it up. Silk Cut Menthol, but it would do. I felt over my pockets for my lighter, then remembered they had taken it. I heard the cop laughing as he walked away.

I couldn't decide whether it was more frustrating or less, having a cigarette, but not being able to smoke it. In the end I put it in my mouth and sucked on it anyway. It did calm me slightly.

I sat down and tried to remember all I could about Prudence Silverstone and her bloody books. Her first ones were out in the early eighties when I was just a little dyklette far from the big city, eager for anything that had a lesbian in it. And here were these books with not just any lesbian but a big, strong lesbian detective out solving crimes. I loved them. They were clichéd sure, but who cared, when Melissa got her woman we all slept better at night.

After about five of them, the style started to wear thin, and the plots and characters began to feel dated. The stories all started to merge together till you couldn't tell one from the other. I hadn't read one for a good eight years, until I scooped the interview. It was such short notice, the usual interviewer had come down with the flu or something, I had twenty-four hours to prepare. So I read her latest offering, and skimmed though her earlier books.

Now, that's a clue, most of her stories are set in America. There is the Australian one, *Murder in the Outback*, a farce about a female rodeo rider and red-neck farmer's wife. Another was on an idyllic Greek island. I wondered if these holidays were tax deductible.

There was another London one too, *Murder* on some famous landmark, and it did have a journalist in it, with a laughable name. If only I had read the book properly. The journalist was tall with long black hair, and piercing blue eyes, she wore designer suits and had slept her way to the top, with women of course. It was *Murder on London Bridge*, that was it! Only the bridge described in it was Tower Bridge – the

Americans could never work that one out.

Well, I had a title and a character. All I needed now was a name, and some idea of the plot. But that feeling that something was about to happen had started again. I heard footsteps approaching. They stopped outside my door and the hatch opened. A woman's face peered in.

'Want a light for that?'

I took the cigarette out of my mouth, the end was all soggy. 'I'm trying to give up.'

The face disappeared and the locks were undone. The woman was obviously a cop, though she was in a very stylish red suit with high heels.

'Come on.' She turned round and walked off down the corridor. I followed after her and couldn't help but notice what a nice shape she had under that smart suit. She tapped impatiently on the door at the end of the corridor and it was opened from the other side. She ignored the stares from the uniformed men and led me through to an interview room.

'Sit down.' She tossed a packet of Camels and a lighter on the table. There was already a cup of hot, black coffee waiting for me.

I sat down. She swung her chair around and sat on it backwards, facing me. Her skirt rode up her long thighs. I pretended not to notice.

'So Pen, why'd ya do it?'

Pen, Pen, that's right. Pen something corny. Pen Scoop? No, Pen Rider, that was it.

The cop was looking at me intensely.

'What?' I had forgotten she'd asked a question.

'Oh, Pen.' She shook her head, so that a strand of her long blonde hair fell over her face. She brushed it out of the way. I reached for the cigarette packet, suddenly aware my hands were shaking. She put her hand down over mine.

'You can trust me.' She leaned forward and her jacket fell

open a little to reveal a glimpse of cleavage. I slipped the
cigarette packet from under her hand and took one out. She
picked up the lighter and offered me a light. I sat back and
chewed on the end of the cigarette.

'Editor Plunges To Death.' A faint idea of the plot was
coming back to me. I could see Melissa on a double-decker
bus somewhere, seeing the sights of London.

The cop flicked the lighter nonchalantly. She was rather
good looking, in a clichéd sort of way. Slim, blonde, smooth
skin. She raised one eyebrow at me.

'Come on, Pen, I just want you to talk to me.' She wet her
lips with her tongue. I realised she was trying to seduce me. I
wouldn't have minded so much, only she wasn't really real, she
was a character in a story. What were the ethics here? If I had
somehow slipped into a piece of fiction, which is what I
thought was going on, was it all right to let her seduce me? In
fact, as the story was already written and I was merely a sub-
character in it, did I have any choice? Would I wake up any
second now and discover this was all only a dream?

I pinched myself, it hurt, and the cop was still there. I leaned
over and pinched her, she felt real enough.

'What was that for?' She looked at me crossly.

'Just checking you were real.' I leaned forward and offered
her my cigarette to light. She paused for a moment and then
lit it, holding my hand steady as she did. Her fingers were
warm and soft, they reminded me of something very nice. I
felt myself start to blush and inhaled deeply. God it felt good.

'I know I hated him, but I didn't do it.' A frown crossed her
face. 'Her.' I corrected myself. 'I hated her.'

I wished I'd read the book properly. It occurred to me that
my character might die, Prudence sometimes did that to stop
them having to suffer at the hands of the criminal justice
system. The word 'cancer' came to mind; I coughed and
stubbed the cigarette out.

'You're lying.' The cop slipped her jacket off and hung it on the back of the chair. She was wearing a sheer blouse with a black bra underneath.

'I didn't do it.' I was blushing again.

'I believe that, it's the hating her I have trouble with.'

If only I knew the plot. 'It's a fine line,' I said, hoping it was ambiguous enough.

'A very fine line.' Her voice was husky and she was pouting. I looked over at the door, nervous about what was going to happen next.

'Don't worry.' She sat on the table beside my chair, her thigh almost touching my arm. 'We won't be disturbed.'

She leaned over me and took two cigarettes out of the packet still on the table. She smelt of vanilla musk, her breasts hovered at my eye level for a moment. She sat up, lit both the cigarettes and handed me one.

'It's not too late for us to try again.' She blew smoke in my face.

'I think it might be.' I had that feeling again, something was about to happen.

'Oh really?' She raised one eyebrow and leaned forward to kiss me. The moment before our lips met there was a bang on the door. She jumped off the table and hurriedly put her jacket back on. I sat in the chair and took a drag on my cigarette. I was quite enjoying this.

Almost before she had unlocked the door, the plain-clothed cop who had arrested me was through it.

'We're going to throw the book at you.' He jabbed his finger at my face. 'We've got witnesses.' He threw a file triumphantly onto the table.

'Yeah, we're going to do you.' A younger cop appeared at his shoulder and leered at me.

Prudence must have been watching *The Bill* for this bit, I thought. 'I doubt it,' I said, taking another drag on the cigarette. 'You're not my type.' I thought it was rather a good line, but then the smoke caught in my throat and I started to cough. I took a swig of coffee and spilt some down my T-shirt. Prudence would have a fit if she caught her hard-nosed journalist behaving like this. I tried to pull myself together.

The cop hadn't noticed. 'Don't play smart with me.' He leaned over the table at me. 'I've got it all here.' He tapped the file.

I thought it could hardly be police procedure to show the suspect the file, but I flipped it open. There was a photo of a well-groomed woman in her fifties smiling at the camera, followed by pages of typed reports and some press clippings.

'You see, we've been keeping our eye on your Ms Forcyth.'

'She wasn't mine.' I picked up the photo to have a closer look at it.

The younger cop snatched it off me. 'That's police property, that is.' He had red cropped hair, and his face was covered in freckles. Prudence always gave the bad guys red hair, sometimes it was the only way you could tell who'd done it.

'You wanted her job.' The older cop sat down opposite me, looking like Columbo without the mac.

'Hardly.' I caught sight of the words *Sun Newspaper*. I hazarded a guess. 'The *Sun* isn't my style.'

'It wasn't her's either. They are suing you both, for everything you've got. The case was due to be heard tomorrow, or had you forgotten.'

'Oh yeah.' I tried to sound sarcastic. A court case? This was more complicated than I had thought.

'She was going to say it was all your story. And that would have ruined you.' The red-haired cop shoved his face in mine.

'You would never have worked again.'

'So I pushed her?'

'Yes!' He punched his fist in the air. 'See, guv, I told you I'd get her to confess.'

'It's a fair cop, guv.' I tried a cockney accent, but it didn't come off.

'You're admitting it?' The female cop spoke for the first time since the men had arrived. She sounded disappointed.

'No.' I had forgotten how stupid the cops in Prudence's books were. I had that feeling again, that something was going to happen. I looked at the door, the cops all turned and looked too. Sure enough, someone banged on it from the other side. The young cop went and opened it, there was some furious whispering.

'You'd better come, guv, there've been some developments.' The men trooped out, the female cop started to follow them, but the older cop stopped her.

'Stay with her, see if you can't get a proper confession.'

When they'd gone she sat down.

'I could make an improper confession if you like.'

She didn't look like she wanted to play, she looked like she was going to cry. 'I didn't push her,' I said, trying to cheer her up. 'She jumped.'

'Because of the libel case?' She sounded like she didn't believe me.

'No.' I paused, something was starting to form inside my head, some vague recollection of the plot. 'She had cancer.' As soon as I said it, I knew it was right, it had a Prudence sort of ring to it. 'Ovarian,' I added.

I felt tears well up in my eyes. I looked at the cop, Lyn, that was her name, we had been an item once, I had left her for another woman.

'What were you doing on the roof then? Witnesses saw you push her.'

'I was trying to stop her. We were lovers, we carried on a public façade of hating each other to hide the fact. It would have ruined us both if it got out. I didn't know she had cancer, I found a letter from the hospital. We had a terrible row, she said she was going out to a meeting, but I didn't believe her, she'd been acting so strange. I followed her to the bridge, I tried to stop her, but she was always stronger than me.'

Tears rolled down my cheeks. 'God I miss her.' I put my head down on the table and sobbed. I should get an Oscar for this I thought, though the grief felt almost real. Lyn patted my shoulder.

'A note? Did she leave a note?'

'I don't know, I think . . .' The feeling something was going to happen started up again. 'I think we're about to find out.' I looked at the door, there was a loud knocking. Lyn went to open it, the older cop came in, followed by Melissa.

'Well, my dear, it looks like you are free to go.' She was carrying a copy of the *Mirror*, which she spread out on the table. On the front page was a picture of a covered body lying beside the river, with the headline. 'Editor Plunges To Death, see page three'. Melissa opened the paper to the editorial and there it was, Erica Forcyth's last column was her suicide note. There was a brief statement about the libel trial, she took full responsibility for the story, saying I was totally innocent. Then Melissa read out the rest.

'As always I want to be in total control of my life, so before the pain gets too bad, I'm leaving this world while I still have fond memories of it, and moving on to the next.'

'How so like Erica.' Melissa folded the paper. I nodded. 'A suicide note for all the nation to read.' I wiped my tears away and smiled up at her.

The police drove us back to Melissa's hotel and we once again sat in her two-dimensional room. She handed me back my bag; my notebook was in there and my list of questions. I thanked her and we shook hands. As we did her hair seemed to lose its chestnut colour and her jaw softened and sagged a little, her voice lost its vibrant depth. I said goodbye and left the room.

Outside I stopped and looked back up at the window, sure enough Prudence was there watching me. She waved. I waved back and headed across the road to Hyde Park. I found a seat and looked through my bag. My notebook was full of illegible scribble. I played the tape I had on during the interview – it was completely blank.

In the bottom of the bag, there was the book, *Murder on London Bridge*. The picture was of Tower Bridge. Bloody Americans, I thought. I opened it and started to read.

Pen Rider sat before me trying to cover her obvious distress. We had met some years before at a writers' conference, now she came to me for help. Her grey eyes were clouded with pain. Her short, brown hair needed a wash.

This wasn't the Pen Rider I remembered. I read on.

Her jeans and leather jacket were crumpled but her Calvin Klein T-shirt was clean.

I closed the book and took a deep breath. *Murder on Tower Bridge* the cover now said, as clearly as if it had always been that. I closed my eyes and counted to ten, when I opened them again it still said *Tower Bridge*. The book flipped open of its own accord, to the acknowledgement page, which I had never noticed before. It said, 'Thank you, Jude, for being my character witness.'

I looked back to the hotel and through the trees it was difficult to tell, but I could have sworn I saw Prudence, still at the window, and from that distance it was impossible to say, but it looked like she was blowing me a kiss.

Murder at the Sales Meeting
Joan M Drury

The worst thing about Peter Suchet's murder was that we all had to spend another couple of days at the flea-ridden Hotel Christie. I never did understand why Suchet Distributors insisted on holding their sales meetings at this rash-producing dump anyway – except for the obvious, of course, that it was cheaper than the stable in Bethlehem – but this was too much. Besides which, Thanksgiving was looming at the end of the week.

My two kids, nine-year-old Jane and twelve-year-old Alleyn, spent most of their holidays with their father and his lovely child-bride, the delectable Lindsay, in East Lansing. Oh I know, that's not very 'sisterly' of me, is it? But then again, I can't imagine a sister as many years younger than me as Lindsay is. She could, almost, be Jane's sister. No matter.

The reason the kids usually spend their holidays with their father, they never fail to remind me, is because the oh-so-perfect Lindsay – just a mere year or two older than them – actually cooks. Real food. Food that neither comes from the frozen food section of the supermarket nor would ever be cooked in a microwave.

Big deal. Is she trying to change the world? Is she encouraging revolution through the publishing of a select group of wonderfully literary and equally political books? Does she even *have* to make a living at all? *No*, Jane and Alleyn would respond, *but she makes real chocolate chip cookies*. And, believe me, my holiday feasts – hot dogs and maybe red jello with bananas or, on a particularly good week, my grand-mother's spaghetti – never resembled Lindsay's. Sigh.

So, maybe the *worst* thing was that I was stuck in New York City, and I was in BIG trouble if I didn't get home to Ann Arbor at once, because this year I had lured my kids into staying home for Thanksgiving by promising them a real holiday feast with all the fixings: turkey, stuffing, gravy, mashed potatoes, sweet potatoes, *both* green and jello salads, sweet corn, cranberry sauce, glorified rice, pumpkin pie with *real* whipped cream, green apple pie – the works! And how was I going to deliver 'the works' if I hadn't even bought any of it yet?

Oh I know. I'm being awfully cavalier about a person's death. But then, it wasn't just *anybody* who had died. I mean, after all, it *was* Peter Suchet. It wasn't as if anyone liked Peter. Oh, I guess that's not fair. There's always someone that likes someone else. Isn't there?

Like PD Marsh, for instance. She adored Peter. Not that anyone else could ever figure that out, but there it was anyway. But then, everyone said they'd been, *you know*, getting it on for years. Of course, that was absurd. I mean, PD *was* a lesbian, after all. And if she was going to do a deviation from her lifestyle, surely it wouldn't be with the likes of Peter Suchet, would it? But then I might not be the best judge because, even if I did sleep with men (which I don't), it certainly wouldn't be a man like Peter.

But I do digress, don't I? Okay. So maybe I should start at

the beginning. You know, like in a crime novel? Who, what, where? Just the facts, ma'am. The where, as I've already told you, was the Christie Hotel in New York City. The 'main' who is me – Harriet Watson – publisher, editor, acquisitions and production and marketing department, and chief (as well as only) bottle washer for the Emma Goldman Press, a small feminist publishing house – translated: a we-make-no-money press. My friends call me Harry, of whom only one such close friend is present and that would be Samantha Mason who holds a similar position at Rhymes-with-Witch Publishing. Really. That's the name of her company. Everyone always thinks I'm making that up.

We were both in New York with some forty other publishers presenting our spring lines to the Suchet sales' reps. After a day of desultory meetings between the publishers and various members of the Suchet organisation, we spent the next two days in ten-to-twelve-minute presentations, attempting to convince the reps that our books were the *only* ones to sell during the upcoming months.

I didn't say it was a perfect system. In fact, it's mostly an imperfect system. But those of us in publishing didn't create the system; we just inherited it. In our allotted time, each publisher or marketing manager had to be so *brilliant*, so *funny*, so *cute* that, somehow, the dozen or so reps would remember us and our books *more* than the thirty-nine other publishers doing their presentations at the same time. Not to speak of the fact that these same reps often were freelancers who worked for other distribution companies and, consequently, spent much of November going from one sales meeting to another.

At the end of these three days, Suchet always threw a cocktail party. Some of us ducked out right after our presentations, heading for home. But most of us stayed. Partly because we figured the bash was our just reward (the food was usually tolerable, sometimes even good) and partly because all the reps attended, and so we had one more chance to imprint ourselves on their memories. Samantha and I always stayed over through the cocktail party and until Sunday, just to catch up with one another.

It was at the cocktail party that Peter Suchet bit the dust, so to speak. One minute he was listening carefully to some-complaint-or-other from an intense Perry Fox of Fox Publishing, the next minute he was lying on the floor, writhing and gasping for breath, turning purple, then blue. I think most of us thought that he'd had a heart attack, although – really – it happened so fast, we hardly thought at all.

It didn't take long, however, once the medical people showed up with the police on their heels, for us to find out that he hadn't had a heart attack, and – in fact – died anything but a natural death: Peter Suchet had been poisoned. And, with a roomful of possible suspects, ranging from forty or so disenchanted publishers to a dozen or more disgruntled employees, the police had their work cut out for them. Probably the only people who would be entirely free of suspicion would be the sales reps as they were mostly the only people in the publishing industry who actually made any money.

By the morning following Suchet's murder, after late-night interviews with police officers who warned us that we were not free to leave town just yet (thus consigning us to more itchy nights), the rumour mill had it on 'good authority' that the poison had been administered through his drink. The likeliest suspect, of course, seemed to be Perry Fox, since he was arguing with Peter at the moment of his demise. But the rumour mill also insisted that the poison could have been administered as much as an hour prior to taking affect, depending on dosage. This, of course, did not rule Fox out altogether; after all, everyone knew that Suchet and Fox had a feud going that stretched over years. But then, who didn't?

Sam and I pondered the possibilities over breakfast. 'If not Perry,' Sam enquired of no one in particular, 'then who?'

I threw my hands in the air. 'Almost any of us, don't you think?'

'Well yes,' she agreed, then added, 'But Harry, much as most of us despised Peter, would we actually murder him? I mean, who would *really* have a motive?'

We looked at one another for a second, then said, simultaneously, 'His wife.'

It was true. Dorothy Suchet put up with a lot. She was his partner in the business, but he treated her like a minion. She always played second fiddle to his 'lord and master'. Also, he did little to hide his womanising, preferring to humiliate her – or so it seemed – in front of everyone.

'And then there's Ham Wolfe,' I said.

'Of course,' Sam concurred. 'Who would be more likely than someone who had to put up with a Peter Suchet on a constant basis?'

We both nodded and lapsed into silence, thinking of Ham Wolfe. He'd been Suchet's assistant forever. As such, he was the buffer, the mediator, the scapegoat for all of Suchet's accounts. No one (except the aforementioned PD Marsh, of course) ever got directly in touch with Peter. We all got Ham who *always* informed us that Peter was 'unavailable at the moment', but he would be glad to relay any messages.

'Did you ever,' Sam asked, 'call Peter and actually get to talk to him?'

We'd had this conversation many times, but I shook my head anyway. 'You know I didn't, Sam. Not once in the five years I was with Suchet did that happen. *Sometimes*, he actually returned such a call but not often. Mostly, like everyone else, I just talked to Ham.'

Sam nodded emphatically. Ham was always in the middle –

we publishers on one side yelling at him for mistakes or problems that Peter was actually responsible for and insisting that he get something done that he often didn't have the power to execute while Peter, on the other side, blamed Ham by pretending that he'd not been informed about our complaints or that Ham hadn't carried through some order he'd been given or for handling a client tactlessly.

All of us, pretty much, liked Ham although we thought he was a bit of a masochist to put up with this good cop/bad cop game that Suchet played with Ham, of course, in the bad cop role. It was a ridiculous effort, actually; although Ham took the brunt of our anger and dissatisfaction, we all knew *he* wasn't the problem. We all knew that the *real* bad cop was Peter Suchet himself.

'It's hard to imagine, isn't it, why Ham would put up with Peter all these years?' Sam asked.

I nodded; this, also, was not a new conversation. 'It must have been money, don't you think?'

Sam agreed. 'Yeah, but can you imagine what *you'd* have to be paid to put up with all that crap?'

I shook my head. 'Peter Suchet could *never* have paid me enough to be his foil. Never.'

'I know, so the point is: why did Ham Wolfe put up with it?'

'I guess,' I answered slowly, just as if we hadn't talked this over many times before, 'he did it because he was used to being "picked" on. You know the kind of family dynamic: a father or mother or sibling always putting you down, needling you until it's so familiar you spend the rest of your life playing "victim" to spouses, friends, co-workers, bosses, whoever.'

'Yeah. It would have to be something like that, wouldn't it? But even a "victim" probably hits their breaking point, don't you think?'

'The final straw?'

'Yup,' Sam nodded, 'Then — WHOOSH!' Her hands indicated an explosion.

'Makes sense to me. *I* certainly would kill Peter Suchet if I had to work with him all the time.'

'Would you?' an unfamiliar voice behind me said, and I jumped — as much from Sam's slightly widened eyes as from the voice. I turned around and recognised the man to be one of the police officers from the night before. 'You startled me, Sergeant . . .?'

'Lieutenant,' he corrected me, as he dragged a chair over to sit down with us. 'Lieutenant Hastings. All right if I join you?' He already had, so we nodded as he indicated 'coffee' to the server. When it arrived, he scrutinised me and said, 'You really think so?'

'I beg your pardon?' I responded.

'You really think you'd murder Suchet if you had to work with him?'

'All the time?' I clarified. 'Absolutely. Or . . .' I hesitated.

And Sam inserted, 'Or maybe yourself?' and we both chuckled.

'Yeah,' I agreed. 'Actually, I hope I'd just have enough sense to quit. Then, no one would have to die.'

'You think someone who worked with Suchet killed him?' I shrugged. 'It makes sense.'

The lieutenant looked from one of us to the other. 'You don't seem too broken up by Suchet's death.'

Sam snorted and I said, 'What can I say, Lieutenant? The man was slime, and we're heartless.'

'Which means you didn't like him?'

'To put it mildly,' Sam offered, and this time I snorted.

'Why didn't you like him?' Lieutenant Hastings had pulled out a notebook and pen and was already writing in it.

'Ah,' Sam waxed rhapsodically, 'let me count the ways.' She put up one finger. 'He was arrogant, slick, condescending.'

'That's three, not one.' The lieutenant was scribbling quickly.

'Nah,' Sam disagreed. 'That's one, part and parcel.'

'Two,' I said, 'you couldn't trust him. He lied as if he were addicted to lying. The truth was alien to him. He lied when it made no sense to lie.'

'And he refused to take responsibility for his mistakes. That's three.'

Hastings looked up and asked, 'Slime?'

'He was a womaniser. Annoyingly so. Thought he was Don Juan, even when he'd been rebuffed. Did it continuously: in front of his wife, in front of his colleagues, in front of ex-lovers. He was slime.'

'Tell me this,' the lieutenant was scratching his nose. 'Why did you do business with this man?'

'Ah,' Sam answered, 'a good question. With a very complex answer.' She looked at me.

'Suchet Distributors have been around a long time. They have a good reputation with booksellers. When a publisher hooks up with a distributor, they usually listen to what booksellers say – because ultimately that's who we are all trying to reach. Maybe Suchet is – was – different with booksellers. Maybe he was different in the past. But now . . .' I spread my hands and shook my head.

'He's an asshole,' Sam finished. 'But – and this is the big BUT – it's hard, once a publisher has a contract with a distributor, to move. It costs a lot of money and time, something that small presses have no excess of. We have a responsibility to our authors, and financial losses and/or "down-time" simply aren't tolerable.'

'In addition, if your distributor is suspect regarding integrity, there's dozens of ways he can "do you dirty" if you decide to break the contract. So, no one breaks contracts lightly. Most of us keep our eyes open for a seemingly better deal – there are few alternatives – and also just hope that things will get better.'

'Who do you think killed him? One of you?' We pointed

to one another with our eyebrows raised, and he said, 'No, I mean one of you publishers?'

Sam and I both shrugged while I said, 'It's possible but doesn't seem like it would really solve the problem. Suchet Distributors would probably continue, although I guess it might be much better without Peter,' I brightened at such a thought.

Then we confided our musings about Dorothy Suchet and Ham Wolfe but cautioned him, too. 'After all,' Sam said, 'it could be any number of other staff members. Peter had a talent for infuriating anyone close to him. You know the phrase, "the buck stops here?" Not so for Peter. The "buck" was like a boomerang for him, he usually turned it back on someone else in his organisation. We were just thinking of Dorothy and Ham because they probably had to put up with the most.'

'And presumably Mrs Suchet would inherit the company, yes?' Hastings asked.

We were silent for a minute, appalled we hadn't thought of that. Finally, Sam nodded reluctantly and said, 'I would guess so, yes.'

'And,' the lieutenant continued, 'it's conceivable that Ham might get promoted to Chief Operating Officer or something, with his experience and know-how?'

We nodded again but said nothing. I did not like the feeling I was getting that the police were tightening a net around Dorothy and Ham. It was one thing for us to speculate; it was entirely something else for the police to be closing in on them. 'But,' I suddenly blurted out, 'it might have been Perry Fox, too. He and Peter had a barely civil relationship for years. And there might have been other problems with other publishers, too, that we didn't know about.'

'Like what with who?' the lieutenant prodded.

I restrained from correcting him – always the editor – and looked helplessly at Sam. 'We don't know,' she said rather sharply. 'But Peter was always borrowing from Peter to pay Paul. He might have overextended in many areas and gotten way behind in his payments to some clients. He even borrowed money from many of them. It might have gotten out of hand.'

'Was he behind in his payments to you two?'

We both laughed. 'Of course,' I answered. 'Suchet was behind to everyone, all the time.'

'He was?' Hastings looked up from his notebook.

'Oh yeah,' Sam said. 'Worse with some than others. We were small accounts. He wasn't behind by a lot with either of us,' we shared these figures with one another easily, 'but it doesn't take much to hurt operations as small as ours.'

'And he borrowed from people, too? Clients? Who else?'

'Not us. We didn't have enough to lend. Plus we wouldn't have lent money to him anyway. But to others, sure. We heard about it all the time.'

'Some names?'

'I don't think I know exactly,' Sam said, carefully not looking at me. 'You'd have to ask each individual, I guess.'

Hastings looked thoughtful as his pen scratched furiously across the paper in his notebook. We offered nothing else, and he asked little else, thanking us for our co-operation. We looked at each other in silence after his departure, and finally Sam said, 'Did we co-operate?'

'I guess,' I shrugged, 'but it feels more like – what? – collaborating?'

'I know,' Sam agreed. 'When he talks about Ham and/or Dorothy, well, it sounds much more menacing than when we talked about them, doesn't it?'

I nodded. 'I know. I mean, if either of them killed Peter, well, would you want them to have to go to prison for that?'

Sam shook her head. 'No, but I guess we won't have anything to say about that, will we?' I shook my head, too. 'Harry . . .' she hesitated.

'Wanna go upstairs and look around?' I supplied, and she smiled at my ability to read her mind.

We expected to find a cop guarding the area outside the hospitality suite on the seventeenth floor where the cocktail party had taken place, but no one was around. The double doors to the suite were closed, and the yellow police tape announcing 'crime scene' and 'do not cross this line' were stretched across the doors. Sam and I looked at each other and immediately divested ourselves of bags and wallets and such and assumed a long-disused but well-remembered duck stance and advanced on the door, 'ducking' under the crime scene tape. But even ducks can't budge locked doors.

'Darn!' I said, 'I really thought we were going to get an opportunity to look around.'

We were sprawled side-by-side on the floor, having quickly abandoned our duck squats when we realised we weren't going to get egress to the hospitality suite. 'Yeah, but we should've known it wouldn't be that easy,' Sam rejoined. At just that moment, the doors of the elevator began to slide open. My body tensed for flight when I realised, where was it I thought I was going to fly to? 'Uh, hi, Lieutenant,' I said as Hastings and another man came into view.

He stepped out of the elevator and stood looking down at Sam and me on the floor. 'You looking for something, girls?'

'A contact?' Sam ventured.

'We are *not* "girls," Lieutenant,' I said severely as I struggled to my feet. Then continued, 'Aw hell,' I stretched a hand to Sam, 'we were going to look for clues. Only you went and locked this damn door.'

'Usual procedure for a murder investigation.'

'Yeah, I suppose,' I agreed. 'We just thought we might be some kind of help, you know? Might be able to see something that you might've overlooked because you don't know the folk involved.'

'Uh-huh,' Hastings said sceptically. 'You might be some kind of help at that. Could you tell me, does Mrs Suchet wear lipstick and if so, what colour is it?

'Lipstick? Dorothy?' Sam said and looked at me.

I furrowed my brow in concentration. 'Not really. If she does, it'd be one of those "natural" colours. I don't remember ever seeing any notable colour on her lips.' I looked for confirmation to Sam.

She nodded. 'I'd have to agree. Why?'

Hastings ignored her question and asked another one. 'Tell me this. Why do you think there might be lipstick on a man's drink glass?'

'Was there lipstick on Peter's glass?' Sam asked, excitement in her voice. Again, Hastings ignored her question and just waited for one of us to answer.

I said, 'Maybe because a woman took a sip of his drink?' But as I said this, a vivid picture lodged in my brain, and I distinctly remembered a voice saying, 'Peter? Let me have a sip of your drink.'

I held my breath for a minute, remembering, and Lieutenant Hastings said, 'What is it, Miss Watson?'

'Ms.' I corrected him. 'Harriet is fine, actually.'

'Well?' he demanded. 'What is it, Harriet?'

I tried to look guileless. 'Oh nothing. Just trying to remember something.'

He looked hard at me but said no more. Sam was staring at me, too. Hastings warned us away, and we got on the elevator. As soon as the doors were closed, I grabbed Sam's arm and said, 'Sam! We've got to find PD! I remember her taking a sip from Peter's glass!'

'So?' Sam said.

'So! Don't you see? That's probably when the poison was added to the drink. I mean, how easy. Just sidle up to someone, simper, "Let me have a sip, darling," then take a sip and slip something in it before giving it back to the original owner of the glass! Brilliant!'

'You think PD killed Peter?'

'She must've!'

'But why?'

'I don't know. Let's go find out.'

'What's the matter with you? Why don't we just tell the lieutenant and let him handle it?'

'Sam, don't you ever read mysteries? She's not going to tell him anything. I'm sure we'll find a way to get her to "come clean".' Sam looked dubious but let me take the lead.

We found PD in the smoker's lounge on the first floor of the hotel, in conversation with another of our colleagues. I sailed up to her and said, 'PD, could we have a few moments alone with you?'

She stared at me, then Sam – we'd never made friendly overtures before – then shrugged and said, 'Sure,' dismissing the other publisher. She added, 'It will have to be here though. I'm not going anywhere I can't smoke. This is too stressful to cut down on smoking right now.'

'Okay,' I agreed, 'but let's go over in that corner.' I indicated an out-of-the-way alcove. She raised one eyebrow and then acquiesced. When we got there, away from other people, I said, abruptly, 'So PD. Tell us all about it.'

'Excuse me?'

'Come on, PD. The cat's out of the bag.' Without looking at her, I could tell Sam was staring at me. 'We know you killed Peter. The police are on their way to your room to question you right now,' I prevaricated. 'We just want to hear it from you directly. What gives?'

She stared at me open-mouthed, then said, 'Harriet Watson, you're crazy, you know that? I have no idea what you're talking about.'

I was either completely wrong or the woman was an

incredible actor. I decided the latter was true and calmly lied
some more. 'Look, PD, you made one fatal mistake. You took a
sip of Peter's drink – so you could slip the poison in – but your
lipstick left its mark on the rim. The colour has been identified
as your colour and probably DNA tests will back this fact up.
The jig's up, Woman. We just want to know why? Of all of us,
you were the only one who even liked Peter.'

Now Marsh looked merely amused. 'Assuming all you've
said is true, Harriet, how does this prove anything? As a matter
of fact, I probably did have a sip of Peter's drink that night. I
don't remember precisely, but I have a habit, as anyone who
knows me can attest, of sipping out of other people's drinks.
So maybe I did that and maybe my lipstick was on the rim of
his glass, but I don't see how that proves anything but that I
took a sip of his wine.'

Uh-oh. I hadn't really thought that through, had I? Should
I quit now while I was ahead or should I lie some more,
believing my theory? While I was hesitating, Sam spoke up,
confidently. 'Well, the truth is, PD, someone actually saw you
slipping something into Peter's drink. The police are looking
to arrest you, not question you.' Oooh, I thought, cool-headed,
Sam.

PD stared at Sam for a moment, then said, 'I don't believe
you.'

Sam shrugged nonchalantly, as if it were no consequence
one way or the other to her. 'Maybe they were right. Maybe
you have been sleeping with Suchet all these years.'

PD's mask slipped as she snarled, 'I never slept with that
bastard,' her hand snaking out to slap Sam, only I grabbed it
and held it in place. She snatched her hand away from me and
went on, as if we weren't actually there, 'That bastard! He
always told me that eventually he would divorce Dorothy and
I would be his full partner. I lent him money, I bailed him out,
I was always there for him in whatever way he needed me to

be. Then you know what he told me? After years of milking whatever he could from me, he told me that Dorothy had gone and gotten pregnant and, really, he just couldn't leave her now! The bastard! The low-life, pond-scum. I was his only friend. You know? His *only* friend! And he basically spit on that, spit on all the promises he'd made to me over the years! Everyone told me not to trust him, but Peter and I – we had something "special," something "different" between us. We were both schemers, manipulators, we were both ambitious. Together, we were going to make Suchet Distributors the biggest and the best! The bastard!'

And suddenly I noticed the cute little gun she'd pulled out of her pocket. 'Come on, you two, we're going for a walk,' she said.

'Oh, I don't think so,' I stalled, 'I don't have my coat, and it's really cold out.'

PD Marsh stared at me and said, 'You know, Harriet, you really are crazy. Or stupid. I've never been able to figure out which.'

'I guess,' I stalled some more, 'when you're going to kill someone, you can say anything you've ever wanted to say to them, can't you?'

'I guess so,' she agreed.

And then Lieutenant Hastings and some other police officers were there, separating PD from her gun and "Miranda-ising" her. When she was taken away, he said to me, 'She's probably right, Harriet. You are a little crazy *and* a little stupid. That was a big risk to take.'

'Naw,' I disagreed. 'I knew you didn't believe me upstairs, and I knew you were going to follow us. So, I knew you were close by to rescue us. And see? I was right. Come on, Sam, let's go pack. I've got to get home and get de-fleaed before I go grocery shopping.'

Four Characters, Four Lunches
Finola Moorhead

Maddy

The mad push of menopause impelled her into the garden. She knew of plants just enough to colour her fictions, as with primrose and gentian.

According to Madeleine Blake she ought to be at the keyboard, creating sentences, but she felt defeated by a succession of computers and software. Huge waves of bitterness and self-disgust swamped her, followed by suicidal depressions. She would wander listlessly through the different green things that were rooted in the earth, stopping, staring down, would curse her ignorance and, vowing to redress this, she would make a beeline for her library to seek out one of the garish gardening books given her as dutiful presents by nieces or nephews. Then she would sit in the armchair, look at the pictures and feel guilty.

Loss like a crash, a psychic pile-up, left trauma. Her precious sentences had been taken off into cyberspace. The poetic moment was gone. That particular dainty insight was lost forever (earth time), because her hand, possessed by the trembling Muse, agitating immediately before placing a word on a page, indeed vibrating with inspiration, shook on the mouse. She could not co-ordinate sufficiently well to click at the right second. So, in answer to the polite, user-friendly question, 'Save changes before closing window?', she clicked 'No'. She couldn't help herself. When she did it, she went bright red with embarrassment, all alone. She felt the shame rise into her cheeks because she didn't do it properly.

One of Australia's most celebrated authors, Maddy Blake had earned her place by working hard at her talent. Naming things. Naming people's foibles. Naming her shrewd observations. She was a craftswoman, as she would humbly say, at conference after conference. She crafted sentences or, if she were doing poetry, words themselves. A word. She crafted a word. Moments of pleasure in literature would alight to be chased away by feelings of worthlessness. Menopause.

Madeleine Blake had protected her mind from scientific facts in the way a mother would protect a child from the truth about father. Generally, she felt they would weigh her prose down to something like journalism. Anger built up in the blood like the blush of shame. Heat flushed her cheeks. Most of her income, ironically, came from newspapers. They sent her books by other female writers. Her skill, fuelled by a passionate rivalry of all except Meredith Heartfelt whom she said was great because she was ordinary, made her reviews sharp and influential.

In her forties, her face went hard suddenly, just as Poppy bright red lipstick became necessary and new wave feminism was in. It accentuated the gaunt lines conscientious thinness gave her face. A look of panic haunted her eyes. She frowned more than she intended, bringing folds into her forehead.

Maddy had come to the country to embrace solitude. The plants, whatever they were, became her friends. She could not tell a weed from a native, admired the flowers and fruit as they appeared and, in this instance, opted for simple wonder instead of finding the word. *Le mot juste*. She got down on her knees, made beds for her vegetables and felt cooler for doing so. To keep trim she went to the local gym and listened carefully to her personal trainer, a Baywatch babe. She felt foolish in her sexual feelings for this moron. To settle her spleen, she went to yoga, taught by an octogenarian whose rude health was testimonial to the efficacy of her Indian practices. In one class, she, contorting like a gymnast, confessed to eating anything and everything that grew in her garden: chickweed, comfrey flowers, dandelion.

In seclusion away from her home, the village of Aus. Lit., Maddy fell in love with a particular plant, whose cluster of four to five white flowers turned into luscious black berries, like blueberries. Maddy felt an affinity with this growing thing that always seemed to be caressing her ankles and knees. She felt it was her totem. Ladybirds affirmed her feeling. They loved it too.

Restless Press
John and Luke wanted to call it 'Restless White Male Press' after a phrase from one of their books: 'beware the restless white male.' Although they loved the idea, and toyed with it all through their discussions of amalgamating their two small, seventies-style concerns, into an incorporated firm, they wisely decided it would offend most of their authors, most especially Maddy Blake.

– She's fifty.

Both had enjoyed her body in University Colleges at vacation times, in convention centres or the expensive hotels of the big cities as the craze for literary festivals blossomed all over Australia.

– Must be, by now.

The latest Blake manuscript bored them both. There were no detailed sex scenes in it. They were what Maddy was good at, in a droll Jean Rhys type of way. Restless would publish it anyway. Their literary good name was based on Madeleine Blake's work. She won prizes frequently and was in the top ten recipients of grants from the Australia Council over the last twenty years.

– By fifty, you've either completely tamed them, or you don't know where they are going to gallop. Mostly, they hobble themselves because it's the pragmatic thing to do. To become and stay mildly mad. Like Merrie Heartfelt.

John frowned at the wall behind his partner.

– Love the equine imagery. Hate the pontificating on middle-aged women. I'm hungry.

The letter fluttered gracefully back into the white, plastic basket on the desk labelled 'Corres. to Resp.'. Although the partners loved their place of work, it was furnished and outfitted with the cheapest products.

– Fifty, the senior end of the baby-boomers, as it were. Baby-boomers fall into two, or three groups. Ages. John continued, intense. – Those born out of desperate post-war marital fucks, in which you cannot be sure the old man will stay around, or be sane, or sober, if he does. Those born in fifties' prosperity as a part of that prosperity, a new lounge suite, kids to go on the Swedish vinyl. Then, those born into a changing world, the Currency[1] kids of the Global Village.

– Let's go down to Scallopini's and discuss the three ages of baby-booming over a pasta and a suitably aged merlot?

– It's only eleven thirty, and I can't afford it. I've brought sandwiches. Sandy and I are house-renovating, don't yer know?

– Just give Gerard O'Dreary a ring. He should have finished his two hours daily drudge by now, always loves a session. Put it on expenses.

---

[1] The 'Currency' lads and lasses were the first children of colonists born in New South Wales, the first white Australians

The partners in this arty publishing house had a long time ago given up any pretence of a relationship between their own capital and that of their company.

The company, although it was themselves, and no one else, not even a secretary, was a cow to be milked, a thing that could go bankrupt or prosper; either way their personal assets and money were not affected.

– The thing about Gerry, the blessed and beautiful thing about Gerry, is his drunken, racist, sexist, poofter-bashing yarns sell! Hello! Gerard! Have to take you to lunch, man, urgent . . . Well, a skip and a jump . . . No, Italian . . . Be there by noon, or twelve thirty at the latest. We need you to discuss the three ages of baby-boomers . . . Oh, you know, on the corner of Charles and Liverpool, the Italian place with the red checked tablecloths.

He pushed down the phone's aerial with a smirk, and clipped it into its holster on his belt like a gun.

– Why didn't you say Scallopini's? The man can read. Have we taken him there before?

– No. Luke shrugged himself into his artily crushed jacket, and looked thoughtful. – I don't know. It sounds neat, younger, not to recall anything that starts with a capital letter.

The bloke from the bush
Gerard O'Dowd was worth about ten thousand a year to each of them in pocket money and free lunches. When Gerard became one of their authors, John and Luke were trooping around the country the Grandma Moses of Australian Letters, Meredith Heartfelt, who had written particularly nasty pieces about younger, or more fortunate, women for fifty years, but had not found a publisher for these works until she was nearly sixty. Restless Press discovered Merrie Heartfelt, groomed her to be a daffy old duck who couldn't find her hotel keys without help, who spoke, for a teacher, annoyingly softly and

dressed like a domestic fowl in an English children's book.
Then the novels came thick and fast off the presses. John and
Luke enjoyed promoting Merrie's work among their friends at
conferences, universities, festivals and on the ABC. They were
genial when the bloke from the bush pushed into their white
plastic office smelling of bravado, whisky on the breath, and
slapped down an armful of foolscap pages. John and Luke were
amused and curious and said they would have a look when
they had a moment.

While they were reading to each other the politically
incorrect rapacious tales of the bloke from the bush, Meredith
Heartfelt found herself an agent who auctioned off her
remaining five novels to competing international publishers
and left their 'stable' without so much as a daffy thank-you
note.

They learnt their lesson.

First, they took him out to lunch. Secondly, at another time,
they asked Gerard for the money to have the manuscripts
typed and made presentable, to themselves as it happened, and
magnanimously gave him a photocopy. Then, with little
deliberation, mainly sniffing the air and discerning the sado-
masochistic trend of postmodernism in Australia, they offered
him a contract.

Gerard, who was too fragile a man to make a fist of the
property his father left him or to stand up to the banks when
their functionaries came in the eighties to foreclose on the
mortgage and possess the farm, had let it be known, at that first
lunch, what he thought of all the big publishers who had
rejected his rough-and-ready tales. Luke was careful not to
place the closely typed pages of clauses in front of him until
the third Benedictine and coffee after a major steak in a place
frequented by City barristers. Gerard scrawled his moniker on
all the papers and a lawyer from the next table witnessed his
signature. Having signed away, for ten per cent of the retail

price of books successfully sold, exclusive rights to this and all his following books for the life of copyright, Gerard blissfully recounted the dramatic incidents of his career, so far. He had started drinking young, never intended to stop, and he could yarn till the Irish blood in him turned cold. He shouted, good-humouredly, across the room to his co-signatory, who was leaving, that he had better have his card in case something went wrong, legally. The would-be counsel went pale, tapping his breast pocket, shaking his head, opening his palms, and, as quick-thinking Luke launched another salvo of flattery, made his escape. John ordered more grog. They had thought the lunching judiciary would give their dealing a kosher feel. They succeeded.

Gerard, in his cups, loved these guardian angels, John and Luke. That he even had publishers gave him folk hero status in his own eyes, but they were mates as well. He would write his heart out for them. He did. His tales of rapine became bestsellers. The thing was he had raped a girl, if 'date rape' was rape. At the time it seemed to him a battle of wills. The thread that ran through the saccharine sentiment and brutal indulgences of his fantasies was his excuse, his justification, his rationalisation. Time and again he proved to himself he was right. And he was damn right. They were buying his books, weren't they?

John and Luke were prepared to bear the humiliations the pathetic excesses Gerard O'Dreary brought upon them at literary gatherings, provided, at the private dinner parties they had with their partners and close friends, they could heap dollops of scorn with ice-cream ladles on his very name and make him the butt of their jokes.

English Mint Relish
Mint reminded Madeleine of her mother, a woman she did not like. Mint, however, brought feelings of warmth and

remembrance of things past, such as roasted leg of lamb. It was not the taste of the meal itself which brought Maddy's emotions close to the creature who had incubated her, it was recall of a Sunday morning hunger redolent with the fragrance of freshly chopped mint leaves. She sat back on her heels in horror and slapped her cheek for forgetting. She, the intellectual daughter who hated cooking, sewing, knitting, all of it, she, Maddy, had been the one who chopped the mint of a Sunday morning when lamb was the roast of the day. Feeling love for this woman she'd loathed all her adult life and blamed for her ills was peculiar. The remembrance was barbed. Madeleine made herself comfortable to reminisce, flaring her nostrils to get the help of the smell of her mint, one of the most virile of the plants in the garden. The body of her personal trainer came to mind, why? Madeleine Blake was a disciplined fiction-writer. Although she did not give too much mind to facts among the thesaurus of detail there, Maddy was strict in chasing the spider-web patterns of logic in her imagination. The answer surfaced She had had to choose between her mother and the sixteen-year-old boy who had taken her virginity. The cat fight had taken place on a Sunday, after lunch. As she had watched the boy run away in terror at her mother's fury, she had screamed, 'I hate you. I hate you.'

What remained now was the image of the boy's tight buttocks and his long, muscled legs fleeing. Her life, her work too, had repeated and repeated the decision made that day. She loved bums and she hated her mother, she would state smugly. It was set in concrete. It was Maddy Blake.

None the less, the Proustian yet menopausal moment electrified her into action. Madeleine must celebrate this mint, this fruit of earth and imagination, this root of her literary angst. She knew there would be a serendipity close as happened in plots when you let the characters take over. Yes. Yes! She ran inside and, anchored with a magnet on the fridge,

curling and yellowing, was a recipe cut from someone else's
Women's Day. 'English Mint Relish'. She studied the words for
several minutes before really absorbing what they said. She
registered that she had plenty of jars and enough mint.
Strangely motivated, she switched on her computer as she
went to the bathroom to splash cold water on her hot face,
came back and drummed out a mad-Maddy letter to her
devoted publishers, John and Luke, inviting them down to her
country abode for a meal and a natter. Then she printed it out,
hurried it into an envelope which she licked with her tongue
and stamped, and sprinted to her car, rattling keys.

A lull in her mood occurred outside the post office as she
stared at the price of petrol, but she waited, cunningly, aware
of the wave motions of inspiration. One came. She drove
around to her yoga teacher's house. She had never been there
before but she knew where it was. The garden was as neat as a
new pin, flowers in the front, vegetables out the back in a
fenced-off yard of their own and narrow concrete strips
leading to the doors into the house. She wondered for half a
second where the dandelion and chickweed and the other
unconventional things she professed to eat were, but there in
front of her was her teacher calling gaily. Maddy felt a sudden,
irrational flash of anophobia, which she swallowed like unwelcome nausea, and, responding fulsomely, rushed into her
request. She had to have home-grown, tomatoes, cucumber,
peppers. It was a writerly thing, she explained. When she left,
only 2 large Granny Smith apples and a bottle of brown malt
vinegar remained to be bought for her adventure in the
kitchen.

The lunch at Scallopini's
Although Gerard O'Dowd, almost solely, was responsible for
their solvency, let alone their financial success, the partners of
Restless Press treated him abysmally. Gerard had one word to

say to their endlessly intriguing gossip of the people in Australian Letters. 'Fuckwits.'

– The whole literary scene is nothing but a bunch of snooty-nosed, hard-faced bitches and pansy fuckwits!

John and Luke ignored him. All three really believed that the Press was paying for their piss-up and pig-out and that it was all right. Belief is a word to be used in cases where to know the truth is too uncomfortable. Gerard could get quite punchy. If he had realised he was paying through the nose for stuff he did not even like, he may have thrown his weight around. John and Luke knew, contractually speaking, they had him by the short and curlies. They let him believe he was a genius in the style of John Shaw Neilson or someone, not a thug who was prepared to voice the alarming rise of neo-fascism in the country. Not only did the successful novels of Gerard O'Dowd make characters who used racist language like 'boongs' and 'slab-heads' sympathetic and heroic in fighting Aboriginal laziness and Asian immorality, there was always murder in them and the victim was always a woman and the circumstances always pornographic. The man's ignorance of life was the grace that saved him from being an enthusiastic apologist for the international sex-slave trade.

– So, what baby-boomers? He burped out his first lager air of the day, interrupting the long-fingered gesturing of his companions.

John and Luke were surprised to find that Gerard was considerably younger than Maddy. He hardly made it into their baby-boom categories at all. They looked warmly into each other's eyes, acknowledging their golden goose was the gander in their midst. Gerard mistook their gratitude for respect of his genius and liking of his person. He ordered spaghetti bolognaise, and more beer.

– A wonderful writer, wonderful. So sharp. Loyal.

Luke began placing Madeleine Blake in the context of the

book world for Gerard. She and he had aged together from the liberating, libertarian early seventies to the middle nineties. The tight-arsed nineties.

— She went into 'sisterhood' for a bit, but kept it ironic. While she needed a man, Madeleine never wanted a child. In fact, Maddy sacrificed practically everything to be the writer she is. Friendship, sport, politics.

— Without Maddy I would never have taken Luke as a partner. Her literary credit was worth my capital. Her knack with words could almost disguise the underlying vulgarity of her work, her craft completely obfuscates her stupidity. She is the most accomplished liar in the country.

Luke laughed while John remained intense and meaningful.

— Lies to herself about her age. I was on a panel with her last September, and I could smell the make-up on her three seats away. And she doesn't love facts. I love facts. Give me a fact and I'll tell you a story, I will.

— But she doesn't make up anything either. It's all personal, as if it really happened. And the immediacy. Like yesterday.

— Yet, it is so calculated Luke was astute with longer knowledge.

— But, bugger me, I liked her.

Both John and Luke looked at him and raised their eyebrows.

— When the flesh is willing, the spirit's weak. Gerard blushed.

— I think she is lonely. Luke put down his glass carefully, so as not to bruise the wine. John, understanding there was much fun to be had as a voyeur, suggested all three visit Madeleine together.

— Well, we did appreciate one another's . . .

— Talents?

— Stature?

— Creativity, finished Gerard.

Al Fresco

Ten days ago Madeleine had roughly chopped the produce from her own and her guru's gardens, boiled vinegar, dissolved sugar and sterilised jars. She had bottled her relish and stuck dated labels on the glass. It was a lovely day. She had dragged the wooden table and four kitchen chairs outside, aiming for a French film ambience for her little literary luncheon. She had popped up to town and bought cold cuts and colourful sub-tropical fruit. A gentle breeze tossed the unnecessary tablecloth about.

As she waited, she sat at her desk, flicking through a couple of slim volumes sent her for reviewing and putting down a note or two on her pad. She had hardly to bother to read the books she criticised to find syntax and words, agreeable in themselves, to put in the article, which would be paid for, which would keep her name up there, and the invitations flowing in. She needed these things to feel decisions she had made along the way were right. Instead of feeling anticipatory pleasure at imminent company, she felt angry. They were five minutes late. She had dashed off a review in her shorthand notebook before she heard the car pull into her driveway. She announced the young had stolen her youth, and she felt she had said something.

All the authors published by Restless Press had a soft spot for Gerard O'Dowd. John or Luke made sure each knew that their own work did not bring in revenue the way Gerard's did. Meagre royalties, and, of course, the flattery of the publishers' attention proved in the quality of the paper used for their literature as opposed to O'Dowd's pulp, were all that separated them from Vanity publishing. Maddy abhorred Gerard's novels, but she had read every word of her gift copies, with a kind of guilty misogyny. She never named it 'self-hatred'. Apart from the beginnings of a solid beer gut, Gerard still had a farmer's body, bow-legged and hard-muscled. He had been drinking on the way down. He kissed her possessively on the lips, to the amusement of John and Luke, who had egged him on earlier. They were more brotherly with their lips and spoke of the wine they brought with them.

Maddy sat them *al fresco* in the long grass of her garden, produced glasses and corkscrew and began the long story of the English Mint Relish, including her first boyfriend and her dreadful mother. As a raconteur, she came into her own.

– So, I shall be deeply, deeply offended if you don't have relish on every bit of cold meat you eat.

– Not me. I don't eat anything green. Gerard leaned back and looked around at the weeds.

– Anyway, I had done practically everything, me, an absolute dolt in the kitchen, when I discovered I had forgotten the raisins. Well, don't worry I rushed up and got some, but, you see, I've fallen in love.

John and Luke were munching away on meat, relish and salad, and swirling full-bodied wine across their taste buds enjoying themselves making faces. Oh?

– Not with a person. With a plant! The ladybirds and I adore it. It's so generous. The flowers turn into this little bunch of gorgeous berries, like blueberries. Racing back with the raisins, I thought why not? So I got a couple of handfulls. As I threw them into the mixture, the hot vinegar etc, I felt this surge of power. Of freedom. An overcoming of my mother. True. Madeleine nodded their agreement.

Gerard snapped his fingers, pleased with himself.

– That's it. Deadly Nightshade. I didn't think I'd ever see a quarter-acre house-block full of it. It could kill you that stuff.

Madeleine Blake sat stock still, having a hot flush.

– Bella Donna.

A Man's Book
Margaret Wilkinson

In the spring of 1870, in the village of *P*, a printer fastened a block of type onto the bed of a huge hand-operated press. She was a muscular woman called Masha, who'd recently inherited the business from her father. Her cast-iron press had multiple levers, ornamented with North American alligators and serpents. A large bird with extended wings surmounted the dark mechanism, grasping in its talons a parcel of thunderbolts and olive branches.

Despite her mighty, modern press, hardly anyone ever entered Masha's shop. People disapproved of a woman printer. They'd rather drive miles out of their way to patronise a traditional male typesetter with a wooden press designed like an olive squeezer in a distant village. 'A printress?' they sneer-ed. Some of the locals believed a female printer was illegal. The reactionary apothecary, for instance, was trying to find a statute or bylaw to this effect in the provincial constitution.

'It was my father's shame,' Masha whispered as she slopped ink onto the forme that held the type, 'that he had no sons.'

Then she rolled up her sleeves and pulled the handle of the press. A system of levers raised the bird-shaped counterweight. The connecting mechanism squealed and the platen came down with a thud, causing an ink bottle on the sideboard to jump. 'This book'll make me rich,' she sang as she removed the printed sheet from the frame.

Instead of the usual wagon repair manuals and religious tracts her father had published, Masha was printing a novel. And not just any novel, a racy man's book. Before setting the type, Masha read each page, blushing frequently.

In the language of the streets, the book described various sexual techniques. It was written by the world-weary Count Anatole Minky. In every chapter there were soldiers with restless hands. Without flinching, the author depicted under-wear and undressing, leading to Viennese embracing.

The little print shop was airless like the inside of a barrel, with only one small window high up on the wall. The dark hand-driven press dominated the floor space. On a small desk, a book of accounts lay open. Masha was going to show the world that a strong woman could operate a heavy printing press, and make money too. Her father's publishing business was nearly bankrupt. He'd spent everything on the elaborate press, which even possessed a cartouche of cast-iron flowers enclosing the engraved nameplate of the foreign manufacturer.

Masha pulled the handle again. She was a bonny, well-developed girl with broad hips, rosy cheeks (although she used no cosmetics) and a pug nose. She wore her hair in a French twist, parted on the side and combed over one eye giving her a coquettish look. Hidden by her long skirt, her calves were muscular and hard as stone from standing for hours at her levers. Despite the fact that she'd only just turned nineteen, she could pull seventy-five pages a day.

With a frown, she examined the first impression and threw

it aside. There was a misspelling.

Gazing at the wildcat of a woman who stood before him, the young Fusilier salivated like a cog, she read with a grimace.

Unlocking the composed type from the forme, she painstakingly replaced the metal letter c with the letter d. Eventually she reassembled the forme, laid it on the bed, put another sheet of paper in place, pushed the bed under the platform and pulled the handle again. She stared at her ink-stained fingers. Every sheet wasted cost her dearly. The small amount of money her father had left her was quickly running out.

Later that evening, by pre-arrangement, Masha waited outside her shop. It was almost midnight. She carried an armful of posters announcing the forthcoming publication of Count Minky's novel.

A few loose coins jangled in a purse she wore around her waist. 'I've got just enough money for one last trip to the Capital to buy ink,' she said out loud. 'Without more ink,' she frowned, 'I won't be able to complete the job.'

Yesterday Masha (who understood the benefits of publicity) had used almost the last of her savings to take out a small advertisement in the local newspaper, announcing the first novel ever to be published in the village of *P*.

CITIZENS! the advert shrieked.

BE ALERTED! A MAN'S NOVEL OF THE HIGHEST STANDARD SHALL SOON BE AVAILABLE IN YOUR VILLAGE. A PREMIER PUBLICATION WRITTEN BY THE INFAMOUS HUSSAR, COUNT ANATOLE MINKY!

READ ALL ABOUT WAR! BETRAYAL! BROKEN SABBATHS! VIOLENCE! STRONG DRINK! HUNTING WITH DOGS AND CAROUSING WITH WOMEN! DON'T MISS OUT. ORDER YOUR COPY NOW.

The street was quiet. Almost too quiet. The roadway was narrow and cobbled. By moonlight, the cramped brick buildings and shuttered shops seemed to lean inwards, oppressing her. Their tottering roofs all but obscured the cold sky. In the distance, Masha heard hoofbeats. She searched the pools of darkness. Somewhere a wagon door slammed. Then a weedy man appeared. He was carrying a sloshing bucket and a brush. When he came up beside Masha, he tried to give her a kiss, but she turned away. His suit of wax-stained clothes was worn and patched.

The candlemaker, alone in the village of *P*, showed a friendly interest in Masha and her printing business. She'd been expecting him. Together they began to flypost the street.

Brushing some glue on the wall below a window from which slops had been recently thrown, the candlemaker took a poster from Masha. Then grabbed her ink-stained hand. 'I know this isn't the time,' he blundered, puffs of breath rolling from his nostrils. 'But have you thought about my proposal?' He held his brush upright like a flower. Glue dripped onto the cobbles. 'I love you,' he said loudly.

Masha looked at his shrivelled face. His expression, far from passionate, appeared crafty. Quickly she withdrew her hand. 'I don't want to marry you,' she told him. 'If that's the only reason you're assisting me, you can depart.'

'But I want to be your helpmate,' he smiled shakily. 'I've told you, novels are good for my business too. It's almost like we're partners already. The more people read for pleasure, after dark, the more candles they buy.'

'Unless they've got a gas lamp,' Masha muttered. She pointed to his waistcoat of brown felt. It was without a watch chain across it. 'Have you pawned it?'

The candlemaker hung his head.

'You only want to get your hands on my business because your's is no longer showing a profit.'

'That's not true,' he protested. He was a young man, but already he looked old. 'Can't I be your Puller, your Beater, or your Fly?' he asked in the language of printing.

'My shop's a one-woman operation. I don't need an assistant.' Masha eyed the candlemaker's withered physique, bowed like a melting taper. Her jaw was set. 'You've already helped me enough,' she softened, 'by forming a literary society. It was a great idea.'

'The first literary society in the village of *P*, to promote the publishing event of the decade,' he enthused.

'I wish I could have been there.'

'Men only,' he reminded her.

'Soon we'll have women's societies as well,' she grumbled.

'It's a new world.' The candlemaker looked over at the recently installed gas lamp at the end of the street and cringed. The bold little gas jet illuminating the desolate corner seemed to mock him. With expenses greater than his income, his traditional business (which included beekeeping) was failing. The new gaslights and oil lamps now available for home use made candles practically redundant. No one but the poor wanted candles anymore.

'All the men who've joined the literary society are looking forward to reading the book you're printing.' He took Masha's hand and guided her along the bare cobbles. 'The first novel to be published in *P*! You'll sell thousands.'

'If I don't, I lose the business.'

Together they walked towards the darkened apothecary's, then stopped. Some of the other shops were boarded up for the night with sheets of tin, but the apothecary's windows gleamed. Clouds, racing above the arched roofs in a strengthening wind, were reflected in the glass.

The candlemaker pressed his face to the front window, and looked in at the dark remedies: a pyramid of Universal Ointment, a single bottle of Good Appetite Syrup on a velvet pedestal, dosage spoons, blistering kits, leeches asleep in jars. With a malicious grin, he adhered one of Masha's posters to the glass. The apothecary, along with other local conservatives (farmers, mothers, etc) was trying to block publication of Count Minky's novel, calling it, 'a Godless book.'

'You can't fail.' The candlemaker turned towards Masha. 'At the first meeting of the literary society we drafted a letter of invitation to the author, begging him to come to our modest village to launch his great work.' He reached into his suit jacket. 'I've got the letter with me. All we need is the Count's address.'

Masha stiffened. 'That's impossible,' she said. 'The Count's an eccentric like all writers. When I accepted his manuscript, I promised complete anonymity.'

'But the literary society is planning a huge event. How many copies are you printing? You'll sell out.'

'I . . . I'm not sure,' Masha said haltingly. Her hands flew to her lips. 'Give me the letter.' She bit her knuckles. 'Tomorrow I'm going to the Capital to buy ink. I'll call on him while I'm there.'

'Without a chaperone?' The candlemaker bent forward and lay his flat cold lips against Masha's. The hard collar of his shirt dug into her chin. 'I insist on accompanying you.'

'Count Minky's a recluse.' She twisted away. 'He won't see anyone but me. Once he was a military genius. Now he shuts himself up like an oyster.' Grabbing the envelope, she turned on her heels. 'I'll deliver the society's letter myself,' she hastily promised. 'But I doubt he'll come.'

'When you get back we'll hold a special meeting of the literary society,' the candlemaker hollered after her. 'You can present yourself and tell us what the Count had to say. I'll arrange it. I'm sure the others will let a woman inside. Just this once.'

Masha faced a room full of men. Sitting on chairs, placed in rows before her, they squirmed impatiently in their seats. They smiled as if they were sneering at her. She noted their starched shirt fronts.

'A woman shouldn't be here,' she heard the blacksmith grouse. He stared at her pillowy breasts.

But then the men of the literary society became enthused by her words. 'I've just returned from the Capital.' Masha held her fists tightly against her hips. 'Count Anatole Minky,' she lifted one hand and waved his acceptance letter, 'will be delighted to attend the launch of his man's book in the village of P.'

The men cheered.

Masha wore a white dress with a blue sash for the occasion. The fabric pulled and strained over her large frame. The dangling ribbons swayed. She stared above the heads of the all-male literary society. There was a dirty moulding of grapes and acanthus leaves around the walls of the high-ceilinged room they'd hired for their meeting.

'Did you see him in person?' the candlemaker got to his feet. His starched white shirt cuffs hung to his knees.

'What did he look like?' the blacksmith cried in a strong bass voice.

'Count Minky's an old man,' she responded. 'But vital. When he opened his door to let me into his apartment, there were hunting dogs yapping at his heels. He asked me to join him for a drink.'

'Noooo.' The men were scandalised and excited.

'He swallowed his vodka straight from the bottle. I was served mine,' she blushed, 'in a horn.'

As they left the meeting, the men gossiped enthusiastically. Soon everyone in the village would be speculating about the renowned Count Minky and the forthcoming literary event. The book was bound to be a success.

Previously scorned and degraded, Masha now found herself

at the centre of the village's interest. Faces peered in at her as
she soaked paper in her trough, dutifully printed pages, and
hung them up to dry. The villagers had climbed ladders to
reach her high window. They stared at her powerful arms, and
waved, distracting her as she tried to work.

Out in the street, her neighbours stopped her, and begged
her to steal chapters for them: out-takes, misprints, or trial
runs. It had been rumoured that there was a step-by-step, easy-
to-follow description of tongue-kissing in the section she was
currently printing. Regularly, her rubbish was rifled.

Most people in the village were anxiously awaiting the
arrival of the author. Two hundred and fifty advance copies of
his novel had been ordered. But there were also ominous
rumours, which Masha appeared to ignore. A large protest was
being planned by the reactionary apothecary and his
conservative minions. It was said that the apothecary would
stop at nothing to ban the book.

Would he stop at murder? The candlemaker told Masha to
lock her doors. He thought she should have a bodyguard.

One afternoon, Masha heard men gathering in the street
outside. She stood on a chair and peeked from her high
window at them. Watching the apothecary's face as he sang
hymns with a crowd of conservative woodcutters, and a
visiting flagellant, who'd come to protest in front of her shop,
she was inclined to agree with the candlemaker. She rubbed
her eyes. The apothecary looked crazy and dangerous. She
could see from his fanatical expression that he was a driven and
determined man. He stood at a portable lectern and ranted
against swearing, filth, and impure soup. All the modern evils
seemed to torment him.

On the morning Count Minky was due to arrive, Masha
waited on the platform of the provincial train station with the
members of the literary society. She held a large bouquet of

flowers for the Count.

A mail train had just departed. Green lamps shone along the line.

The candlemaker, who wore a coat with tails dropping mothballs, unrolled a red carpet. At once a hapless commuter stood on it and was shooed away. A welcoming band, consisting of a local horn player and an accordionist, began to tune up.

Behind the band, a disgruntled group of farmers carrying pitchforks and mothers carrying brooms, had formed under a banner declaring FAMILY VALUES: NO GODLESS MAN'S BOOK IN OUR VILLAGE.

Masha shrugged. 'Any publicity is good publicity,' she said to the candlemaker. The reactionary apothecary was noticeably absent. She looked around for his familiar skulking figure, but couldn't see him anywhere.

Even though there was plenty of time before the train was due, the candlemaker kept checking the large station clock. Soon he began to tap his foot. It was a chilly day. He'd brought a cloak for the old author.

'What does he want that for? He's a soldier,' the blacksmith complained. 'A retired Hussar.'

Some of the literary society sided with the candlemaker, others with the blacksmith. Tersely they argued amongst themselves about the degree to which retired Hussars-turned-authors felt the cold.

Masha stared off into space. The platform began to fill up with people. She shifted her feet and made her shoulders twitch. Her usually lively eyes had a dull lustre.

'What's wrong?' the candlemaker hissed.

'I don't know.' She gave him an exhausted smile. 'Lately I've been having trouble sleeping. I didn't sleep last night, or the night before. Soon I'll have to visit the vodka traders,' she joked, crossing her eyes and staggering in front of him.

The candlemaker stared at her as if she were mad. Then he glanced over his shoulder.

A ranter, standing on a crate, started to lecture those waiting for trains about the evils of book-reading, card–playing and sprawling in chairs.

'Another one of the apothecary's conservative league,' Masha complained. She looked up at the roof of tar paper and wood. She looked down at the plank floor. In the distance, she heard a high pitched whistle. She squinted along the track. Tendrils of hair fell over her eyes as she leaned forward. Then the platform began to vibrate.

All at once, the air filled with steam and smoke, and a train slowed into the station, braking with a deafening roar. Masha lifted her bouquet. The men alongside her slicked down their hair. The blacksmith, who was going to make the welcoming address, cleared his throat. Then the band struck up with a rendition of the village anthem: *Stalwart Men*. But as the passengers departed the carriages, coaches and private compartments, they could not see the Count anywhere.

Masha stood on tip-toes. A tailor carrying a sewing machine emerged from one carriage, a blind man was led from another. In front of the luggage van, a well-dressed woman with a lap dog engaged a porter. A youth with a newspaper brushed past. Behind him, a man of great bulk wearing smart clothes, paused for a moment at the door of his compartment, before stepping onto the platform.

'Is that the Count?' The candlemaker tensed his shoulders.

'Nah, he's too young.' The blacksmith shook his head.

When the whistle blew, signalling that the train would soon depart, the candlemaker pressed forward, pulling Masha along with him. 'There's an imminent author on board,' he cried to the guardsman.

'You mean eminent.' Masha clutched his wrist. The swing barrier was already raised.

'You can't leave!' The candlemaker ignored her and continued to argue with the guardsman. 'He's supposed to get off at this station. We're here to meet him. He must have fallen asleep on the train. We've got to find him.'

Three members of the welcoming committee, dressed in their best clothes, with Masha holding the flowers, were allowed briefly onto the train to look for the author. Systematically they began checking carriages and opening doors.

The first thing Masha saw in the last compartment she entered, was a pair of feet in military boots, dangling over the side of the upholstered seat. She screamed and mussed her hair. He'd fallen backwards, his limp body slumped against the window of the otherwise empty compartment, his eyes staring crookedly at the ceiling. Swaying she grabbed the doorframe for support. His crumpled face was ashen, his blue lips contorted in a twist of pain. One hand, frozen in a claw, clutched at the collar of his uniform. A gold braid dangled from his shoulder.

'It's Count Minky!' the candlemaker screamed. Pushing Masha to one side, he bent over the old man's lifeless body. The close smell of almond bread clogged the air.

One moment Masha was standing in the compartment, the next moment she was running. She stumbled down a narrow corridor inside the train. There were tears in her eyes. She covered her face with her hands. Through her fingers she could see startled passengers standing in their seats. She moved her lips but made no sound. The stationmaster dashed past her carrying a stretcher. A guard holding a cannister of smelling salts gestured wildly in the confined space.

When Masha jumped off the stalled train, she was surprised to see the candlemaker following close behind. She quickened her pace.

As she hurried along the platform, Masha nearly collided with the apothecary. He was walking furtively towards the exit. 'Grab him!' Masha heard the candlemaker cry. Briefly she turned to look at the crowd that had gathered behind her. At first they stared dumbly at the scene. Then they took up the cry. 'Grab him! Stop him!'

'Let him go!' the protesting farmers and mothers shrieked.

'He's killed Count Minky,' the men of the literary society countered. A farmer threw a hayrake at a society member. 'Somebody call the police,' his comrades hollered as hoes and harrows rained down upon them. The mothers hurled milk bottles.

Hearing their angry voices, Masha leaned against a pillar and threw up. 'This is all my fault,' she groaned.

As she ran back to her shop, Masha tried to calm herself. Once inside, she took a deep cleansing breath. The air smelled comfortingly of paper dust. Purposefully, she printed a single sheet of type with the word *influenza* on it, although her heart was still thudding. Then she hung the paper up to dry.

When the members of the literary society, the manacled apothecary (chained by his hands and feet), and a policeman carrying a bayonet arrived, she ceased her work and opened the door.

'You're the only one to have seen Count Minky before today,' the candlemaker yelled from the doorstep. His eyebrows appeared overgrown and wild. 'Why did you run away?'

'Is it that women have no stomach for viewing dead bodies?' the policeman standing alongside him asked.

'You've got to come to the morgue right now and make a formal identification, so that the police can charge the apothecary,' the candlemaker pulled Masha's sleeve. The policeman jabbed his bayonet in the air.

'Count Minky's not dead,' Masha backed away from the men. She still held an ink dauber in her hands. 'He cancelled.' She waved a telegram at them. 'It was just delivered. The poor man has influenza.' The paper in her hand rustled.

'He's dead,' the candlemaker insisted. 'The apothecary poisoned him. You saw his body on the train. The apothecary hated him. He was trying to get his novel banned. He killed him. He was probably going to kill you next.'

'No.' Masha tore at her bodice. There were tears in her eyes. 'It was me.' She clasped her chest.

'You killed Count Minky? But you were with us all along.' The candlemaker drew his wild eyebrows together. 'On the station platform.'

'There is no Count Minky.' She breathed heavily. 'I faked his acceptance letter, intending to cancel the visit at the last minute. The telegram's a phoney too. I printed it myself.' Masha burst into tears.

'But you hand-delivered the invitation. You took it to the Capital. You met him. You drank out of his horn.'

'I only pretended to meet him.'

'But you described the Hussar we saw dead on the train.' He looked at her with good-natured reproach. 'Your description fit him perfectly.'

'I made it up.' She lifted her arms, and let them fall. 'One lie led to another. There is no Count Minky. It's all a horrible misunderstanding. A series of coincidences . . . Why did you have to make such a fuss? Forming a stupid literary society? Inviting him here? It was me . . . I wrote the book!'

'You?' The candlemaker's face went stiff. 'You're a woman.' His eyes were crazed and full of horror. 'What do you know about dogs and war?' He stuck out his bottom lip. 'What do you know about French kissing?'

Masha hung her head in shame. 'I needed the money.'

Later it was discovered that the soldier on the train was not murdered. He was a military suicide, of which there were many in those days. A note was found in one pocket, and a

packet of cyanide in the other. As Masha had said, his
appearance on the train was merely a coincidence.

But no one in the village of *P* cared anymore. They had a
new scandal. Buzzing with excitement, men armed with
cabbages gathered in front of Masha's boarded-up printing
shop (which the candlemaker was trying to purchase at
auction, having withdrawn his offer of marriage).

When he saw her coming down the street, the apothecary
(now released from police custody) threw the first cabbage.
The candlemaker swore at her. But Masha didn't twitch. She'd
gained a certain daring notoriety in the village. The woman
who wrote a man's book was secretly, and openly, admired. Her
face was calm and indifferent. Young ladies copied her hair-
style. Dubbed *The Bad Girl of P*, her doings were highlighted
in the centrefold of a local tabloid beside a glamorous
daguerreotype that many readers cut out and hung on their
walls.

It was rumoured she'd placed the feature article herself
because she'd become a publicist. (Some say she invented the
profession.) After a while, she moved to the Capital where far
more people wanted their names and deeds in lights.

HAVE YOU BEHAVED SCANDALOUSLY? NEED HELP AND
ADVICE? GET A PRESS AGENT, her new business cards read. They
were printed (by Masha herself) on creamy white stiffened
paper of the highest quality, satin-finished, with an embossed
typeface like a wedding invitation.

STET
Barbara Paul

Julia Cutler stared gloomily at the edited manuscript on her desk. She'd flipped through the pages to see how many times the word 'stet' had been written in the right-hand margins; there was at least one on every page, frequently as many as six.

Some writers couldn't *stand* to be edited.

Martin Klein was one such. Martin was a shallow writer, but until recently a popular one; his books were action-filled and entertaining in an old-fashioned macho sort of way. His mystery plots were full of holes; and he had a stable of about six characters he drew upon regularly, changing their names from book to book. Still, as long as his books kept selling, Julia would keep buying them for Gotham House.

But even that was becoming problematic; Martin Klein's last two books had been disappointing, with fewer sales and higher returns than ever before. The kind of book Martin wrote had been in decline for years, and Julia was vaguely surprised that he'd managed to hold on as long as he had. The handwriting was on the wall, though.

With a sigh she got to work. Her rule of thumb was to give the writer his or her way in every instance that was not an outright violation of usage, spelling, or factual accuracy. But Martin tended to get sloppy about grammar – right there was an example: 'She was one of those women who always has to have the last word.' The copy-editor had correctly changed 'has' to 'have'; but Martin had written a big red 'stet' in the margin – let it stand as it is. Julia drew two blue lines through the 'stet'.

It was dark and the other Gotham employees had gone home by the time Julia finished. Martin's new book was called *Swimming in Blood*; the word *Blood* appeared in every Martin Klein title. Another Martin Klein trademark was an extended scene in which his private-eye hero got beaten to a pulp. Usually the scene appeared about halfway through the book so Martin could show his hero struggling valiantly on, even though in great pain. Real he-man.

Julia had meant to run a couple of errands before she met Dan for dinner, but there wasn't time now. She wrapped up warm against New York's harsh January winds and took a cab to Three-Card Monty's on Fifty-seventh Street. Dan was sitting in the bar area, waiting for her.

Julia sank down on the bar stool beside him. 'Martini,' she told the bartender.

Dan grinned and said, 'No need to ask what kind of day you had. What happened?'

'Martin Klein's new book happened, that's what.' The bartender brought her Martini and she took a sip. 'No real problems – just tedious work.'

Dan grinned. 'And does good old Whatsisname get the stuffing knocked out of him again?'

Martin's fictional detective. 'Of course he does,' Julia replied with a smile. 'And of course Martin won't allow a word of his precious prose to be changed. So, what about you? Catch any bad guys today?'

Dan Bernhard was a police detective working out of New York's Midtown South Precinct. He claimed Midtown South was too big a precinct for only twenty-three detectives to cover; moreover, he didn't like his lieutenant and he had little respect for his partner. Still, he insisted he liked police work. Julia didn't know him well enough yet to question him on the point.

She listened carefully as he told her about a new gang war that had broken out in the project houses along FDR Drive and was spreading uptown. It was a territorial thing, Dan said. Who had the right to sell drugs on what streets. America's future lies in its Youth.

It was a depressing subject, but Julia didn't have to fake an interest. Like everyone connected with mystery writing, she had a certain degree of curiosity about police work. Dan was a bright, college-educated go-getter who'd been partnered with an old-time street-tough cop who was barely literate. The two men tended to look down on each other, not an easy situation.

They went into the dining room and ordered. Julia couldn't imagine doing the kind of work Dan did and still remain a nice guy, but somehow Dan had managed it. They'd met when Gotham House had been broken into the previous week and Dan and his partner had been sent to investigate. One computer had been taken, nothing else. The thief had not been caught.

Dan was still thinking of Martin Klein and his fictional detective. 'The trouble with Klein's books, he always makes the police out to be stupid or corrupt or both. I haven't read all his stuff — did he ever write a cop who was good at his job?'

'Not that I recall.'

'I'd like to see him spend a couple of days in Midtown South and learn something about how cops really operate. Open his eyes a little.'

'It'll never happen,' Julia said with a rueful smile. 'Martin's writing a fantasy series – one strong man taking on the establishment and always coming out on top. A series like that can't stand very much reality. He makes the cops stupid because he doesn't know any other way to make his private investigator look smart. Martin's hardboiled detective is an anachronism.'

'Then why do you publish the books?' Dan asked – and laughed at the expression on her face. 'I know, I know. Money. But doesn't it bother you?'

'I can't afford to let it bother me,' she said crisply, not quite yet willing to admit that Klein's days with Gotham House were coming to an end. 'And you'd be surprised at the number of people who take Martin Klein seriously. There's someone in Texas writing a Master's thesis about him right now.'

'Good God. But why? What's the appeal? Why do people read junk like that?'

'Don't ask me,' Julia replied. 'I'm only his editor.'

At that point they dropped the subject and enjoyed their dinner.

Gotham House published a number of authors like Martin Klein, less-than-Nobel-quality writers whose sales kept Gotham in business. Taken as a whole, they even brought in enough money to let Julia take a chance on an unknown writer now and then.

The next morning Julia eyed the stack of manuscripts on her desk that had made it past the first readers. The stack had been there for ten days; she couldn't put it off any longer. Editors don't read manuscripts, Julia thought gloomily; they just talk on the phone and go to meetings. But her first meeting wasn't until two that afternoon, and the telephone was strangely silent.

She spread out the manuscripts and skimmed through the readers' evaluations. The sixth one she came to made her

pause. It was a rave. That was unusual, made even more so by
the fact that the evaluation had been written by Rosemary
Vance . . . who never raved. Ever. Rosemary was Julia's editorial
assistant who helped out with the slush pile when she could,
and she'd turned out to be Julia's hardest-to-please reader. But
she'd been pleased this time. 'A new female investigator,'
Rosemary had written, 'that will put all the others to shame.
With the proper promotion, we could have a bestseller here.'
She'd gone on about the author's lively style, her sense of
humour, even her humanity.

Julia felt a stir of excitement. She opened the manuscript
and began to read.

And was appalled.

The heroine spent the first three pages worrying about her
appearance. By the end of the first chapter she'd gotten herself
into a spot of trouble that required her rescue by a stalwart
boyfriend. She'd inherited her father's detective agency but
didn't want to do investigative work; what she really wanted
was a home and babies and a strong man to take care of her.

Julia read on. This new female detective that was supposed
to set the world on fire conducted an investigation based solely
on hunches and wild guesses. When she discovered a dead
body, she fainted. Julia glanced again at Rosemary Vance's
neatly typed evaluation sheet: 'A new, sensitive woman
detective just in time for the new century.'

This was the wave of the future? More like a retreat to the
fifties. Julia leaned back in her chair and tried to think. The
story wasn't meant to be a parody, she was certain of that. The
name on the manuscript was Amanda Forrest, a name unknown to Julia, as were all of the names on the unsolicited
manuscripts that came to her office.

Amanda Forrest, whoever she was, was a throwback. But
what had Rosemary seen in that manuscript that made her
think it was a winner? Only one way to find out. She pressed

the button hand-labelled 'Rosemary' on the phone.

And got the voice-message service. Annoyed, Julia went looking for her. And found that no one had seen her assistant that morning. Had she called in sick? No one knew.

Her annoyance giving way to concern, Julia dialled Rosemary Vance's home number but reached only the answering machine in the apartment in the Village that Rosemary shared with two other young women. Julia looked up Rosemary's cell phone number and called that.

It rang four times and then a male voice answered. Julia could hear street noises in the background. 'Yeah?' the voice said.

Somebody else had her phone? 'I want to talk to Rosemary,' Julia said almost belligerently.

'Who's calling?'

'Julia Cutler. Who's this?'

'Julia! It's Dan Bernhard. Who was it you wanted to talk to?'

Dan? 'My assistant, Rosemary Vance. Why – '

'Describe her.'

'Dan, what's going on?'

'Please – describe her.'

Julia took a deep breath. 'She's twenty-five years old, about five-four or -five, a bit on the plump side. She has thick, shiny black hair that she wears very short.'

There was a brief silence. Then Dan said, 'I'm afraid I've got bad news.'

Julia listened in horror as Dan explained that her assistant had been stabbed and killed. Her body had been found in a dumpster behind a café, on Fourteenth Street. No purse near the body, so they hadn't known her name until Julia called. Rosemary had been wearing her cell phone clipped to her belt under her coat, so the killer hadn't seen that. Dan wanted to know if Rosemary Vance had any family in New York.

'Ah, no,' Julia said, trying to marshal her thoughts. 'She came here from Iowa. She was mugged? She was killed by a mugger?'

'No family,' Dan went on. 'Then I'm going to have to ask you to do something. We need a positive ID. That means viewing the body, Julia. They're taking her away now, so could you come down to the morgue? The sooner the better. Can you do that?'

Julia stammered out agreement, and forced herself to focus while Dan told her how to find the city mortuary on First Avenue. She hung up and just sat staring at nothing, trying to absorb the news.

She was still sitting like that when a familiar voice rang out, 'Ah, there she is, the dishiest editor in New York! Do I have a proposition for – God, Julia, what's the matter? You're white as a sheet!'

Not for the first time Julia wished that Martin Klein lived in Hawaii or some place equally far away. Stocky, short neck, a face he liked to describe as 'lived-in', Martin seemed to take up three-fourths of the space in her office. 'I've just been talking to the police,' Julia said. She explained about Rosemary Vance and watched his mouth work wordlessly as he tried to take in what she was telling him.

Finally he said, 'Rosemary? Rosemary's dead?' He swore. 'A mugging! When did this happen?'

Julia stood up and got her coat. 'I don't know, Martin. But I have to go down to the morgue now. They need someone to make a formal identification.'

Martin gave himself a little shake and said, 'I'll go for you. That's no job for a woman.'

She bit back a retort; he was trying to help. 'Thanks, but they're expecting me.'

'Then I'm coming with you. Don't argue, now.'

She didn't; for once, Julia didn't mind Martin Klein's company.

★

It was even worse than she'd thought, looking through the glass window at Rosemary lying on that gurney, so obviously naked beneath the concealing sheet. Julia and Martin both identified her quickly and left the room.

Dan Bernhard followed them out to the hallway in the city mortuary, along with his partner, a fiftyish cop named Finelli who had a strangely oversized head. Dan murmured a few perfunctory words of condolence and asked, 'Do you know if she had any enemies?'

'Enemies?' Martin exclaimed. 'Wasn't she killed by a mugger?'

Finelli shook his big head. 'That wasn't no mugging. Muggers don't hang around and try to hide their victims. Perp took the purse to make it look like a mugging.'

Another shock. 'Why would anyone want to kill Rosemary?' Julia protested.

'That's what we're trying to find out, lady. *Did* she have any enemies?'

'Not in the office,' Julia answered. 'I don't know about her private life. Her roommates could tell you – she shared an apartment with two other girls.'

'Got an address?'

Julia told him the number on Bleecker Street. 'When was she killed?'

'Coupla hours ago,' Finelli answered. 'She goes into the caff for breakfast, she goes out, and . . . *zap*! Somebody lets her have it.'

Dan promised to keep her informed. The cab ride back uptown to Gotham House was a silent one, both Julia and Martin lost in their own thoughts.

But she was surprised when Martin didn't get out of the cab. 'Aren't you coming up?'

'I don't think this is the best time to pitch an idea,' he said. 'I'll come back in a few days.'

Julia hesitated. 'I think I need something new to concentrate on, right now. Come tell me what your idea is.'

It was an invitation she was soon to regret. Martin wanted to edit an anthology of short stories based on various characters in his books, all the stories to be written by other writers. Julia wasn't enamoured of the idea; characterisation wasn't Martin's strong point.

His eyes were glittering with what Julia at first thought was eagerness but soon recognised as desperation. Martin started talking more and more rapidly, dropping names of bestselling mystery writers he claimed he could get to contribute to the anthology . . . as if Lawrence Block or Sara Paretsky would put their own work on hold to write about Martin Klein's cardboard characters. Martin wasn't stupid; he could see his series was in trouble. So he'd come up with this cockamamie scheme to keep interest alive by recruiting good writers to do his work for him. Julia finally got rid of him by promising to bring the matter up at the next sales meeting.

Not much work got done at Gotham the rest of that day. Julia had to force herself to inform the rest of the staff of what had happened to Rosemary Vance; inviting Martin Klein up had been a delaying tactic. Following the same stunned disbelief that Julia herself had felt when she first heard the news, all the members of the staff had questions, questions that Julia didn't know the answers to.

She met Dan for a quick drink after work. 'We haven't learned a damned thing,' he told her. 'She had breakfast alone, read the *Times* while she was eating. Nobody saw anything, of course . . . they never do. Medical examiner says she was killed by a long, thick blade. Her room-mates don't know nuttin' about nuttin', as Finelli says. Vance had no boyfriend at the moment, no financial problems outside the usual, and her health was okay.'

'So what do you do now?'

'Have another go at the room-mates. Lieutenant Larch is already hollering at us to put this one away.'

The lieutenant that he disliked. 'After only one day?'

'Yeah, well, most killings are nailed down right away or not at all. She doesn't like long investigations.'

'She?'

'Yup. Our lady lieutenant.' Dan laughed shortly. 'Who just loves to give orders. Oh boy, does she love to give orders! Bossiest broad I ever met.'

Julia didn't care for what she was hearing. 'And you don't like taking orders . . . from a woman?'

'Oh, hey, come on, Julia! I don't like taking orders from *that* woman. And I'm sorry I said "broad" – okay?'

They smiled and talked of other things, but neither of them was comfortable after that. They finished their drinks and went their separate ways.

Julia finished the soup she'd picked up at a deli and opened her briefcase. Inside was a manuscript: *Flowering Evil*, by Amanda Forrest. Julia had given the book only a hasty reading, and an incomplete one; she'd quit after Chapter 4. But *Flowering Evil* was the last book Rosemary Vance had recommended before she died, and it deserved a good, close reading because of that. Julia settled down to work.

It wasn't until Chapter 6 that Julia began to suspect the truth. One sentence read: 'He was one of those men who always has to be right' – an all-too-familiar verb error. Certain other turns of phrases sounded familiar as well. She'd seen some of the characters before, using different names in a different set of books. Julia wondered whether the heroine would get beat to a pulp halfway through the book.

She did. In Chapter 13.

He wasn't even a good enough writer to disguise his style; but what capped it for Julia was the fact that at the end of the manuscript, 'Amanda Forrest' had attached a sheet proposing further books in the series – *Flowering Avarice*, *Flowering Violence*, *Flowering Lust*. The same naming gimmick he'd used in his hard-boiled series (and not an original one at that).

Julia had underestimated the extent of Martin Klein's desperation; she should have seen it coming. The mystery field was once dominated by men – men got the bigger advances, the bigger cut of the advertising pie, the more reviews. The women, for the most part, had to take the scraps. Then came the Revolution, and the new spate of female investigators that appeared on the scene had pretty much pushed the old-fashioned, trench-coated, tough-talking male private eye right out of the market. There were a few years there when no new male detectives at all were introduced to the reading public; they were poison at the bookstores. Many of the male writers were resentful, never sparing a thought for how the women had felt all those years when *they* had been shut out.

A few of the well-established older series had managed to hang on, Martin Klein's among them. But Martin had understood his time too was drawing to an end, so . . . if you can't lick 'em, join 'em. But whatever had made him think he could write from a woman's point of view? A lot of men could – but not Martin Klein. All the women in Martin's books were either Delilah or Little Nell, evil temptresses or helpless victims.

But where did Rosemary Vance fit into all this? Rosemary was a sharp reader; she would have recognised Martin's style just as quickly as Julia had. Yet Rosemary had written that glowing evaluation; had Martin gotten to her and bribed her? Julia couldn't believe that; for one thing, Rosemary could be stubborn and self-righteous about even the most minor things – a point of grammar, for instance. Rosemary Vance, Julia thought, had probably been the most *un*bribable member of the Gotham House staff.

Oh, what a mess. Julia gave it up for the night and went to bed.

Dan Bernhard staffed one desk in an open squadroom on the second floor of the Midtown South stationhouse on West Thirty-fifth. The place was busy and the noise level just short of deafening. A couple of homeboys who'd been arrested – at nine in the morning? – were mouthing off at the detectives leading them none too gently to an interrogation room. The phones never stopped ringing. Julia caught a glimpse of the lieutenant Dan disliked; she was just an ordinary-looking woman, one who gave away nothing about herself.

Dan's partner was sitting at the desk facing Dan's. 'So you're saying this Martin Klein killed Rosemary Vance? Because she didn't like his book?' The scepticism was heavy in Finelli's voice.

'It's more than that,' Julia said. 'His livelihood's at stake.'

Dan picked up the evaluation sheet for *Flowering Evil*. 'She says here that the book's a winner.'

'If she wrote that. I don't think she did.' Julia sighed. 'That just isn't her language, Dan. Rosemary wouldn't be that enthusiastic even about a good book, and *Flowering Evil*, well . . .'

'It sucks.'

'Does it ever.'

'So Martin Klein wrote this evaluation himself? And somehow substituted it for the one Rosemary wrote?'

Julia nodded. 'This morning when I woke up I remembered the break-in we had last week – when the computer was stolen? That must have been Martin, sneaking in to substitute his own evaluation for Rosemary's. He'd have taken the computer to account for the jimmied door.'

Finelli frowned. 'And Rosemary was there working late? She caught him in the act?'

'I don't think so. She would have said something to me.'

Finelli snorted. 'He bought her off.'

'You don't know she was even there!' Julia flared.

'That break-in ...' Dan was counting back '... that was eight days ago. Where's the evaluation sheet been all this time? And the manuscript?'

Julia smiled wryly. 'On my desk. Waiting to be read.'

He picked up the manuscript. '*Flowering Evil.* Cribbed from Baudelaire?'

'Who?' Finelli said.

Dan ignored him. 'Julia, are you absolutely certain this book was written by Martin Klein?'

'Yes, absolutely.'

Finelli's big head wagged back and forth. 'It'll never stand up in court.'

'It's admissible,' Dan said quickly. 'Expert testimony.'

Finelli wasn't buying it. 'That ain't *real* evidence. The way a guy writes. Shee-ut.'

So scornful. 'Look, Detective Finelli,' Julia said, 'I know this isn't the kind of detective work you do every day, but it *is* detective work. I see the clues, and I recognise the style. I can go through that manuscript page by page and show you parallels to Martin Klein's other books.'

'You may have to,' Finelli muttered.

Dan shrugged. 'If that's what it takes.'

'Yeah, but will a jury believe her? You know what the lieutenant'll say if we go to her with this kinda evidence, Danny Boy.'

His partner shot him a sharp look and turned back to Julia. 'There's one way we can get Klein. We put a wire on you.'

Julia's eyes widened. 'I go meet him alone while you sit in a place of safety and listen in? No, thank you. I've read too many books where too many dumb heroines confront killers alone.'

'You won't be alone,' Dan said hastily. 'We'll be right there in plain sight. You can meet him in some public place. A restaurant. This is a team effort, Julia. You help us, we help you.'

'But I don't *know* that he killed Rosemary!'

'Then mebbe we eliminate him as a suspect,' Finelli said. 'Either way, we learn something.'

'It's the only way to be sure,' Dan added.

Reluctantly, Julia agreed. 'But how can I get him to give himself away? I can't just come right out and ask him.'

Dan loosened his tie. 'That's what we need to figure out right now.'

La Feria was a Peruvian shop/eatery on Broadway. The shop took up all the ground floor area and sold only small items – some Peruvian apparel, painted trays, colourful knick-knacks. Overlooking the shop was a balcony housing a small dining area and, at the rear, a bar. Julia's table was at the frontmost part of the balcony where she was visible from the street through the two-storey glass front, about as 'public' as she could get. Dan was sitting at the bar; Finelli was at a nearby table demolishing a plate of *ropa vieja*. Outside in a parked car were two other detectives who'd record everything she and Martin Klein said.

From her table by the wrought-iron balcony railing Julia could see Martin enter the shop area and head for the open staircase. He looked up and saw her and put on a big artificial smile. Julia clasped her hands in her lap to hide her nervousness.

'I hope this summons to lunch means good news,' Martin said as he sat down.

'In a way,' Julia responded noncommittally. 'Let's order first.' They spent a minute studying the menu and gave their orders to the waitress.

Julia took the manuscript of *Flowering Evil* out of her briefcase and put it on the table. A tic appeared in Martin's cheek, but he made a show of reading the title page. 'Amanda Forrest? One of your new discoveries?'

'One of Rosemary's discoveries. I don't think the book's much good, myself. But Rosemary wrote a glowing evaluation . . . and since it's the last book she recommended, I want to give it a chance. It needs a professional hand, though, and I thought of you. The rewrite should be a breeze, and you'd get a nice chunk of the royalties.'

It had been Julia's idea to throw Martin off-balance by asking him to rewrite himself – and now she watched as he struggled to keep his composure. 'I don't do rewrites.'

'I know, but I thought you might make an exception in this case. At least read the manuscript.'

He decided to bluff. 'What is it, some pushy female investigator who needs to be rescued every other chapter?'

Julia leaned forward in her chair. 'How did you know she needed to be rescued?'

'Well, they all do, don't they?'

'No, Martin, as a matter of fact they don't. Female private investigators are able to take care of themselves. Haven't you read any of the women's PI books? You should have done your homework before you tried to cash in.'

'What!?'

'I know you wrote *Flowering Evil*, Martin. And I think Rosemary knew it too.'

The waitress arrived with their food; her two customers stared at each other without speaking until she'd left. 'You're out of your mind!' Martin hissed.

'Oh, stop it!' Julia said impatiently. 'I'm prepared to offer you a deal, but I can't if you go on claiming to know nothing about *Flowering Evil*.'

He looked at her sceptically. 'What kind of deal?'

'I'm willing to let you get away with this pretence in exchange for fifty per cent of the advance and the royalties.

The series will be controversial, because it's so obviously
written by a misogynist. We milk that controversy for all it's
worth and split the take right down the middle. You write the
stuff, I'll see that it gets published and promoted.'

'Fifty per cent!'

'Which leaves you with fifty. As opposed to the zero per
cent you'll have otherwise. You can try taking that piece of
crap to other publishers if you like. But I can tell you what will
happen – they'll laugh you out of the office. No, Martin, it's
Gotham House or nothing. That's the deal.'

A small smile appeared on Martin's face. 'Well, well. So
Queen Julia is on the take. Whoever would have thought it?'
He was silent a moment. Then: 'Very well, I accept your deal.'

Julia saw Finelli get up from his table and go downstairs to
the shop area; through the front window she could see it had
started snowing. Dan was still at the bar, carefully not watching
them. Julia said to Martin, 'But first, you have to tell me about
Rosemary.'

'I don't know anything about what happened to Rosemary!' he protested.

'Then the deal's off. I've got to know what I'm getting into
here.'

He stared. 'You're joking.'

Julia looked down at her untasted lunch. 'She figured out
you had written *Flowering Evil*. Did she call you? She didn't say
anything about it to me.'

'Yes, she called me.' Martin made a sound of exasperation.
'She was working late – you and everyone else had gone
home. That bitch took a great deal of pleasure in reading me
the evaluation she'd just written. Then she oh-so-sweetly
advised me not to try writing from a woman's point of view
again. She said I "didn't have a clue".' His face darkened.
'Rosemary never did appreciate my work. It was just my luck
that *she* should be the one to read *Flowering Evil*.'

'So you broke into our office later that same night — to substitute your own evaluation for Rosemary's? And stole a computer to account for the break-in?'

He looked surprised that she'd figured that part out. 'There was no talking sense to Rosemary, you know, once she'd made up her mind. Pig-headed young woman. I found the manuscript on your desk, with the evaluation sheet clipped to it. I made the switch and put the manuscript about halfway down the stack.'

'But surely you knew Rosemary would speak up when —'

'It was a stop-gap measure, Julia, for Christ's sake!' he snapped . . . and then remembered to lower his voice. 'Of course I knew I had to do something about Rosemary. She was standing between me and publication.'

Julia's mouth dropped open. 'You were that sure I would buy the book?'

Martin shrugged. 'You've always bought my books before. Look under the table.'

'What?'

'*Look under the table.*'

Wondering, Julia bent sideways and looked . . . and saw a long knife clasped in Martin's hand. Slowly, she sat back up. She cast a sidelong glance at the bar.

Dan wasn't there.

Stay calm. For the benefit of the microphone taped to her breastbone, she said, 'You have a knife. A *long* knife. Are you going to kill me too, Martin?'

'I'm hoping I won't have to,' he said. 'I was able to keep Rosemary quiet for a few days by scaring her — she didn't like the sight of a knife any more than you do. But I was losing her. It was only a matter of time before she told you what was going on. But you — you're an even bigger danger than she was.'

'I offered you a deal,' Julia said quickly. 'I'm willing to stick by it.'

He snorted. 'I'll bet you are.' He looked around; every table in the dining area was filled. 'Leave some money on the table and put your coat on.'

'Where are we going?'

'Someplace less public.'

Even with Dan and Finelli mysteriously gone, Julia knew she was safer right where she was. 'No. I won't do it.' Suddenly she felt a sharp pain in her left knee that made her gasp.

'That was just a sample,' Martin said. 'Remember, a knife doesn't make a noise when it goes off. Don't make me kill you, Julia. I need to think. Get up – we're leaving.'

She did as he said. When she stood up, she saw a red spot on the left knee of her pants. Going down the stairway, she glanced around the shop area but couldn't spot either Dan or Finelli.

Outside, she turned the collar of her coat up against the wind; Martin grasped one arm and held her close beside him. There was an air of unreality about the scene; the grey sky, the swirling snowflakes, the pedestrians hurrying by with their eyes on their feet – none of it seemed to have anything to do with her. *Is this how Rosemary felt the last moments of her life?*

'You know the drill,' Martin muttered. 'One false move and you're dead, sister.' He waved at a cab that sped right on by.

In spite of the danger, the editor in her couldn't help thinking: *What dreadful dialogue.* 'What turned you into a killer, Martin?'

'You did. You and your kind. You women have taken over everything. All the editors are women now. Who the hell do you think you are? You couldn't write a book if your life depended on it, yet *you* decide whether *I* get published or not.'

Julia saw red. 'So it's all *my* fault?'

'You're spoiling everything. Why couldn't you just let things stand the way they were? Taxi!'

This time a cab stopped. Martin dragged her into the street, but Julia was so outraged she could barely see where she was walking. 'I will not be your scapegoat!' she yelled.

'Shut up! And get in!'

'I'm not getting into that cab with you!' The cab driver, seeing what looked like a fight about to break out, hit the gas pedal and sped away. With a cry Julia twisted around and kicked Martin as hard as she could behind his knees.

His knees buckled and he went down flat on his back. Without stopping to think, Julia flung herself full-length on top of him. She knew she wouldn't be able to hold him down, but it was all she could think to do.

'He's got a knife!' a passerby cried out.

'Nemmind, I got it,' a familiar voice said. A big foot stepped on Martin's wrist and Finelli twisted the knife out of his grasp. 'Okay, Superwoman, you can let him up now.'

Julia scrambled to her feet. 'Geez, Finelli, where were you?'

'In the Peruvian shop – where you couldn't see me.' He hauled a swearing Martin to his feet and turned him over to two men Julia didn't know, presumably the detectives who'd been recording everything. Finelli said, 'Why dincha just run, when you knocked him down?'

She shrugged. 'Where would that get me?'

He gave her a lopsided grin. 'You're fierce when you're riled.'

Uh-huh. 'Where's Dan?'

As if on cue, Dan came bursting out through the doors. 'Julia? Finelli? What happened?'

'We got 'im,' Finelli snarled. 'No thanks to you. Where the hell you been? It wasn't supposed to go this far. What if she'd gotten into a cab with him? Where were you?'

'Uh, I had to answer a call of nature.'

'You couldn't hold it, fer Chrissake?' Finelli was disgusted. 'How can I depend on a partner who endangers a civilian because he has to go pee?'

'Put a cork in it, Finelli,' Dan said testily. He turned to Julia. 'Are you all right?'

No thanks to you. 'Whatever happened to the team effort?' she asked. 'I help you, you help me.'

He wouldn't meet her eye. 'Yeah, well, you know how it goes, team effort. Sometimes it doesn't work out.'

'I've noticed that.' *Not even an apology.*

'Thanks for your help,' Finelli said to her.

'And for yours.' She meant it.

'It wasn't as if I left you on your own,' Dan said. 'Finelli was there, and you did all right.'

Excuses? Julia looked him straight in the eye. 'Goodbye, Dan.'

He didn't try to stop her as she walked away.

For Your Eyes Only
Penny Sumner

Death doesn't occur instantaneously but by degrees, it's multi-layered. When I first read this (in a well-thumbed text lent by a friendly coroner), it came as a surprise. I'd thought of death as a curtain falling: the end, *finis*. I hadn't thought of it as something you slowly sank into. But that's how it happens, the organism as a whole dying – somatic death – followed by the death of individual cells and organs, starting with the brain. There are stages of *mortis* as well: *algor mortis, rigor mortis, livor mortis*. First the body loses temperature, then the skeletal muscles stiffen, then the blood pools on the underside, causing discoloration. (Funny, isn't it, that blue-red, the colour of a hickey, is also the colour your body turns when it's ceased to function.)

Inebriation, for me at least, also comes in stages although this does depend on what it is I'm drinking. Wine, for instance, gets to work on my brain first whereas a gin-and-tonic starts at my fingertips, which go – I must confess not at all unpleasantly –

numb. And so it is with pleasantly numb digits (I've only had one, Marty's away for the week and I'm not in the mood for reaching stage two solo), that I study Charlotte Trewluv's photograph in the light thrown by the bedside lamp.

She's twenty-eight, striking, with good skin, a full mouth, cropped dark hair. On the back of the photograph there's a date – '14 February' – written in Ms Trewluv's own hand and followed by the words, 'I'm yours, for always.' Always, however, doesn't have to be synonymous with forever, or even with for very long at all. Thus in Ms Trewluv's case 'always' had, apparently at least, lasted only another three months; terminating as, dead smack in the middle of Chelsea Bridge, her front bicycle wheel lost its grip and veered under a red, double-decker bus.

(At which I suggest that when you do this scene in your mind – the silhouette of bike and rider poised against a Thames the colour of blood velvet; the slow skew sideways into metal and *mortis* – you shoot it not at the normal speed of twenty-four frames a second but at three, even four, times that.

So that when it plays, it plays slow.)

'So you see,' my new client had said, very, very slowly, 'I quite believed Charlotte had died.' At four on a dull Monday afternoon Richard Mayson was looking ill at ease in a long cashmere coat and Gucci boots. Or, rather, he was looking completely at ease in his upmarket clothes but less comfortable at finding himself in a verging-on-downmarket agency in Ladbroke Grove. In fact he looked like a man who was about to say he'd never done this before, consulted a private detective; which I could quite believe because although I hadn't previously met my client I'd recognised his name straight away. Richard Mayson, thriller writer, with at least a dozen novels under his belt and not one, that I'd seen at any rate, suggesting the writer had ever contemplated any serious research.

'But you didn't check?' My eyebrows arched to indicate an amazement I didn't actually feel.

'Why no,' a hint of annoyance entered his voice. 'There seemed no need. The woman who rang to tell me about the accident said she was a friend of Charlotte's, and she sounded completely genuine. More to the point, I hadn't heard from Charlotte for ten, blissful, days and that seemed proof enough. Of course I appreciate now,' his smile was grim, 'that I was more than willing to believe she'd died because that was what I wanted to happen. After all, I'd been fantasising her death for over a year. More than fantasising it,' he narrowed his eyes and leaned forward, 'I'd been *writing* it. Over and over. Charlotte being blown up by a terrorist bomb. Charlotte in a plane accident. Charlotte swallowed by Jaws.' His eyes, I'd already noticed, were a mixed pair, one blue, one brown. 'The only scene I hadn't written was Charlotte going under a bloody bus.'

Lilith carefully pushes the plunger into the cafetière. 'So this Trewluv woman stalked Mayhew for a year?'

'Thirteen and a half months. And it's *Mayson*.' Lilith had her nose pierced last week and it's looking sore. I know from things overhead that that's not all the piercing she's had done by any means, but I haven't enquired further. Don't ask, is Marty's credo, if you don't really want to know. I strongly suspect I don't. 'You must have seen his books. In WH Smith's, train stations, airports . . .'

'Not that I can remember. Here comes my dose of caffeine for the day.' She takes two mugs from the filing cabinet that functions as the office kitchen, then reaches into a Tesco bag for a carton of semi-skimmed. I know it will be semi-skimmed because Lilith's been nagging me about my fat intake. Not that I have a weight problem but because of what horrors might be happening to my arteries. Lilith has been my business partner for three years, actually choosing to become a private detective rather than, like me, merely falling into it. And she's been my daughter for twenty-five. Not only that but by August she'll be a mother herself. Which means that by forty-five I'll be a grandmother.

I reach for the coffee. 'Thanks. She was supposed to have had her run-in with the double-decker almost two years ago. And then, on Sunday night, she rang from beyond the grave. All she said was, "I'm back Richard, and I'll be seeing you very soon." At which point he dropped the phone.'

Lilith's warming her hands around the mug; she's always had cold hands. 'You know it mightn't be her at all, it might be someone trying to spook him.'

'He's convinced it was her, and he's desperately worried. Which isn't surprising because by the sound of it she made his life hell. Abusing him at readings, disrupting signings.' Many writers would welcome the excuse to give up such activities of course.

'Weird or what?' Her legs are long – much longer than mine, she's almost six foot – and as she crosses them the new red mini, bought before she knew she was pregnant, rides even higher. 'I mean, why would someone ring to say Trewluv was dead if she wasn't? And, if she wasn't dead, why did she disappear out of his life only to reappear again now? Unless,' she glares at me, 'she really is dead. I mean, he's not a nutter who thinks we're ghostbusters? I hope his cheque doesn't bloody bounce!'

'He paid cash.' Could I do that, a skin that short? Not red, but maybe black; with black, ribbed tights? Or would I merely look ridiculous? 'I can't say I like him, but he seems sane enough. However, just in case she did die and someone's putting the wind up him, I'll go along to St Catherine's this morning and check the death certificates.'

She yawns as pink as a cat. 'What else do you have in mind? A computer search?'

'Hopefully not. Mayson's supposed to be part of a panel discussion at the South Bank tonight; it's been well-publicised and he suspects Trewluv might stage her comeback there. And if she does I'll follow her home. Case closed. That's all my brief is, to find out where she lives.'

The yawn turns into a frown. 'Mum, what if he gets up on stage and she shoots him? This whole thing sounds just crazy enough to be dangerous.'

'Uh, I really don't think there's any risk involved, she was never violent. All Mayson's frightened about is the publicity. Particularly at the moment because he's on the verge of signing a new contract and the publisher will be expecting him to do lots of public events. He doesn't want anyone in the book trade to know Trewluv's resurfaced.'

'Which will be hard to avoid if she disrupts tonight's performance.'

'Oh, he's not going to appear tonight. He cancelled late yesterday and is on a plane for New York this morning. There's a publisher who's read his new book and wants to meet him. He'll be back Thursday afternoon. But the general public won't know he's not going to show of course.'

She nods, 'Sounds reasonable. What about relationships? Married?'

'Divorced. No kids that he mentioned. I don't know if he's with anyone at the moment.'

'And they never did it at all?'

'Who?' I take a sip. 'Did what?'

Her eyes roll. 'Sex, Mum. Did Mayson and Trewluv do the sex thing? He's at least twenty years older than . . .'

At which she breaks off and I know exactly what it is she's thinking. Which is, *Oh shit, what have I just gone and said?*

'Well if they did he came to regret it,' I burble through a

mouthful of coffee. (If Marty could only see us now!)

She manages to avoid eye-contact by standing up and tugging at her hem. 'Once he's got her address what's he going to do?'

'He's a tad vague on that. I suggested he should get his solicitor to put on the frighteners. Now the law's got a bit more bite he might be able to stop her before she starts.'

She nods, walks to the door, then turns back. 'Tonight's discussion is about?'

I pass over the flyer.

'"It's Genre, Jim, But Not As We Know It: Popular Writing And The Millennium."' She passes it back.

'Interested?'

'Thanks, Mum, but Lee's cooking, and I've been feeling so damn tired.'

Under Waterloo Bridge the winter Thames is black ink run with orange and blue. I start the shot in my mind's eye from twenty metres, the young woman in a long coat, poised like a dancer against the night sky. And then the fall, shadowing the Jodhi May character in *The Last of the Mohicans*: a small, quiet step into space. She makes eye contact and you cannot believe, refuse to believe, that she'll do this thing. But she does.

'Be cold, eh? Down there.' The boy holding out his hand at the end of the bridge must have been watching as I stopped to look over the edge. Next to him a girl and a dog huddle under a tartan blanket.

'Very.' I take off a glove but my fingers are so numb they can hardly tell what the coins are in my pocket. 'But better than going under a bus.'

'Geez lady, I dunno.' The pound coin disappears.

From under the blanket the girl speaks dreamily. 'It'd be so cold, down there in the water, I bet you wouldn't feel nothing. Nothing at all.'

Charlotte Trewluv isn't dead. At least not according to the records at St Catherine's House. But then again, according to those same records, she isn't alive either. No death certificate, and no birth certificate. Which means, (1) she never existed and Richard Mayson has invented her, or (2) surprise, surprise, Charlotte Trewluv isn't her real name. For the moment I suggest we run with number two.

I take up position at the top of the stairs in the hope that, if she does make an appearance, I'll see her straight away. I've checked out those already seated in the hall; faces are something I'm good at and I'm sure I've remembered her photograph well enough to recognise her. You can't go by hair, she could have a blonde bob by now, but I can picture the nose and the cheekbones. Full mouth, wide eyes, good skin, light on makeup. Height, according to my client, around five-eight, the same as me. Slim build. Now thirty years old.

A big contract, he'd said, a special deal his agent had been working on. But I'd had no idea how big. At least, not until I'd rung Debby, who works for Waterstone's. Debby's one of the best networkers I know and when I sounded her out on Mayson she was full of the latest trade gossip.

'A million pounds?' My jaw dropped so much it hurt. 'But Debby, his novels are crap! You know I could write . . .'

'I know that. Ten years ago he was promising to be hot property but his recent stuff hasn't sold well. However he must have got his act together coz publishers have been falling over each other to bid for this latest book.'

'I've read a couple of things by him in the past and they were just violence splattered with sex; the violence dull and the sex conventional.'

'Yeah well conventional is how some of us like it. And, speaking of sex, how's Marty? I was thinking about you guys the other night; you must have been together three years now.'

I wonder how Debby brackets Marty and me, as

conventional or un? 'Three and a half, and he's fine. Doing a stint on the northern comedy circuit, so he's in Newcastle until the end of the week. Now, Debby, I can't tell you what this is about, but if you do hear anything of interest about Mayson I'd be extremely grateful.'

Things aren't due to start for another ten minutes but I go into the hall because I want to make sure of a seat in the back row, near the exit. 'Excuse me,' a middle-aged man in a suit squeezes past, followed by a teenage girl who appears to be his daughter. I'd say we're heading towards an audience of sixty to seventy, more than I'd expected, the problem being that most of them are coming in now and I'm not getting that clear a view.

And then I spot her, a woman with waist-length black hair, long fringe, and ruby-red lips. My eyes slide over her at first, but then there's something about the way she hangs back in the doorway, not looking for a seat but studying the stage. Her hair couldn't have grown that much of course and she's too tall. Hang on, those are platforms; the hair could be a wig. She's wearing a great deal of makeup so it's hard to tell from her face, but there's a definite likeness. And the age is right, as well as the build. She sinks into an aisle seat three rows in as a woman on the stage taps at a mike.

'Good evening!' The woman thanks us for coming and then starts to introduce the panel, which includes a publisher, an academic, a television writer and – instead of Richard Mayson, thriller writer, who unfortunately cannot make it tonight – Benedict Plowden, prize-winning writer of science fiction, who has kindly agreed to stand in.

At which the woman with the black hair slides back out of her seat and, smiling, heads for the door.

It's the smile that clinches it, because it's a smile of triumph. She's smiling because he's chickened out.

*

The couple and their dog have gone from the bridge, replaced by an older man selling *The Big Issue*. I'm a good twenty metres behind my quarry but that's fine because there's no one between us except for three teenage boys on line skates. Not that she'd notice me anyway, people never pay that much attention.

'Whoa!' One of the skaters swerves in my direction before crashing against the side of the bridge. For a moment I think I see sparks. 'Be careful lady!'

'Why . . . ' I'm startled into saying out loud, before finishing under my breath, 'the fuck don't you watch where you're going?' I skirt around him, beginning to hurry now because if she's heading for the tube I need to get in the same carriage. Without warning, however, one of the other skaters is directly in front of me, spinning out of control. As he catches onto my shoulders we both slam into the railing.

'Jeezus!' I'm winded.

'You okay? Hey I'm sorry.' He's half holding me up, half supporting himself.

'She all right?' a nearby voice asks, like it's not terribly interested.

'She'll live.' He abruptly pushes himself away and in a flash the three of them are gone.

It takes a few seconds for it to sink in that I've lost the black-haired woman. A few seconds after that I realise my bag's been opened and I've lost my wallet also.

Okay, so it's a big city, and it happens. What doesn't happen is that you get into work the next morning and find your stolen wallet nestling safely in the post box.

'No note?' Lilith asks for the second time.

The nose stud is still looking sore and I find myself wondering if she's had her nipples done. What about breast feeding, has she thought about that? 'No note.'

'And you're sure it's all there?'

'As far as I can see. Credit cards, cash. Even the stamps and library tickets.' I glance up at the window where there's a desultory flurry of snow.

'Well then, I guess this goes to show there are still some honest punters.'

She doesn't sound convinced, and neither am I. 'Not only honest but clairvoyant. How did whoever it was know where I work? And why would those punks rob me then have a change of heart?'

'Maybe they dropped it and someone else was honest.'

'Which still leaves the question of how it made its way back here.'

We stare at each other for a moment then give up. 'Right,' I shrug, 'I'll get on to the bank and tell them my cards have found their own way home.'

After dealing with the bank I fill the electric kettle and wander across to study the wall calendar, which was a Christmas present from Australia. It's of paintings by Brett Whitely and the picture for February is of a large brown rat, with flames shooting out of its mouth. Well, that's what it looks like. The print at the bottom indicates it's a Tasmanian Devil.

Why did this woman, who called herself Charlotte Trewluv, stalk someone so assiduously, and then simply vanish? And who was it who rang to say she was dead? Poor Charlotte. It happened so quickly she didn't feel a thing, the bus took her and now she's out of your life, for ever.

The rat which is really a Devil gives me a fiery grin. That's it! Someone – her friend, her therapist, her *mother* – finally says, come on Charlotte, enough's enough. You have to leave this man alone. I'm going to ring him and say you're dead. That way you're out of his life. For ever. And Charlotte – who's getting the slightest bit tired of all this herself – says okay, tell him I went under a bus.

The phone's ringing.

'Hello!' I know I'm right, but the question still remains of why she's suddenly resurrected herself. 'Can I help you?' On a notepad I scrawl *For ever* . . .

'I hope you might be able to answer a question.' It's a woman speaking.

'What question is that?' Divorce is the guess I make in the short pause that follows. I'd like to be able to say sorry Madam, divorce is something We Don't Do. But the truth is we have mortgages, so we do do it. Often. Where we draw the line is at cases of child abuse, and rape where the defence is consent.

'Why it is you're working for an arsehole like Richard Mayson.'

At which I blink down at the number recorder, where the screen reads *number withheld*. 'What?'

'Because he is an arsehole, believe me. Which, in my experience, is what many men are. And that's been your experience too, hasn't it, with two divorces?' She laughs, her tone more amused than malicious, but I don't feel inclined to laugh along with her. 'I must say, however, that I think you've got the right idea now, settling down with a much younger man. And I do admire the way you and your daughter have sorted things out. Because they were living together, weren't they?'

I'm about to hang up but she beats me to it.

'Mum?' Lilith's peering at me, shaking out an umbrella. 'Are you okay?'

I'm fifteen years older than Marty; who was never Lilith's lover although they did share a flat. 'I'm fine. But my wallet . . .'

'I knew it!' she yelps. 'They used your cards!'

'No, but I don't think the punter who returned it was quite as kosher as we thought.'

Scopophobia: the fear of being watched. The opposite is

scopophilia: the erotic satisfaction gained from watching. Things or, better still, people. It's a psychoanalytic term that's become important in film theory. 'It's a buzz watching people, isn't it?' That's the message I found on the answer machine when I got home last night. My home number's ex-directory but that's no problem if you've hired a professional. Which Trewluv clearly has. It's obvious now that she guessed Mayson wouldn't turn up at the South Bank, and that he'd have someone waiting for her. So she decided to play the same game. She hired a private detective – one of the dodgier variety, with numerous contacts and fewer scruples – and my wallet was lifted. Then they checked me out. The wallet was returned to emphasise the message that it wasn't my money but identity they were after. Something I should have understood at once. When I got into the agency this morning there was another small present in the post – a somewhat unflattering photo of me slushing homeward in my wellies last night.

'Oh great!' Lilith groaned when I showed her. 'Now she's stalking you!'

No, what she's doing is stalking Mayson by proxy. He employed me to stalk her. Fine, so she'll stalk me. To show she can.

'I know you get a buzz out of it,' Trewluv's message went on, 'because I do too. The difference between us though is that you're a professional *eye*, while I'm merely a gifted amateur!'

The first thing I did this morning was to arrange for a computer check to be run in the name of Charlotte Trewluv, in case that's the name she's still using. And then I followed a whim and hiked myself over to the Central Library in Kensington, in order to leaf through back copies of the *Evening Standard*. During the week Charlotte was supposed to have died a pair of gangster twins had been murdered outside their

Gran's house in Putney; there were reported sightings of a white seal in the Thames; a holy man arrived in Kensington, having rolled all the way from Delhi. But there was no news involving a bus, a bridge and a bicycle.

On the Wednesday of the previous week, however, there was a short piece on a cyclist – who fell under a bus on Chelsea Bridge and lived. 'True Love Conquers Double-Decker': beneath the headline there's a picture of the cyclist, a man in his sixties, and his beaming fiancée of the same age. 'When I saw the double-decker coming at me I was sure I was a gonner. But as I went under it I thought of how much I loved Audrey, and I'm sure that's what pulled me through.'

'Come on, Charlotte,' someone had said, 'I'm going to ring him and say you're dead.' And Charlotte remembered the article about the miracle of true love, smiled an ironic smile, and said, 'Tell him I went under a bus. On Chelsea Bridge.'

'Mum,' in the doorway Lilith's face is a pale oval above her black sweater, 'Debby on the phone. Would you like some passion-fruit tea?'

Something rather stronger is what I'd really like, but there you go. 'Please.' I pick up the phone, 'Hi Debby. What's news?'

'Don't ask. You would not believe the management meeting I was in this morning.'

'Lilith and I don't bother with those.' I like Debby; a lot. I'm not, however, in the mood for a chat.

'But what I'm really ringing about,' she lowers her voice conspiratorially, 'is your case. I've contacted a few people, discreetly I promise, and *get this*. A couple of years back Richard Mayson was being stalked! By a woman! Did you know that?'

'Uh, I had heard something . . .'

'Amazing, eh? My friend Frank told me about her. He organised a weekend of crime readings and Mayson was one of the writers. Then this woman turned up and sabotaged Mayson's reading, launching into this amazing routine about how he ought to learn to love people, how he ought to love her. Mayson was furious but Frank said the audience was enthralled. Apparently she was young and very attractive.'

With an appalling taste in men. The results of the computer search should be ready any time now although it's unlikely anything will come up.

'Frank thought she was rather funny actually, and that she was wasting herself on Mayson. Anyway she must have come to the same conclusion because she quit stalking him shortly after that.' She laughs, 'It's like *Fatal Attraction*. Or what's the Clint Eastwood one? *Play Misty For Me*! Jessica Thingy is the stalker.'

'Walter.' With Eastwood directing for the first time.

'It is *so* scary, when she comes after him with the knife . . .' There's a pause, after which she asks, 'So you going to tell me what your case is about?'

'Sorry but it's confidential.' I can hear the fax machine running in Lilith's office; that's probably the report coming through now.

She sighs. 'Frank says he's sometimes tempted to ask her what on earth she saw in Mayson.'

'Mmm. Look I've got to go now Debby but . . .' Frank says what? Was that really in the present tense? 'Debby, are you telling me that Frank knows where this woman is?' I take a deep breath. 'He knows where she is *now*?'

'Why yes,' she sounds surprised. 'About a year ago he went to visit a small publishing company that had started near the arts agency where he works in Camden, and he recognised her as one of the owners. She didn't recognise him and he didn't think it would be polite to mention Mayson. He sometimes sees her on the tube and says hello.'

'Yes!' I yell, startling Lilith as she comes in with the tea.

'Debby my love, you are bloody brilliant!'

I hate wigs, they make me itch. But Lilith beat me to the woolly hat.

'They don't have a big list, but it's nicely done. Manuals on yoga and tai chi, guides to herbs and herbal medicines, a series of self-help books.' My daughter ticks a list off on her fingers, in much the same manner that I would myself. After Debby's call Lilith dashed off to reconnoitre the publishing company while I rang Companies' House and persuaded a clerk I know to do a quick check in the register for names and addresses. It turns out that there are three owners of the publishing company, two men and a woman named Charlotte Selffe, who lives in a ground-floor flat in a semi-detached building in a quiet side street in Brent Cross. I know it's quiet because Lilith and I are currently parked in it. The time is seven pm and we've been here since four. My bladder has never been cut out for this job; fairly soon I'm going to have to go in search of a loo.

'There was a manual about natural childbirth,' Lilith continues, 'which I might order at a later date.'

As well as the wig I'm wearing a pair of glasses. 'I'll buy it for you. Anything about how to cure yourself of stalking?'

'Not that I could see. Thank God it's stopped raining.'

I've adjusted the rear-view mirror and peer into it again. I spy. The building looks well-cared for, with the door and window frames painted a bright blue. There's a low hedge along the pavement and a short front path. To the left of the house there's a high wooden fence and gate.

'Hey, Mum, I think it's her.' Lilith forgot to put in her contacts and is squinting into the side mirror. 'Can you see?'

I turn and lean over the back seat, ostensibly reaching for a scarf. Out the back window I can see a woman with short dark hair, wearing an ankle-length red coat and striding confidently along the pavement. She looks straight at me for a moment and yes, it is her. She's carrying a black shoulder bag and a yellow plastic bag that looks like it's full of books.

'It is, isn't it?' Lilith hisses.

'I'd say so.'

She reaches her front door, gently puts down the yellow bag, searches through her bag for a key and lets herself in. A moment later a light goes on in the front room.

'Whew!' Lilith sags back against the seat.

Why? I ask myself. Why does she bother with Mayson?

'You might as well ring him now. He was due back this afternoon, wasn't he?'

'Uh-huh.' Reaching into my bag I take out the mobile.

'And I suggest that after you've finished speaking to yet another satisfied customer we go do dinner. You would not believe how hungry I am.'

Lilith's strictly orange juice these days, which cuts down on any debate as to who's drinking and who's driving. Tonight she ate for two; and I drank the equivalent. Which makes me sound like a soak while I'm not. The truth is that it doesn't take more than a few glasses of wine to send me well on my way. A bottle and I'm under the table. Or, as I am now, on the sofa, with a cushion under my head – obligingly positioned by my only child, who'd insisted on escorting me inside – and the lights down low.

'Excellent.' That's what Mayson had said when I told him the address. 'That really is excellent. She's not half as clever as she thinks.'

In the corner of my eye there's a dancing light: the answer machine. Haven't checked for messages have we? Rolling slowly onto my chest I fumble for Play.

'Hi there!' The voice is recognisable straight away. 'I'm absolutely thrilled because I've just found out who you . . .'

I manage to hit Off. 'You can go and play your games with someone else Charlotte,' I say out loud. 'I'm off your case now, so you can fucking well get off mine.'

Fast forwarding there's another message, the voice male. 'It's so cold up here my earrings hurt!' Marty. 'The audiences at the Comedy Café are utterly fab. I'm booked on the ten o'clock train on Sunday and should be back home mid afternoon. Have you solved the stalker thing yet? Kisses!'

'Case solved,' I announce to the room at large. I also blow a kiss.

Next on the line is Debby, sounding excited. 'Are you there? No? Oh well. It's five o'clock and I've just heard another piece of Richard Mayson gossip.' Which, thank God, I no longer need. What I am in need of, so my body is telling me, is sleep. 'Do you remember my friend Alison? You know, the blonde who goes out with Beth. Well, Alison's ex writes for the *Bookseller* and apparently details of Mayson's megabuck deal are going to be announced in the next couple of days. And you'll never guess what his book is about! It's entitled *For Your Eyes Only*, and it's the diary of a woman stalker! I think we know where he got the idea for that from, don't we? Alison says it's supposed to be absolutely brilliant.' She grunts, 'I'm surprised he could pull it off actually, his women characters aren't exactly deep; they're only there for sex. And to get murdered. Anyway, I thought you might be interested. Do let me know if this is of any use. Bye!'

As I roll onto my back the pain that's begun in my left temple shoots into my left eye. A stalker's diary. Mayson is such a jerk! He thinks she's dead so he writes a book like she's not a real person at all, just a piece of fiction. No wonder she's come back to harass him.

Which it is, isn't it? I close my eyes and watch as another piece falls into place, like a young woman calmly stepping from a bridge. She works in the book world and has heard on

the grapevine what he's bringing out next. So she's come back
to punish him. She got out of his life entirely, and now he's
raked over everything that happened and is going to make a
mint out of it. Oh God! I laugh and my head throbs. Bloody
serves him right! He could never have written anything like
that if it hadn't been for her – he ought to give her a cut.

I've been dozing and my neck hurts. My head hurts too, but
adjusting the cushion won't fix that.

I sit up gingerly, a dim reflection in the mirror next to the
doorway. You, I console myself from across the room, will feel
a lot better if you go up to bed. And on the way you could
make yourself a nice cup of Earl Grey, and take a couple of
painkillers.

Instead of pushing myself into a standing position, however,
I remain seated, because there's a voice somewhere in the back
of my head saying that it's not just that I've had too much to
drink. Something else is bothering me.

What?

Mayson. Something Mayson's done.

What's he done?

Ah, now I remember. He's written a book. A diary by a
woman stalker.

But? The voice in my head asks.

Although I'm aware that I don't really want to think about
this I do it all the same. After a few minutes thinking I whisper
aloud. 'But I don't believe it. I don't believe he could write
something like that.'

So if he didn't, who did?

For Your Eyes Only. She must have written a diary and sent
it to him. An entry every day. (*This is for you, for your eyes only.*)
And then he thought she'd died (. . . *that was what I wanted to
happen . . . I'd been fantasising her death for over a year . . .*) so he
claimed he'd written it himself.

Very good! And now what's happened?

She's come back, and is threatening to expose him. And he's very angry, and very frightened.

Exactly! Though there's more, isn't there?

Is there? My gaze shifts uneasily from the mirror to the doorway. She'd put the yellow bag with the books on the top step and searched for her key.

Dear God, I've told him where she lives.

'This is the number. That'll be seven . . .'

I thrust a ten pound note at him and clamber shakily out of the mini cab. 'Hey thanks!' he calls.

It's past midnight but there's a light on in her ground-floor flat, while from the first floor come the sounds of a very loud party.

The front gate's open and I walk carefully past the hedge and up to the door. After I take my glove off it seems a long time before I can find the bell, but when I do I press it. Hard. No one comes. I lean on it again but it's impossible to hear if it's ringing inside. Moving my fingers up I hold them on the upstairs button.

'You're gor-geous!' A window opens on the first floor, and a head appears along with a blast of music.

I call up, 'Hi, do you know . . .' But the head disappears again and the window slams after it. Shit.

She mightn't be in. Or she might be at the party upstairs. Or he might have got here first. He'll try to make it look like suicide of course. I can picture it now, Richard Mayson, established author, explaining to the police that yes, he had gone to visit her and had told her there was never any chance of a relationship. She must have finally accepted he meant it, and tragically taken her own life.

'You bastard!' I wipe my eyes with the back of my sleeve, catching sight at the same time of the gate next to the house.

The back door, I could go round and try that. Stumbling past a rubbish bin and a pile of garbage bags hidden behind the hedge I push at the gate. It's locked.

Over. I'll have to go over. I haul the bin against the fence and clamber onto it. I'll be able to pull myself up, but my shoulder bag's in the way so I take it off and drop it down the other side. Then I grip the fence with both hands, and heave.

'Hey lady!' A voice comes from the pavement. 'You pissed or what?'

'Or maybe she's a lady burglar!' There's a burst of laughter and they move on.

As I straddle the fence it starts to spit rain. I pull my coat up, throw my left leg over, and slide clumsily down.

The side of the house is in darkness but there's light at the back. I cautiously make my way towards it and turn the corner into a small, bricked yard. The light's coming from a pair of French doors, at the bottom of two or three steps. I peer down to see if anyone's inside. There is. A man in a grey suit is standing in the middle of the room, in front of a sofa. He turns side on and I see he's pouring wine into a glass. There's someone sitting on the sofa, I can see the back of their head. And then the man puts the bottle down and picks up another glass and offers it to the person sitting in front of him. It's Mayson, the man is Richard Mayson.

'No!' I hear myself yell. 'Don't drink it!' All at once I'm slipping, the glass doors rushing towards me as I fling up my arms to protect my eyes.

They've put me on the sofa. The woman from the photo, Charlotte, is squatting on the floor, positioning a pink flannel on my forehead.

'You're not cut,' she says soothingly. 'Just stunned. How do you feel?'

Like a bit of an idiot to tell the truth: shock is a great

soberer. I have no idea what's going on here, but I no longer suspect attempted murder. 'Fine. I feel fine.'

Her smile is relieved. Then she looks up over her shoulder. 'Well, aren't you going to tell her who I am?'

Mayson's face is almost as grey as his suit. He nods curtly in my direction, 'Not that it's any of your business, but this is Charlotte.'

'Who is?' her voice acquires a distinct edge.

He's obviously struggling. 'Who is,' he manages to force it out, 'my daughter.'

'Daughter!' The flannel falls off as I struggle to sit up.

'What else?' she laughs. 'You know it's a good thing you're a better crime writer than you are a detective.'

'Crime writer!' Mayson sounds as bewildered as me.

'I had a feminist thriller published two years ago,' I inform him. 'Under a pseudonym.' Then I look back at Charlotte. 'But how can you be . . .'

She cuts in, taking both my hands, 'I'm truly sorry about your wallet and the phone calls, it wasn't meant to be *personal* you know. I love *Dying By Degrees*, it's great. I read it when it first came out, so I was gobsmacked today to discover you're Tallulah Bioletti! I was always hoping there'd be a sequel.'

You know, I don't think this woman is so crazy after all. 'Well, thank you, but since *Dying* I've been trying my hand at screenwriting.'

'Oh yes!' As she leans closer I observe that her eyes are the same as his, one blue, one brown. 'I'm sure you could write the most wonderful film.'

'Ow!' I wave a hand in protest.

'Oh come on, Mum, they're only splinters.'

Charlotte was right about my not being cut but when I ran my fingers through my hair this morning I could feel minute pieces of glass embedded in my scalp.

'So the book's going to be published under both their names?' Lilith probes with the tweezers.

'Uh-huh. His agent's going to present it as a publicity coup, a secret father–daughter collaboration. If I were Charlotte I'd want him brought to book, humiliated, but I guess she's more subtle than that. She's demanding eighty-five per cent of the dosh and, of course, is getting what she's always wanted, public acknowledgement as his child. Which is all she was after when she first started to follow him around. Her mother got pregnant while she and Mayson were students, and he simply denied he was the father. Her mother left university, had a breakdown, and went on to live unhappily ever after. Charlotte was obsessed with the question of her father's identity, but didn't learn his name until her mother died and a relative told her. She contacted Mayson, who promptly told her to piss off. So she stalked him. Partly to avenge her mother, and partly, I suspect, in the hope she could turn him into a nice guy after all. She never announced publicly he was her father because she was determined to make him do that. By the way, she used the name Trewluv because that's his real name. I guess he figured Trewluv wasn't macho enough for a thriller writer.'

We're in my living room and as Lilith turns sideways in the mirror I can see a slight bulge under her red jumper. My breath catches. A baby. My daughter is having a baby.

'Was Selffe her mother's name?'

'No, by this stage she was in therapy and the therapist kept stressing she should forget about her father and be true to herself. It was the therapist who rang with the news of her "death".'

'Ah!' She straightens her back. 'Can't see any more but you'd better check.'

I carefully run my fingers through my hair. 'When she heard he was publishing her diary she was furious, and determined not to let him get away with it. She decided that if she threatened to stand up and expose him he'd be so frightened he'd agree to a deal. He had to find her first of course. She knew we would trace her but wanted to make him sweat.'

'I can't believe he was pleased to think his daughter had died. He's vile.'

'Completely and utterly.'

'Well,' she drops the tweezers back into my makeup bag, 'I for one am pleased this case is over and we can forget about it.'

Forget about it?

It's a pity Tim Roth isn't older, otherwise he'd be perfect for Mayson's part. And I'm going to have to completely rewrite the beginning, doing away with the bicycle altogether. The opening shot will be of the young woman on the bridge. She's silhouetted against a night sky and, just as it looks as if she's about to step into space, a bus passes. So for most of the film you're wondering if she really did it or not.

It also needs a more dramatic end. In which, I'm afraid, he does kill her. The detective knows it's murder, not suicide, but can't prove it. It doesn't, however, take her long to decide on how to exact revenge.

After all, stalking is her business.

(CUT TO the detective's face. Full frame. DISSOLVE TO CLOSE SHOT of her eyes, which reflect a scene from the mean streets, people and cars passing, a bus . . .

The closing credits roll. FADE OUT. THE END.)

Contributors' Notes

Melissa Chan grew up in the Western Australian wheat belt, then moved to the Eastern seaboard where she works (mainly in Melbourne) as a lawyer. She is the author of *Too Rich, One Too Many* and *Guilt*, novels featuring the independent feminist detective and film critic Francesca Miles, and of two books of short stories, *Getting Your Man* and *More on Getting Your Man*. Together with J Terry she is editor of the Artemis crime anthologies: *A Modern Woman and Other Crimes, Calling Up the Devil and Associated Misdemeanours, Don't Go Near the Water and Additional Warnings, Spies, Lies and Watching Eyes* and *Public Hangings, Private Executions and Every Associated Barbarity*.

Joan M Drury is the publisher of Spinsters Ink and founder and executive director of Harmony Women's Fund and Norcroft: A Writing Retreat for Women. Her Tyler Jones series consists of *The Other Side of Silence* (1993), a Minnesota Book Award finalist, and *Silent Words* (The Women's Press, 1997), a Midwest Book Achievement Award finalist, an Edgar Allen Poe Award finalist, a Small Press Book Award finalist, a Benjamin Franklin Book Award winner, a Minnesota Book Award winner, and a Northeast Minnesota Book Award winner. She wishes to thank Zad for her help in creating the story-line for 'Murder at the Sales Meeting'.

Stella Duffy was born in England and grew up in New Zealand. She has written four novels, *Calendar Girl*, *Wavewalker, Beneath the Blonde* (all published by Serpent's Tail), and *Singling Out the Couples* (Sceptre), as well as a musical cabaret *Close to You*, a radio play *The Economies of Justice*, and *The Hand*, a dance/theatre piece for Gay Sweatshop. She is a writer and actor with the comedy company Spontaneous Combustion, and teaches improvisation as a creative tool to writers and actors and in the corporate sector. She lives in London with one girlfriend, and no cats.

Susan Dunlap is the author of seventeen novels, and her short stories have twice won Anthonys, awarded by the Bouchercon world mystery convention, and a Macavity award from Mystery Readers International. Born in New York City, Dunlap has a BA from Bucknell University in Lewisburg; and a PA and an MAT from the University of North Carolina, Chapel Hill. She worked as a social worker, and also studied hatha yoga in India which she then went on to teach in California. She completed the Berkeley Police Department's Civilian Academy course and was a speaker at the Investigation Seminar of the National Association of Legal Investigators. Dunlap was a founding member and president of Sisters in Crime, an international organisation of 3600 members who support women's contributions in the field of crime writing.

Dale Gunthorp says that 'Pikeman and the Bagwoman' might be her biography: 'if Pikeman represents reason and

Bagwoman the slightly-crazed imagination, then I am a disciple of Bagwoman.' She has two published novels, *The Flying Hart* (Sheba) and *Looking for Ammu* (Virago), and is working on a third. She was born in 1941 in South Africa, and now lives in East London.

Christina Lee's story was awarded the 1996 Scarlet Stiletto Award by Sisters in Crime Australia for the best overall short story. She is an academic who specialises in the psychology of women's health, and works at the University of Newcastle, Australia. Although she wishes her job gave her more time for crime she has (writing as Judith Guerin and in collaboration with Catherine Lewis), published two crime novels in academic settings.

Finola Moorhead, who was born in 1947, is a full-time writer. In 1991 she won the Vance Palmer Fiction Prize for *Still Murder* (The Women's Press, 1994). Her other books are *Remember the Tarantella* (The Women's Press, 1994), *Quilt* (1985), and *A Handwritten Modern Classic* (1985). She is a radical feminist fiction writer. She lives in the country in Australia, where she plays golf and tennis; has a horse and a dog; and does handy-person-type things because she has to, rather than wants to.

Millie Murray, a freelance writer, was born in London. She has four published novels for teenagers: *Kiesha* (1988); *Lady A – A Teenage DJ* (1989); *Cairo Hughes* (1996); *Sorrelle* (1998) (all published by Livewire Books, The Women's Press), as well as a number of short stories. She created the comedy sketch show *The Airport* for Radio Four.

Barbara Paul formerly taught at the University of Pittsburgh before quitting to write full time. She is the author of seventeen mystery novels, five science fiction novels, and about fifty short stories. Her most recent book is *Full Frontal Murder*.

Robyn Vinten came to England from New Zealand in the mid-eighties, and forgot to leave. She lives in an unfashionable part of North London with her two cats. She has had two other short stories published, one in The Women's Press anthology, *Reader, I Murdered Him, Too* (1995).

Margaret Wilkinson, who is new to crime, originates from New York but now lives in the north-east of England. She teaches creative writing at undergraduate and postgraduate level, as well as running women's writing workshops. Her short stories have been published in magazines including *Stand* and *The Printer's Devil*. She has written a creative-writing workbook, *Mothers of Invention* (Virago and the National Extension College), and a novel, *Ocean Avenue* (Serpent's Tail). She is currently working on a new novel.

Barbara Wilson is the author of several novels, most recently *If You Had a Family*, and a childhood memoir, *Blue Windows*. She has written five mysteries, the last two (*Gaudi Afternoon* and *Trouble in Transylvania*) featuring translator sleuth Cassandra Reilly. Stories with Cassandra Reilly have appeared in many anthologies and have serialised on the internet by the on-line travel magazine *biztravel.com*. She lives in Seattle.

Mary Wings began her writing career with *She Came Too Late*, winner of the *City Limits* Best Novel of the Year Award, and first published by The Women's Press in 1986. *She Came Too Late* launched the bestselling career of intrepid detective Emma Victor, and was followed by *She Came in a Flash* (The Women's Press, 1988), *She Came by the Book* (The Women's Press, 1995) and *She Came to the Castro* (The Women's Press,

1997). Mary Wings has also written the bestselling Gothic detective novel *Divine Victim* (The Women's Press, 1992), which won the Lambda Literary Award in 1993. Her books have been translated into Dutch, German, Japanese and Spanish. Mary Wings has been nominated for the Raymond Chandler Fulbright in Mystery and Spy Fiction and lives in San Francisco, California, with various cats and a Shetland sheepdog.

Penny Sumner
The End of April
A Victoria Cross Mystery

Victoria Cross, archivist and professional PI, returns from New
York at the request of her aunt, an Oxford professor, to
transcribe Victorian pornography . . .

Then she meets the gorgeous April Tate: law student, lesbian
activist and anti-pornography campaigner. But April is in grave
danger and, when death intrudes, suddenly and violently, Victoria
Cross realises it could soon be the end of April . . .

**'Deftly written and cleverly crafted . . . We will hear
more of Victoria Cross.'** *Gay Scotland*

Crime Fiction £5.99
ISBN 0 7043 4358 4

Penny Sumner
Crosswords
A Victoria Cross Mystery

London in January is cold and wet. Business is slow. And Victoria
Cross is only too happy when a seemingly plum job lands in her lap.

Her assignment is to recover a valuable item of property – a
Chinese vase stolen from a swinging Mayfair nightclub twenty-five
years ago. But what part did this play in the collapse of a major
gangland empire? And just how involved was her client? Before
important questions can be answered, murder intervenes – and
Victoria's own life is placed in deadly jeopardy.

For her partner, April, it's an open-and-shut case. Either Victoria
drops what could be a fatal investigation or April drops her. As
tensions mount – at work and at home – January in London
becomes a very hot month indeed . . .

'Draws on the spirit of Dorothy Sayers' *Gaudy Nights* **. . .
All the women are interesting, even the villians.'**
Mystery Review

Crime Fiction £5.99
ISBN 0 7043 4448 3